California plains in the 1850s. After
cholera on the wagon train out west, E...
fends for himself in the boom town
where he and his busy and ambitious father settle.

Coming of age for Emmet means hiding in the corners of his
father's new saloon, scrounging for food in the local brothels
and finding refuge in tunnels underneath Colusa's Chinatown.

While fighting off town bullies, an evil Irish stepmother, and
his own learning disabilities, Emmet struggles to find his
footing but never loses his curiosity about the world around
him and the people in it.

When forced into a court case to establish his identity and
rightful inheritance after the untimely death of his father,
Emmet must find family and identity in places he might not
have reckoned for. But can he?

With equal measures of the dark and the light, Campbell's
boy is a tender tale about a boy whose fractured beginnings
lead him on a journey through life that reveals what it can
mean to be human.

Early Praise

"In *Campbell's Boy*, Mary Kendall expertly paves an odyssey
of Dickensian proportions, taking us deep into Colusa
tunnels beneath the Chinatown of Emmet Campbell's
childhood and across the tumultuous plain of an
extraordinary life."—*Robert Gwaltney, award winning
author of The Cicada Tree*

"Tender, charming and emotional. This inspiring story of
Emmet Campbell, Campbell's Boy, tugs the heartstrings and
immerses you in the sounds and smells, hardships and
adventures of California in the 1850s."—*Kate Braithwaite,
author of The Girl Puzzle: A Story of Nellie Bly*

i

"An engaging read about an historic case of social injustice…. Can Emmet Campbell rest in peace now?"—*Cathie Dunn, author of Ascent, House of Normandy*

"With a deft hand, author Mary Kendall brings to life the heartbreaking story of Emmett Campbell and the gritty world in which he lived."—*Jean M. Roberts, author of The Angel of Goliad*

A hand whipped out fast and grabbed his wrist pinning it down to the table. Emmet craned his neck and found himself under the baleful gaze of Old Man Chung. The man's voice came out in a high sing-song tone. "You drink it!" Emmet tried to work his wrist out from under but the man was stronger and kept it down. "You drink it!" he said again.

Emmet shook his head frantically and came out with, "No! I won't drink it!" Suddenly his wrist was free and the old man began to cackle, his body shaking with mirth and the effort of the cackle. Emmet swiveled away from the old man, the drink and the room. He ran into the tunnel with the cackle echoing louder and louder in his ears as he fled.

CAMPBELL'S BOY

Mary Kendall

Moonshine Cove Publishing, LLC

Abbeville, South Carolina U.S.A.

First Moonshine Cove Edition NOV 2022

ISBN: 9781952439452

Library of Congress LCCN: 20229xxxxx

Copyright 2022 by Mary Kendall

Front cover image by Hannah Linder Creations LLC; cover and interior design by Moonshine Cove staff.

About the Author

Mary Kendall lived in old (and haunted) houses growing up which sparked a life-long interest in history and story-telling. She earned degrees in history related fields and worked as a  historian for many years. Her fiction writing is heavily influenced by the past which she believes is never really dead and buried. Fueled by black coffee and a possible sprinkling of Celtic fairy dust, she tends to find inspiration in odd places and sometimes while kneading bread dough. She resides in Maryland with her family (husband, three kids, barn cat and the occasional backyard hen) who put up with her mad scribbling at inconvenient hours.

Campbell's Boy is her second novel. Her debut novel, *The Spinster's Fortune,* was published in 2021. She is also a contributor to Darkstroke's anthologies for charity with short stories included in *Dark Paris, Dark New Orleans* and *Dark Venice.*

Acknowledgements

This book has been many years in the making (eleven years, in fact). A great deal of assistance, input and help from others was picked up along the way. Alongside of those years, I was raising my three kids (Mack Lavin, Desmond Lavin and Lucia Lavin) who I thank for teaching and inspiring me every day, then and now.

At the start of this journey were those who assisted me with my research endeavors:

At the Columbia Maryland Family History Center, Dottie Aleshire, was an invaluable resource as I maneuvered this particular genealogical hunt.

Mimi Woods Ringstad, friend and colleague extraordinaire, indulged me early in the game of figuring out the peculiarities of this genealogical puzzle on long walks around Centennial Park in Maryland. (We call that multi-tasking.)

John Morton, Colusa historian, provided me with documents, photographs and maps from the area that would have been difficult to procure otherwise. (An aside: John also played the part of John Campbell in the town's reenactment of the real-life event of the celebration of Lincoln's assassination depicted in the novel.)

Halfway into this project, I was very fortunate in being able to visit Colusa, California, the setting of this tale. I made advance contact with Resa Lynn, the historian and researcher at Colusa County Library. Resa went above and beyond, digging up valuable information for me in my too brief time there. She has continued to provide me with anything related she comes upon.

Next up for huge applause are those who supported my writing:

My long-suffering beta readers have been through more renditions, variations, points of view and drafts than I care to confess. I owe them---Nigel Lavin and Dart Clancy. Dorrie Clancy also provided a critical reading from the young adult perspective.

About eight years into this project, I was able to consult with Nathan Bransford. After following his eponymous blog on all things writing for years, I just happened upon the fact that he is coincidentally a native son of Colusa. I am thankful for his willingness to take a look and his advice which led me to take the manuscript in a different direction---where it is now.

The wonderful M.M. Finck at the Query Quill provided astute guidance in perfecting my query, the same query that ultimately led to a publishing contract.

It was a red-letter day for me when Emmet's story struck a chord with Gene Robinson and Moonshine Cove Publishing after being passed over by countless others. I will forever be grateful.

Most of all, I have such gratitude for Emmet Campbell, the inspiration of this tale. His life was really something.

Dedication

For the ancestors (of course).

CAMPBELL'S
BOY

"Every man has two deaths, when he is buried in the ground and the last time someone says his name. In some ways men can be immortal." Ernest Hemingway

PART ONE: BEGINNINGS
Chapter One

Emmet Campbell opened the dirt encrusted palm of his hand and stared at the penny candies in swirling colors of reds, greens and yellows. He didn't know numbers but he knew there were enough to keep him happy for a while. Sticking them deep into the pocket in his pants without the hole, he gazed out onto the empty street. He could almost taste the sweets melting in his mouth. But not yet...he would wait until the tunnels.

Mid-day he had the town of Colusa to himself as most slumbered inside after their noon meals. With the exception of a lone rider in the distance heading away from town, it was just him, the blazing hot noonday California sun and the dead still air. He sniffed that air smelling manure and river rot with an overlay of fragrant blooms. Then he bared his teeth like he had seen his father's plow horse do, exposed his upper gum line and neighed out into the empty town. He got nothing back.

Turning to face due west, he began to half skip and half hop his way down Market Street, the dust kicking up under his boots. His mind picked over the sights and sounds of the town he considered his own. He hummed as he took in the ground underneath, keeping an eye out for any treasures. But there was only a dead frog, sticky due to being squashed by a wagon wheel.

Around the corner at Fifth Street, he slowed his pace nearing Campbell & Sons, Dry Goods and Sundries, his father's store. Right before the storefront, he skulked down to move past. Popping his head up just enough to sneak a peek through the window, his breath caught at the sight of the tall figure with a thatch of salt and pepper hair that stood on end from running a hand through it. His father's concentration was on a customer and Emmet let his breath out after passing by safely and turning onto Main from Fifth.

If John Campbell caught him, he would get a whupping or worse. At eight years and some change, Emmet was supposed to be sitting in that classroom over on Tenth Street learning numbers and letters. But...he didn't want any parts of that. And as long as his father didn't know Emmet wasn't there, he didn't bother none.

He moved quicker down the street towards his destination where Main Street cleared out to an empty lot. The wooden buildings beyond the empty lot shrank in size, becoming narrow and short, as they lined up snug next to each other like the sugar cubes Emmet stole from his father's shop. Colusa was different looking in this block-long part of town and, with that difference, came a distinct smell, leftover cooking layered with something else. Something he had never smelled elsewhere. Emmet had reached Chinatown.

On the side of the last building in the row, the way in was disguised by a large clump of tarweed that bloomed yellow. The plant grew everywhere it could find purchase throughout the town. Brushing the plant aside, Emmet slipped through and headed down a wooden staircase that creaked and moved more than not taking him seven steps down. At the bottom, he stood on hard-packed earth.

He carefully pushed onto the wooden door that barely hung on its hinges and found his way into the narrow channel that went on for about a hundred paces. His hand touched the wall's brick that sweat with moisture. Walking deeper in, he felt his body immediately begin to cool. This was what he sought. Relief from the burning sun aboveground. And, because all the Chinamen were out laboring, he would have the place to himself.

Emmet first heard about the tunnels one night listening in on one of the many long-winded conversations between his father and Dudley Shepardson, his father's friend. There had been a tone of respect when the two men discussed the tunnels. A respect for people who looked so different and came from somewhere else but managed to carve out their own secrets underneath the town.

Sometimes Emmet tried to imagine the place where they came from. What it looked like and how far away it was. But his thoughts would eventually venture into whether they could shoot a marble farther than him or why their foods smelled so funny and other questions. No white folks had gone through the tunnels as far as anyone knew, according to Dudley Shepardson. But Emmet latched onto the idea of finding a way in.

On many evenings late into the night, Emmet watched from his chamber window as the majority of the inhabitants of Chinatown returned from the ranches or the railroad sites. Emmet had never been in the spaces above the shops where they all bunked up together, magically fitting somehow. He imagined them lined up like the cordwood laid out at the river a short distance away to fuel the steamboats. Taking a few hours of rest before the sun rose, they repeated the same process all over again the next day, and the next and the next.

Now that he was inside, the channel opened up into a room. As Emmet felt along the wall where torches were kept, he could hear a steady drip of water from somewhere deeper within. He lit a torch and cast it around to see the space. A crude table strewn with chairs along the sides held the remnants of leftover activities from the previous evening. Cups, cards, dice and smoking apparatus.

With the torch illuminating the area, he picked his way over to the far end of the room, his boots making a scuffling noise against the hard packed dirt floor. A niche dug into the wall contained a bench. That was Emmet's spot.

He made himself comfortable, propping up his body with boots pressed against the wall in front of him. Pulling out the candies from his pocket, he popped the first one in his mouth. As he worked his jaw this way and that, the sugar filled his mouth. His eyes half closed at the sensation. The coolness of the tunnel room and the sweetness of the candy lulled him into almost a trance-like rest.

Getting the candies and other rewards was his main activity during the days. He had proven himself to certain folks that he was quick on his feet and reliable despite his short stature and young age. His mind ran through his routine of errands and chores with its varied prizes. With Mr. Ware at Ware's Mercantile, it was the penny candies. With the saloon owners, it was coins thrown his way which he learned to catch every time. With those ladies on the streets at night, it was bonbons and sometimes fancier chocolates from foreign parts. What he didn't consume right away, he stored in his own private stash kept well hidden from his father.

He kept other things well hidden from his father. His thoughts went back to his first time in the tunnels. He had finally gotten up his courage one night and laid in wait outside, hidden behind a trash hill, while the men filtered down. When they were all in, Emmet moved over to the tarweed plant as he had watched them do on so many nights. Pushing it aside, he climbed down, his spine tingling with anticipation and a good measure of fear.

Once in the tube-like channel, he crept along as a sickly, sweet odor assaulted his nostrils. A smoky haze became thicker as he made his way to the edge of the open room. Pressing himself back against the wall, he looked over his shoulder and peered in.

What he saw that night was not too unlike the scenes he spied on aboveground at the saloons, aside from the color of the skin of those who participated. Some men sat with cards or dice, playing out a game of chance. Others sat at a separate table passing around a huge pipe with smoke drifting out of its top end, the source of the sickly, sweet smell. The haze in the air was not cigar smoke like in the saloons but this other smoke that he didn't know too much about. Others in the room just sat and talked. All by his estimation seemed tired and worn out. Maybe even beaten down. Since that first time, he came back often in the daytime hours. That was when it was empty and he had the run of the place.

He now drew out the experience of eating his penny candies for as long as he possibly could. As he was jawing on the last piece, a thud suddenly came echoing down from the entry tunnel. He felt the lump of sugar from the last candy stick to the side of his throat as his guts clenched. He drew himself as tightly as he could alongside the niche hoping to go undetected. Someone was coming.

His heart thumped in his chest as he watched to see who it would be. A shuffling sound got closer and closer, ramping up his heart beat, until the figure came into his direct view. Emmet recognized him as Old Man Chung, or at least that was what folks called him. The elderly man's canvas slippers continued to make the whispery sounds on the floor surface as he moved closer.

With the long, thin, white beard that hung to his chest and the face crunched into a thousand wrinkles, everyone said he was the oldest man amongst the Chinese in town. Everyone also, white and of color, gave him a wide berth when he walked through the streets because he had powers beyond nature. At least that is what Emmet heard more than one time.

Emmet had never been this close to him. Now, though, he could study more closely the scraggly beard and the agate stone eyes that shone in the man's crumpled up face. Even though he was afraid, he could not take his gaze away. What kind of magic did this man have? How did he get it? Was he just born that way? Could Emmet get some of it for himself?

Old Man Chung murmured to himself as he walked over to the table and sat down with a groan. His eyes fell to half-mast and he shook himself. Getting up with some effort, he went over to the cook stove and lit a fire. Emmet could just make out that he was heating water. He began to fiddle with a pile of small leaves sorting and discarding as he went about it. After placing his careful selections in a bowl, he poured the heated water on top and sat back down in front of the now steaming bowl. It baffled Emmet that the man would want to drink something made out of those leaves. But he was also curious about what that would taste like.

Emmet watched and waited and eventually the man's eyes fell all the way closed and his head drooped over to one side. When gentle snores came out of his mouth, Emmet knew his opportunity had come. Moving slowly, he untangled himself and stood out of the niche. On tiptoes, he moved away over to the exit but then stopped. He couldn't resist the urge. He had to see what was in the open bowl.

Creeping over to the table, wary of any change in Old Man Chung's snoring, he peered down into the bowl. All manner of leaves, other debris and maybe even some skunk cabbage like he saw out in the wetlands formed a thick and slimy liquid. A smell rose up from the bowl and hit his face. Unlike any other smell he had known...bitter, acidic, sweet and noxious all rolled into one.

A hand whipped out fast and grabbed his wrist pinning it down to the table. Emmet craned his neck and found himself under the baleful gaze of Old Man Chung. The man's voice came out in a high sing-song tone. "You drink it!" Emmet tried to work his wrist out from under but the man was stronger and kept it down. "You drink it!" he said again.

Emmet shook his head frantically and came out with, "No! I won't drink it!" Suddenly his wrist was free and the old man began to cackle, his body shaking with mirth. Emmet swiveled away from the old man, the drink and the room. He ran into the tunnel with the cackle echoing louder and louder in his ears as he fled.

Chapter Two

Making it to the top step of the tilted wooden stairs, Emmet pushed his way out into the yellow tarweed, thrusting it aside. Back aboveground, he ran down Main Street and away from Chinatown before stopping a block away. Bending over with hands on hips, he gasped for air with the stench of the noxious drink still filling his nostrils.

With the bright sun on his back and the familiar sights and sounds of Colusa, he could barely believe it had happened---Old Man Chung trying to force him to drink that muck. He shook his head to get the smell out, thankful for the reprieve. Maybe the old man wanted to punish him for being in the tunnels or maybe he was just crazy.

He stood up and righted himself. Looking over towards the Sacramento River where a row of palm trees softly swayed along its edge, he could see activity had picked up on Main Street. A steamer had docked and, with it, the hustle and bustle of moving goods off as folks headed to the landing to procure what they needed.

He kept moving, no one paying him any mind, but he did glance over his shoulder now and then for Old Man Chung just in case. Once in the alley space between Fifth Street and his father's store on Market, he climbed up the staircase hanging off the back of the store and leading to the rooms above Campbell & Sons that served as home. The door closed behind him with a dull thud as he walked inside. The musky, manly odor that he associated with his father replaced all the other smells of the day.

The room held the barest of furnishings, just a table and two hard back chairs. Over on one wall, the cooking area was arranged with the basics. Emmet walked over to see if his father had put up any supplies or foodstuffs. Rifling through the empty shelves, he gave up the endeavor and sighed. He would figure something out later he told himself.

Emmet moved to the end of the room to the open doorway that led to the one chamber where he and his father slept. A straw tick mattress was pushed into one corner with some bedcovers strewn on top. One window provided light and a glimpse out onto Market Street. He peered out the window to check out the activity generated by the steamer, horses and wagons moving to and fro and a number of people walking about. He plopped down onto the mattress and stared around him at the mostly barren space with the exception of one corner where his small pile of treasures formed a stack on the floor. Things of nature that included tree branches, bird nests, stones and some feathers.

There was also his painting stuck onto the wall with a tack nail. One day, he found some paints in his father's storeroom and put down the Sutter Buttes on the paper. The buttes lay outside of town some distance away but they drew him in every time he saw them. There was some magic in the shape of them and in the way they loomed out of the flatlands rising above all else. He eyed his painting again, always comforted by the look of the buttes, even if it was just from his imagination and not in his direct field of vision.

This place was so unlike Malinda Cooper's house outside of town apiece where he spent his earliest years. His mother had died of some sickness that he always forgot the name of on the wagon trail when they came out west. He had no memory of her. None at all.

Too little to be left alone, Campbell shuttled him out to the Cooper homestead on most days. He remembered those early morning rides with the sun coming up, snuggled against his father on top of the Spanish horse that Campbell kept in the nearby livery.

Days were spent rambling around the Coopers' ranch with the Coopers' granddaughter, Mary Benicia, who lived there along with her widowed mother, Fanny. She was a couple of years older than Emmet and, with her at his side, they had the run of the place. They would play games all day long amongst the almonds, filberts and other nut trees and also too amongst the carefully tended lanes between the numerous figs, oranges and other fruit trees. Once spent, they would return from their adventures to sprawl on the big front porch with Sarshel, the eldest son, and Major Stephen Cooper, when his day's work came to a finish.

The Major would sit and talk about everything. By contrast, Sarshel mainly sat in silence. Sarshel was not like everybody else and did not say more than a few words a day by Emmet's guess. Emmet heard somebody talking about Sarshel as "not right in the head" but he didn't know what that meant.

Emmet missed it. All of it. The pungent tang of citrus in the air. The creak of the floorboards on the porch that ran the length of the ranch house. The warmth of being folded into Malinda Cooper's ample bosom with Mary Benicia for a hug with the scent of freshly baked bread always wafting over her and on her.

But he especially missed being side by side with Mary Benicia. She taught him to talk when he couldn't and the words were trapped in his head. She taught him how to ride the mules, stubborn as they were. She taught him to mind her when his tendency was to run into the trees tripping and falling along the way. But he became too much for Malinda Cooper, getting into everything after Mary Benicia moved out when her mother remarried. His time was up.

He walked out sometimes to the Coopers' ranch. If his father caught him making the long, hot trek, he scolded that Emmet was wearing out his welcome. So, he only went out sometimes... because he never wanted to see a look of unwelcome on the Coopers' faces.

Still thinking about Mary Benicia and the Coopers' ranch, Emmet drifted off to sleep with a hunger in his gut despite being a bit sour from Old Man Chung's tea smell. A voice bellowing brought him out of slumber in short order. "Emmet? Emmet? You here?"

Before Emmet could lift himself up off the straw tick mattress, John Campbell strode into the back chamber, his presence filling up the space. Dusk had set in and Emmet could barely make out his father, the tall lean form with the craggy lines on his face partially covered by his beard. The sharp dark eyes looked down at Emmet briefly with the same slight questioning gaze they usually held...or so it felt to Emmet. "I got some supper," he said.

His father turned on heel and Emmet scurried to meet him in the other room. Campbell was flinging some supplies on the small table. Emmet recognized the waxen paper from Heeps and Hale Grocer. His hunger came back in force and he salivated at the thought of the cheese that it held. At Heeps and Hale, they kept the cheese out on a wooden butcher block where it would sweat throughout the day and customers would cut their own piece with the attached blade that hung beside the block. A cooked-up sausage was in the other wrapped paper and Campbell sliced it into several large pieces. A loaf of bread that Emmet looked at with suspicion for freshness also lined up with the cheese and sausage. Lastly, a glass bottle of ale sat prominently in front of his father.

As they ate in silence, each concentrating on the meal, Emmet was aware that his father's thoughts were far away. He wished he could know these thoughts, tap into them. He thought about how different it felt to sit with Sarshel without talk. How it felt comfortable and right. Not like when he sat with his father. At mealtimes, he felt the pang of not being at the Coopers' the most.

As though his life depended on it, his father took deep gulps from the bottle that dripped with condensation. Emmet stared at the froth that dribbled into his father's beard. It was a scruffy beard that matched his salt and pepper hair color and hung several inches below his chin. When he took his last pull of the drink, even more froth got hung up in the beard's wiry bristles and threatened to plop down onto the table top. Mesmerized by the sight, Emmet felt mirth rise up in his belly and he couldn't stop the high-pitched giggle that erupted out. His was a distinctive and unique laugh. He knew that.

Campbell gazed at the boy in front of him and his face cracked into a half smile moving the froth off to one side which made it an even more hilarious sight to Emmet. The father began to laugh with the son. A deep laugh seldom heard by Emmet. Almost rusty from disuse.

After Campbell's laughter and Emmet's giggles tapered off, Campbell wiped his eyes. "I haven't laughed so hard in a while. I remember the first time I heard that crazy laugh of yours..."

Emmet looked expectedly as his father's eyes gazed off probably to that earlier time that Emmet did not remember.

"It was on the trail. At the Sink of Humboldt. That dried out lake bed..."

It felt to Emmet that his father was telling a story more to himself than to Emmet but he soaked up every word and the rarity of it.

His father's eyes turned back to him and his voice became softer when he said, "I had just buried Amanda. Your mama. After the damned cholera took her."

Shaking his head at the memory, he said, "You were sitting in that pile of dirt while I finished cleaning up. And I heard that sound out of you for the first time. That laugh of yours. I looked over and you had found a stone. There you were, holding that stone up and laughing at it."

He shook his head again. "There I was. On my own all of sudden with a young'un to raise. A young'un that didn't even have words. And you start laughing."

Emmet took a leap and asked, "What'd she look like?"

Campbell focused back on his son's blue-eyed stare and said "What?"

"What'd she—"

Campbell cut him off saying, "Finish up now." Emmet stared down at his remaining bits of food.

After they finished the meal off in silence, Campbell let out a big sigh of breath. "We got some changes coming soon, boy." Emmet looked up at his father's face to see what he could read on his expression. If the changes would be good or bad.

Campbell nodded almost more to himself than to Emmet and continued. "I'm getting us a mail-order bride. That's what they call it."

Emmet's face scrunched up, puzzled by the term. "A bird gets sent in the mail?"

Campbell gave a snort. "Bride. Not bird. And I'll go fetch her probably."

Emmet pondered all of it and a hundred questions swirled around in his mind. He came out with, "Well...where you going to put her?"

"She'll be here. With us. She's going to be your new mother. "

All Emmet could think to respond was, "Oh." He would have to sit with this awhile and figure it out. A mother that looked like a bird? It was a lot to take in.

Chapter Three

It awaited a woman's touch according to his father. Emmet had wandered south from town the three miles to the Campbell ranch to see if he could understand what a woman's touch meant. A mail-order bird would be coming to Colusa soon and, in anticipation of that event, his father started construction on a ranch building with a low-pitched roof sitting squarely on the plot of land. Between running his store, his saloon and now setting up his farmland, the construction of the house was slow to happen, largely left for last.

Standing in the middle of the building's footprint, Emmet gazed around the skeletal pieces in place to be fleshed out and become their house. He could make out the place for the hearth on one end and where the windows would be situated. But the rest would wait for her touch, he guessed.

Outside, he edged his way closer to the field where Campbell's hired hands were threshing winter wheat. He found his favorite field rock to perch upon and pulled some candies out of his pocket. While sucking on the sweets, he watched the men with the equipment hitched to the oxen move up and down through the fields, the process tedious and slow going. After a bit, he worked up a ball of spit to see how far he could get it. He snorted when it did not go far enough. Nowhere near as far as his father could spit.

In the distance lay the Sutter Buttes, poised like sentries and casting long shadows. Emmet's eyes moved from the men to the buttes, watching those shadows shift as the clouds stirred in the sky. It calmed him. Made him forget about whatever was gnawing on his mind.

His very first memories were the colors. When he watched the colors ripple with the winds on the plains, he saw them as one complete wave. He didn't know their names back then. Now he did. The purple sage, the yellow tarweed, the blue-green June grasses, the pink wildflowers. He saw the colors on people too. In time, he got the words for the feelings, piecing it all together. The red that lit up on a person meant anger; the blue meant sad; the green, jealous.

He remembered the day his father bought the ranch a couple of years earlier. Emmet followed along behind him, curious about what brought such life to John Campbell's face. He stood right by his side in line for the big event in town. A gentleman surveyor with a bolo tie from a place called Denver sat behind the makeshift table set up on the courthouse square, selling plots to anyone who could plunk money down on the table. Emmet had been fascinated by the man who swatted flies away and wiped sweat off his brow while working through the long line in front of him with haste, clearly wanting to be on his way.

His father was coiled tightly that day like an animal ready to spring on its prey. Emmet stepped away from him a couple feet because he didn't like the way it felt. When Campbell's turn came up, his father stood in front of the man and studied the dotted lines delineating the portions left for the taking on the map. Emmet peered around his father's hand to see the rectangular pieces, some regular, some irregular, like the jigsaw puzzle Mary Benicia had at the Coopers' ranch. The one her granddaddy, the Major, made from leftover wood scraps.

The man impatiently brushed off another fly buzzing about his pomaded hair, attracted no doubt by the scent. "Well, what's it going to be for you, gent?" he asked Emmet's father.

Campbell's stubby forefinger danced in the air for a second before landing on a spot on the map. "This here. Looks to be about three miles south. Two pieces. How many acres is that?"

The man pulled the map back towards him and frowned at the area. Turning it this way and that, he finally said, "Two rectangles at one hundred and sixty acres a piece. Three hundred and twenty acres. A man named Powell got these pieces here."

He pointed at the pieces which again reminded Emmet of Mary Benicia's jigsaw puzzle before adding, "Work it out with him and buy those bits to fit it together better would be my advice."

After his father signed some papers and counted out gold coins from his small leather bag, the fancy man deftly bound the sheath of paperwork in twine and handed it over saying, "There you are, sir. Done!" Looking past Campbell and Emmet, he called out, "Next!"

Campbell walked away and several patted him on the back as Emmet trailed behind. They went straight to the livery. Riding out to the claim south of town, the setting sun cast its rosy hue in front of their path. Getting closer to their new ranch, Emmet looked over and set his gaze on the Sutter Buttes which became nearer out in the open plains, away from town, abiding and comforting in their bulk.

His father pulled the horse to a halt where a stake was planted. "This is it, boy. Can't you just see it?" Campbell, squinting one eye, pointed to different sections saying "There, we'll put the dwelling house and, over there, will be the stables and supply sheds."

His father's voice vibrated with his excitement. He was getting back to the land. Emmet was his silent audience of one, even though his gaze was fixed on the buttes. At times like these, it struck him that he saw things in a different way from his father.

Shaking his head out of his musings of that long ago day, Emmet now stood up and dusted his hands off on his dungarees. The walk back to town was three miles, flat and true, and it would be getting on dark if he left it too long. He moved one foot in front of another and settled into a rhythm passing by vast wet stretches of land and newly planted crops on Jerry Powell's ranch both accented with wildflowers and lively birdsong.

Once on the outskirts of town, small farmsteads with associated outbuildings began to pepper the landscape. Eventually, the road forked into two choices, the main road to Yuba City or straight on into Colusa proper. Sometimes, Emmet wondered what would happen to him if he just kept walking on the road to Yuba City. Sometimes, he wanted to. Instead, he kept on the road most familiar as Colusa opened up to reveal itself with houses on town lots. In time, he reached the Sacramento River that abutted Main Street and there he sat on its bank as the sunset unfolded.

That was his mistake. To sit on the river bank and take a rest. The Gunderson brothers grabbed him from behind when he was immersed in staring at the river, unaware of their close and looming presence.

"Look who it is. Emmet Campbell. Just staring off into space as usual. The town idiot."

They had found him like they always did. Emmet wondered if their noses were like the bloodhound dog he saw once. His scent being detected by the brothers.

Emmet looked at the snarl that was on Freddy Gunderson's face. He pondered what he had ever done to bring that snarl about on that face, homely as a badger. Meanwhile, his brother, Hiram, was lighting a smoke that looked almost used up. As Emmet squirmed, the older and bigger Freddy kept a tight hold on him although he hardly exerted himself to do so.

Once lit, Hiram handed the smoke over to Freddy who immediately pressed it into Emmet's arm. Emmet let out a screech at the sizzle of the burn and the boys started up with howls of laughter. Freddy was laughing so hard that he let his grip on Emmet go. Emmet ran as fast as his legs could take him with the horrible sound of the Gunderson brothers' glee behind him. They called after him with a volley of names. Idiot, ninny, coot.

He kept running all the way down Main passing by his father's saloon and all the way to the tunnels. He stopped just outside of them, bent over with a stitch in his side and the burn on his arm smarting. He brushed the yellow plant aside and stumbled down the staircase.

Making his way the hundred paces before it opened up into the first room, he realized too late that the light emanating out meant that some were already gathered. He came to a halt as several Chinese men at the table looked over his way. They all spoke to each other in rapid fire cadence at the sight of him. Emmet had heard that angry cadence above ground but never directed his way before.

One man stood up and pointed a finger into his chest. Speaking loudly in a guttural voice, spit came out along with the force of his words. In broken English, he made himself clear. "Why you come here? This place not for white boy."

Emmet stumbled back when suddenly a voice rang out, shouting a word he did not know. The man in front of him stopped his barrage of words mid-stream and sat back down at the table. Looking in the direction of the voice ringing out, Emmet saw Old Man Chung. The dark, stone-like eyes gave him a long stare before he turned away and fiddled with the pipe that sat in front of him. "Sit," the old man said. Emmet let out his breath. He could stay.

Emmet crept over to the table and did as he was told, sitting on one of the half broken chairs around the beat up table. As he perched on the edge of the chair, Emmet kept his gaze to the side not directly looking at the man next to him.

Taking a puff from his pipe, Old Man Chung breathed out and turned his stare to Emmet. The strange, sweet odor from the man's breath emanating out into the room made Emmet's eyes smart. The man's gaze moved down from Emmet's face and caught sight of the fresh round welt on his arm. He reached over with a talon-like grip and picked up Emmet's wrist, turning his arm to get a closer look. "Who?"

Emmet looked down in shame and embarrassment. How could he possibly explain to this man who did not know English words about the boys who tormented him above ground? The elderly man dropped Emmet's wrist and spoke Chinese to one of the other men. A pot of what looked like animal grease was brought over to the table.

Old Man Chung daubed the mixture onto Emmet's wound. At first touch, it felt like the sizzle from before and Emmet scrunched his face up at the feeling. But a cooling sensation took over and the burn began to subside. When Emmet opened his eyes, he looked down at the skin on his arm which did not seem as angry looking.

As Emmet sat still, he took in the scene around him. A couple of men played a game with dice. One man sat on his own with a pipe like Old Man Chung's with a plume of smoke curling upwards.

Old Man Chung stood up abruptly and brushed off his hands, the chair making a scraping noise with the suddenness of his movement.

Grabbing Emmet's arm, he led him across the room. Emmet felt a creeping sensation along his spine not knowing if this was right.

On the table at the far end of the dimly lit room sat the pot that Emmet had seen before and he realized too late Old Man Chung was going to make him drink it. He squirmed from the man's grip but, just like the first time, it was steel-like and he could not get away despite how old the man seemed to be. Another Chinaman, the one who had yelled at him, came from behind and helped the older man restrain Emmet.

As they got closer to the table, the smell migrated into his nasal passages and his stomach immediately rolled in protest. Once standing next to it, the old man took a cup and gestured to Emmet a drinking motion. Emmet began to shake his head vigorously saying, "No, no, no..."

"Yes. Good for you," the old man said.

Using a wooden ladle that sat next to the pot, he scooped some of the oozing liquid into the cup, debris hanging off the sides. Emmet took the cup and the now familiar smell flew up in his face. Seeing no other way around it, Emmet slowly brought the noxious liquid to his lips and sipped. His taste buds immediately were on fire but he managed a swallow without gagging it back up.

The two Chinamen leaned into towards him, staring, and he knew he must drink the rest. After drinking the entire cup, he felt rumblings as it splashed around in his gut. But then a settling followed and a strange feeling of ease came over him. He looked up at the two men in wonder. What had he just drunk?

Old Man Chung nodded at him as though he knew exactly what Emmet was thinking. The other man grabbed Emmet's arm and yanked him towards a small door on the back wall. Emmet had never noticed the door but found himself at the bottom of another rickety wooden staircase. An exit to the outside that was an even bigger secret...

After climbing up, he looked around to get his bearings. He found himself almost at the edge of the river where the banks were especially high and Main Street had ended a block or so to the east. He closed his eyes and again felt that strange sense of ease in his gut.

Chapter Four

The sliver of moonlight from the night sky cast shadows around the room. Sleep would not come as Emmet fingered the faded blue threadbare piece of cloth by his side. He didn't know where it had come from. He just always had it.

In the nights, Emmet felt the twinge in his right arm bone more than in the days. He had broken it at Coopers'. One of his last weeks there...his mind went back to the memory of it all. He had climbed up a dwarf pear tree, up high and almost to the top. From his perch, he could barely make out through the lower branches Mary Benicia's form standing below with arms positioned on her hips. She said with indignation, "Emmet Campbell! Get down here right now! You're too high up!"

Emmet shook his head even though she couldn't see that response. He couldn't find the words to tell her how he felt about her leaving him. He only had action...climbing the tree.

"It's not that bad...I'll come back a lot."

But it won't be the same was his silent answer back.

"Come on. Let's go down to the henhouse and poke at that jackass rooster."

Nothing will be fun anymore without you here was his unspoken response to that.

"Aww...When are you coming down out of this tree, Emmet?"

I don't know...I'll never feel right about this was what he wanted to say aloud.

"Well. I'll just sit here I guess...bored out of my mind." She added with no small amount of irritation in her voice, "We could be having a good ol' time you know."

He heard her give a loud sigh and plop down under the tree. Eventually, he could hear her humming and he knew she figured out a way to occupy herself. Probably she strung some weeds together to make a necklace was his guess. She liked to do that. His mind whirled around the fact of her departure. Which was soon to happen. Going over and over it like a sore spot hot to the touch but too hard to resist.

One of his legs started to cramp up from the awkward shape he had pulled himself into. By his estimation, he was up in the tree about the distance of two quarter horses if put atop each other...maybe a little more than that. He decided it was time to work his way back down.

He untangled himself and worked one leg at a time from branch to branch. Mary Benicia stirred below at the sound of his movements. "Finally! I thought I'd be sitting down here for the rest of my life."

Emmet half smiled at her dramatics but put most of his attention on his movements. As she continued to yammer on, he kept on his way until he put weight on the next branch and felt it give a bit. He heard the sound of the crack first before the feeling of it splitting through. Losing any grip or hold he had, he was flying all of a sudden in a freefall.

When he landed, the air felt sucked right out of him in one fell swoop. Mary Benicia was struck silent. He tried to shift to one side but saw his arm turned out at an impossible angle. It felt like it wasn't the same piece of him anymore. Her voice came out shrill and scared. "I'm getting Granddaddy. Stay put." He watched her skirt fly up in the air in a swirl of red and white as she scrambled away from the tree.

Sarshel and Major Cooper carried him back to the house in a two man hold. He screamed with the pain while Mary Benicia held his hand tightly and they slowly made their way. Once Doc Robinson got there, Mary Benicia insisted on being right by his side even through the agonizing sounds of his bone being set back in its rightful place.

Later, they put him in Sarshel's bed and Sarshel took Emmet's usual place out on the hearth in the bedroll. After Malinda Cooper gave him a dose of some sort of syrup which she said was a draught for sleeping, Mary Benicia tucked the blanket around him with gentle care.

Even though the pain of the broken arm had been tremendous, it was a memory he held close because it turned out to be his last day at

Coopers' with Mary Benicia. Shaking it off now, he sighed and brought himself up to sitting, staring out the window at the sliver of moon and giving up on the sleep that would not come. He decided to do what he generally did on nights when sleep escaped him. Sneak into his father's saloon, the Mount Hood Saloon.

After pulling on his shirt and trousers, he picked his way through the dark room out to the main one. He made as little noise as possible like mice did when poking their tiny heads into the pantry searching for vittles. Emmet discovered early on that watching animals gave him some bright ideas about how to conduct himself, the mice included. No one would hear him moving about since the store below was closed but it was always good practice to be careful.

The door opened with its customary creak. He gently shut it closed behind him before making his way down the outside stairs. Once in the alley, he could see light at the end where it emptied into Market Street. He did not go in that direction. Instead, he moved towards Main which was less traveled at night, sticking to the shadows alongside the buildings and pausing if he heard any sounds.

A block down, he slipped into the passageway behind his father's saloon. It provided a small entrance for some of the deliveries and also provided an escape hatch for those inside who might need it. A screen door hung heavy on its hinges. Emmet pushed it in slowly hoping that his father and Florian, the barkeep, would be at the bar. Gauging it was safe, he quickly opened the pantry door directly to the left.

The pantry was overflowing with supplies. His father often said he didn't want the well to ever run dry. Emmet did not know exactly what that meant but he too liked the abundance it provided. With the little light that came through the door vents, he looked around to see what was there and smiled when he spied his favorite. Dried fruit wrapped up in muslin.

He plopped down on the bit of floor space and got busy with the treat. When he had his fill, he edged over to the other pantry door. The pantry had two doors, one by the back and one that opened at the bar counter end. When Emmet peered out of the slits of the bottom vent, he could make out who was there.

He saw the fancy silver buckles on the boots first and knew right away that Dudley Shepardson sat at the end of the bar. People paid attention to Shepardson, his father especially so. He was the person that John Campbell seemed to trust the most in town. Emmet positioned his body to look up towards the man.

Shepardson possessed a head that seemed too large for his short height in Emmet's estimation. His face was adorned with thick dark mutton chops, long lashes around light-colored eyes and a moustache that dangled down equally but maybe farther than necessary on either side of his lips. Sometimes he played with the sides of the moustache.

His ears tuned in and picked up the thread of conversation between Shepardson and somebody he could not see. "...I'm from Kentucky and a lot of folk from home are here. We got the best folk in the world in Kentucky."

"Is that right?" the disembodied voice said, sounding none too interested. Emmet could relate as he had heard Shepardson talk about Kentucky too often himself.

"Hmm...I started out on the American River in El Dorado looking for the gold, no different from all the others maybe. But I struck out and now I got my sights here. There is a lot to be had here my friend. I'm trying my hand at the law now."

"The law?"

"Sure. All you gotta do is read some books. They don't got anyone lining up to handle all the legal trouble folk get up to here. So...why not me?"

The other man made a grunt.

Emmet could see a set of boots arrive behind the bar back and recognized them as his father's. "How you keeping tonight, Campbell?" Shepardson asked.

"Fair to middling, Shepardson. Yourself?" Emmet could not see his father from his angle in the pantry but he recognized the gravelly timbre of his voice. He could see the bottle of liquor that Campbell placed on the bar in front of Shepardson.

"Ah...Kentucky bourbon. The finest around. Good man." Emmet could hear liquid being poured into glass.

Shepardson pulled some papers out of his waistcoast pocket and waved them around saying, "We got some takers, Campbell."

What takers, Emmet thought.

He heard his father gulp down his drink as Shepardson said, "Well, what are you waiting for? Open them up."

Emmet heard the crinkling of paper and then his father gave a long sigh. "Huh. This one is a 49er's wife. Says she had lost her husband in one of the mines and is looking for a safe place to land. And she's got five young'uns.

"Her mistake for being honest," Shepardson said. "Read on."

His father read the next one aloud:

Dear Mr. ?,
I am interested in learning more about the arrangement you seek. I am recently located in Sacramento after venturing over from Sligo, Ireland. A strong and hardy worker, I am 24 years of age, good in teeth and bone. My first husband sadly passed on and I am a widow woman. Most would say I am easy enough on the eyes.
Sincerely,
Mrs. A. Ginty

There were two others, one that his father called an 'upstairs woman" trying to change her ways---and her fortunes. And one that his father said he couldn't make out the writing.

Emmet watched Shepardson stroke one side of his moustache after all were read. "I think you may want to start a correspondence with this Widow Ginty. She's probably a Catholic and not much can be done about that given where she's from. But that's okay, you can work around it." He paused and then added, "In the meantime, I'll try to find out through some folks in Sacramento if she's on the up and up."

"You going to write it up for me or…"

"Nah. It's up to you now."

"Fair enough." Emmet could hear more liquid poured into glasses and his father said, "You are a good friend to have, Shepardson." Then he added, "You gonna get a bride like this?"

"When the time is right, Campbell. When the time is right."

Emmet saw Shepardson tilt his glass, staring into its empty bottom. Emmet sat back on the floor and pondered what he had just heard. He stumbled out the other pantry door to the outside, his belly filled but his mind bogged down with questions.

He was so lost in thought he did not notice the big, dark and hulking figure until it was right in front of him and alcohol fumes filled his breathing space. Doc Robinson, holding a liquor bottle. In his cups again, Emmet assumed, as his father would call it.

"Who dat?" the man asked with a slur in his voice.

"Emmet Campbell."

"A lad your age should be abed at this time," Doc attempted a weak scold as he took in Emmet with bleary eyes under spectacles tilted to one side. His overcoat hung askew off his tall frame. Emmet sighed inwardly. He would have to help Doc to his house again. Something he had done other times.

Aloud, he said, "Come on, Doc. Let's get you home."

Emmet reached behind the older man's lower back to keep him from stumbling and nudged him towards Main Street. They made slow progress with Doc stopping to belch and cough every few yards. Emmet felt the sweat start to drip down his back as he supported the man's weight. They made it finally to the National Hotel and Doc grabbed the hitching post in front for support as he took a step up. He looked up at the sky and said, "See it up there? The moon?"

Emmet nodded in response, wanting to get on with the walk and finish his duty to the doctor. But Doc continued talking. "Did I ever tell you about the time that I met up with an Injun tribe on the trail?"

Without waiting for Emmet to answer, Doc went into a long-winded tale about Indians, buffalo and the like. Emmet waited for him to wind

35

down by hopping on one foot then the other. Doc broke off the tale and suddenly focused one bleary eye on Emmet with the other eye in a squint. "Boy, you were in the saloon again tonight, weren't you?"

Emmet gave a shrug in response, looking to the side. Doc looked up into the nothingness of the night and then looked back at Emmet saying, "Well, did you hear something you wanted to hear?"

Emmet thought about it and answered. "I heard some things I didn't want to hear."

Doc nodded. "That's usually the case when you listen in where you shouldn't." Then he took a faltering step off the National Hotel's porch with Emmet grabbing his arm just in time.

They continued all the way down Main toward the bridge across the Sacramento River where Doc's house sat. His office was attached to his residence with a shed roof. Once there, Emmet helped Doc up to the entrance of the house and grabbed the marble door knob to open the door. Doc stood in the threshold with a confused look as though he could not remember something. He rubbed on his bewhiskered cheeks before walking past Emmet and into the house, still unsteady on his feet.

Lurching his way to the dining room, he landed on a chair that creaked in protest. Emmet followed behind him and saw evidence of his earlier evening activities sitting on the table, numerous empty bottles and smoke butts smudged out on a plate.

Doc looked up at Emmet and said, "Did I ever tell you how I ended up in this place?"

Emmet shook his head.

"I came here like most people come to Colusa. To start over. Get away from that half-ass town in Missoura that I was from. They said I hurt that boy...but I never hurt him! I helped him is what I did."

His eyes blazed at the memory of whatever had happened to make him leave his home state. Emmet began to edge out of the room to make his escape. He knew from experience that if he didn't, he would be listening all night to Doc rail on. There was not much more he could do for the man now that he was safely back in his house.

As Emmet walked back to the rooms above the store, he thought that Doc was a good man but should probably hold off getting into the cups like he did. Once behind the store, he placed one foot to climb up the stairs but heard a low growl. He looked over to see the store cat, one-eyed with buff orange fur more torn up than tended to. "Ah, don't be like that, Sampson. Come on...you wanna come in?"

His father had told him Sampson was not allowed into their rooms but Emmet took the risk. Once Sampson settled in, Emmet looked at the glint of the cat's one gold eye reflected in the moonlight on the mattress. He had a lot of questions left in his mind.

Why was Dudley Shepardson involved with getting his father a mail-order bird? What was this place called Ireland? What did "easy on the eyes" mean? And what was a catholic? It would probably be better if he and his father could just go along as they were without all this aggravation. As Sampson's rough-sounding, ragged purr cut in, Emmet's mind let the questions drift off and finally found sleep.

Chapter Five

Emmet felt that sensation that Mary Benicia called butterflies build up in his stomach while he waited in the alley for his father's return from Sacramento. His father made supply runs to the big city about once a month but this run was different. This run would include the mail-order bird on the return trip.

He still had no idea of what kind of bird she was going to look like. Was she going to be like the robin with the red chest that sung by his chamber window in the mornings? Or one of those brown birds with the dark orange streaks on either side of their heads that he saw out at the ranch? Or maybe just a common field crow, black as night, that picked at the plowed fields? He shivered a little at that thought.

From his hiding place, he could peer out and watch the passersby, studying them in turn to relieve the boredom of waiting. Emmet liked to watch people when they didn't know they were being watched. They revealed more of themselves and he could understand who they were better.

Doc Robinson bustled down with his scarred leather bag filled with medicine slung over his shoulder. With his determined stride, Emmet figured the Doc was on his way to a house call. No falter in his step on this day. It was better to see him like this than the way Emmet encountered him in the nights.

He studied two women, Mrs. Smith and Mrs. Cheney, walking down the street each holding shopping bags chattering away like womenfolk always seemed to do. Women were mysterious to him, despite his time at Coopers' with Mary Benicia, her mother, Fanny, and her grandmother, Malinda. He was used to just living with his father for the most part. But now...that was changing with the bird's arrival.

Florian, his father's barkeep from a place called Germany, sauntered by with quick strides and a towel around his neck. A dapper man, he kept himself to himself, as Mary Benicia would call it. Emmet knew he took a morning bath in the river long before his shift at the Mount Hood Saloon.

Then there was Dudley Shepardson. When Shepardson stopped right outside the alley near the storefront, Emmet shrunk himself smaller. Leaning against a hitching post, Shepardson struck a match and lit one of those cigarillos he was so partial to. Maybe, like Emmet, Shepardson was waiting to catch sight of his father's bird.

Even though Emmet had known Shepardson as long as he could remember back, he had never liked the man. Emmet discovered early on that there were some he took to and some he didn't. Just like with animals.

Finally, he could see his father's wagon in the distance heading down Market from the east. As it came into view, he spied the woman seated next to his father. She sat straight with a ramrod spine and no hint of a smile anywhere near her face. Her dark hair was pulled back tightly behind her head and her eyes were squinty. He knew, of course, she wasn't going to be a real live bird but he half hoped she might look a little like one. But she didn't look like any of the birds he had ever seen. Not one bit.

As they pulled up to the store, Emmet hung back and watched as his father helped the woman down. She reached behind and pulled out a big wrapped bundle from behind the seat. Lifting the bundle up, some of it became uncovered and revealed a baby with its mouth opening into a big yawn. A baby. The bird had brought a baby with her.

Emmet caught the woman's stare at the building that was to be her home. While his father tied off the reins, he said in a voice that Emmet was unfamiliar with, "This is just temporary like. I'm working on my ranch house out on the farm land. You'll see it soon enough."

Emmet wondered why he lied like that. The house out there was not even close to being finished. As his father talked, the woman gazed around not saying anything. She stood a couple heads shorter than his tall father and it looked odd, the two of them standing next to each other.

Emmet crept backwards into the alley not knowing what to think about this new turn. As his father, the woman and the baby went into the store, his mind raced. Was he going to have to sleep with the baby? Was it a boy baby or a girl baby? Why had his father not told him about this?

He heard his father's voice bellowing for him in front of the store. "Emmet! Emmet! Emmet Campbell!"

He stood still for a second and then took off running down the other end of the alley to Main as though his life depended on it. He concentrated only on the feeling of his legs pumping harder and harder, nearly a tangle his appendages, until he reached the tunnel entrance. All he could hear was the sound of his beating heart as he worked his way into the underground room.

Old Man Chung sat alone in the room. He cast a doleful eye over in Emmet's direction. Emmet stood with his hands on hips while he caught his breath. When he was able to speak, he spit it out. "John Campbell brought a bird home from Sacramento and she's got a baby. The bird's got a baby."

Old Man Chung stared at him for a long second and gave a loud sniff. He rose stiffly and walked over to the side of the room. Pushing on the wall slightly, it opened to reveal a hidden niche of space. The niche sat back far enough so that anyone walking by would not notice. It was kitted out with a straw mat on the floor. "You stay here."

Emmet stared at the space. Should he do that? Leave his father? Maybe he should. Maybe he could move into the tunnels. But Old Man Chung added, "When you ready, you go back." When would Emmet be ready? That was the question.

After a night in the tunnels, loud with activity and uncomfortable, Emmet made his way back to the center of town when the sun began to rise but most of the town still slept. He snuck in the back door of the store and sidled into the storeroom. He sighed with relief as he curled up on the storeroom floor. Much better than the tunnels. He fell to sleep almost at once.

From the depths of his slumber, he heard voices talking in the store. He tried to shut his ears to the intrusion but eventually the talk seeped into his brain.

"I need some supplies to prepare our dinner, you understand. Not much to be had in the rooms upstairs..." The voice was female and strange sounding to Emmet. An accent he thought it was called. Not at all like the way people spoke in Colusa.

"Yes, I should have lain in more provisions. Time got away from me before going to get you in Sacramento. Too busy it seems." His father's voice. Again, it sounded unfamiliar to Emmet's ears. He was more careful with his words than normal. Not the way he usually talked.

The woman proceeded to tell his father what items she needed for the evening meal. They agreed that he would bring up the items and she would begin her preparations. Emmet stretched out one leg that had become stiff and it hit the door with a thud. The talk stopped.

"Do you have rats in here?" the woman asked.

The storeroom door was flung open and Emmet cowered, looking up at the face of his father on which so many emotions passed over at once. "This where you were all night?" his father said tersely, more in his regular voice.

Emmet looked up, saying nothing in response.

"Why didn't you come home last night? Well, never mind...come on out. Your new mother... and new sister are here."

Emmet did not move. Campbell raised his voice saying, "Come on, boy." He grabbed him roughly on one arm.

With Campbell's firm grip on his shoulders, Emmet was not able to squirm away. He brushed his hair out of his face and looked at her straight on. She sized him up with a critical gaze.

She reached out and touched the top of his head. "Look at the crop of hair on you! Hiding those big blue eyes. Never you mind...we'll fix you up."

Emmet looked at his father in alarm. His father's expression was neutral. What did she mean? He flinched under her touch and saw the corners of her mouth turn down before she quickly changed course and picked up her baby.

"So...It is nice to finally meet you, Emmet. I am...I am...your new mother. And you may call me that." She looked down at the baby in her arms and said, "And this is my little baby...uh...your new sister. Mary Ann is her name. Isn't she a prize?"

Emmet stared down at the baby with its large grey eyes and open gaping maw. She did not look like a prize to him. He turned to his father and asked, "Why she talk funny?"

The woman gave a cough that covered up maybe something else.

"She's got an accent that's all, boy. She came over from the old country...like Mrs. Walraith over on Jay Street."

"She done talk funnier than Mrs. Walraith."

The woman spoke up. "He doesn't favor you much, does he?"

Campbell scratched a spot on his neck and said, "Well, I guess he does...and he doesn't."

There wasn't much more to say and the new little family all looked in opposite directions wondering maybe what was to come next...

Emmet waited in the alley again until his father took the bird and her baby out by wagon to the ranch. He had managed to shrink away back out of the store. Once they were gone, he headed up to the rooms.

At the threshold, he stopped dumbstruck. Everything had shifted looking smoothed out and neatened. A mop and bucket were propped against one wall. The main room almost sparkled with clean.

He moved into the back room and a squawk came out of his mouth. All his things...his bird nests, his spider webs, his rocks...gone. The only thing other than the mattress that remained was his painting. He quickly tore it down from the wall and clutched it to his chest, heart pounding. The bird must have done all of it. Was this what his father meant about a woman's touch?

Back in the main room, he gazed around. The eating area was straightened and organized too with everything perfectly lined up on the shelves. There was even an odor in the air that smelled of freshly washed linen like he used to smell on Malinda Cooper's drying lines.

His eyes caught sight of a steamer trunk pushed off to one wall and he went over to it, lifting the brass clasp on the lid. Once opened, the fabric lining on the top and bottom brought a bit of color into the room. He ran his fingers over a faded, ornate pattern of geometric designs. She must have brought this with her from that old country his father talked about.

He began to pick through the items. Bits and bobs. Some jewelry and a tin photograph. He studied the image, a woman of some age who had the same eyes as the bird. Maybe it was her mother. The thought occurred to him that her mother might be dead like his. He shook the thought aside and kept digging through the trunk, not really knowing what he was looking for.

So distracted by what he was doing, he heard too late the sound of the door creaking open followed immediately by a voice shouting. "Emmet!" and "How dare you?" Her voice. That weird lilting tone called accent.

She strode into the space with her baby slung across her front. He looked up with a piece of satin cloth held in one hand and gaped at her. He knew what the color red coming off her and around her meant. Pure rage. He felt fear but, overlaying the fear, was a mild fascination at an ugly mole that was situated where her earlobe connected with her face.

Scrambling like a cornered animal, he skirted around her to the door. As he almost half-tumbled down the staircase, she yelled and screeched after him. At the bottom, he broke into a dead run.

Running away from the store toward Chinatown, he cast a look behind to see if she was following him. He got to the yellow plant and headed down into the tunnels. Early in the day, he knew he would be by himself. Making his way to the hidden niche that Old Man Chung had shown him and where he had slept some the previous night, he plopped down, alone at last.

The bird was now ensconced in his space. With her baby. Situating himself in the niche, he thought about the look on her face when she caught him going through her stupid trunk. It took a lot to scare him, but that look had done it. Who did she think she was? Going through all his things, throwing them away, rearranging and the like but yet he could not go through her things. It wasn't right.

He had seen something hard and cold in her eyes though. He knew she wasn't there to be his mama as sure as he knew the puffy smoke that he smelled down in the tunnels was not quite right. He sighed and picked some candies out of his trouser pocket. He tried to rub the dirt off before popping them into his mouth. Maybe she wouldn't last long. Maybe his father would become dissatisfied with her.

Chapter Six

The new makeshift family sat at the dinner table when a rap at the door caught everyone's attention. Prior to the rap, there had only been the sound of eating utensils hitting plates and the baby's gurgling noises. Emmet's father stood and the chair legs scraped along the floor. Opening the door, he let out a chuckle and said, "Well, look who it is."

Dudley Shepardson took his hat off and entered the room. Emmet took a sideways glance at Shepardson and noticed that the bird did the exact same. Shepardson broke the silence and bobbed his head saying, "Ma'am."

John Campbell stepped in the space between the two. "Mrs. Campbell, you remember Mr. Shepardson. Dudley Shepardson. He was at the store the other day."

"Mrs. Campbell" nodded with a thin smile.

"Have a seat, Shepardson," Campbell said, pulling up the only other chair available.

"Mighty kind of you."

The bird added, "And a plate too." She spooned out some of the hash onto the only additional plate in the house and placed a biscuit on the side.

"Much obliged...I'm glad for the opportunity to finally chat with Campbell's bride."

Emmet saw the bird look at Shepardson as though questioning what he said. She answered, "Yes, it is very nice here in Colusa. I'm well pleased to be here."

Emmet's father, as usual when he was around Shepardson, had a bemused look on his face. "What's the news?" he asked.

Before answering, Shepardson picked up a biscuit and examined it as though he had never seen one like it before. "Huh? Oh, not all that much. Mainly the arrival of Mrs. Campbell I would say."

He looked again at the bird and added, "So how long have you been in these parts, Mrs. Campbell?"

"Oh please, call me Ann. I don't stand on ceremony."

Emmet was taken aback. "Ann" was the bird's actual name...he didn't know anyone named Ann.

Shepardson nodded. "Okay, Ann. So..." She looked at him with inquiry on her face. He repeated his question. "I wondered how long you have been in California."

"Oh..." Her answer seemed to take some thought and an odd silence filled the room. Finally, she said, "Some years now...I think all total it has been eight."

Shepardson raised a brow. "Surely, you remember the year you hit the trail?"

"Well, I came the sea route, didn't I?"

"Cape Horn or Panama?"

She hesitated slightly. "Yes, it was down south that way, it was. Really quite something...But yourself, Mr. Shepardson...How did you come to be here?"

Emmet inwardly groaned knowing that Shepardson would take this opening to rail on with one of his stories. And he did begin to regale them with a tale of a group who had barely made it through the Isthmus, maybe forgetting or maybe not that the bird had not really answered the question.

Emmet let Shepardson's voice fade away into the background and instead concentrated on picking apart the stone hard biscuit that lay on his plate, layer by layer. He became so engrossed in the endeavor that he almost missed it when Shepardson brought up the fire.

"...so these are all new buildings down here since the fire. Yep...happened in September of '56. What a night that was..." He paused as if thinking of that night. "It wasn't all that long ago but we rallied and fixed up everything. What you see now is a whole different town."

"Hmmm..." the bird said as if she was imagining a different town, a different place.

46

Talk of the fire always brought it right back to Emmet. That horrible night where he felt as though he were clawing for breath. The big arms reaching down and scooping him off his straw tick mattress and away from all of it. His father's arms. He looked over to his father and saw him too shaking his head at the memory of it.

"Campbell here had to rebuild the whole store. Everything from the ground up again just as if he was back in town for the first time. Ain't that right, Campbell?" His father just gave a nod.

Shepardson gestured to Emmet and added, "And he almost lost this imp over here. Barely got him out of the building in time."

Again, the feeling of the scratchiness in his throat and the billowing smoke filling the room overcame Emmet. He stood up abruptly and made his way out of the rooms. His father called after him but he kept going. As he left, he heard Shepardson comment to the bird. "That boy..." And it hung behind him.

He walked the short distance out of the alley and across Main Street to the river. There was enough moonlight to see the ripple of waves battering into each other from the current. He stood just like that, listening.

After some time, he heard what he needed to hear. A meow. Getting louder and closer. Sampson had been immediately banished when the bird arrived. Emmet had not seen him since and feared the worst. He got down on one knee. "Come here, Sampson. Come here..."

He felt the cat first, slinking around his leg and twitching its tail. "Hey buddy. You're okay. I'm glad you're okay."

When the cat looked at him, his one gold eye glittered in the moonlight and it looked to Emmet like a smile. "Where you been anyways? I about gave up..." Emmet started a one-sided conversation, filling in Sampson on the events he had missed.

Sometime later, he reluctantly left Sampson at the riverbank and made his way back, saying in parting, "I'll bring you something to eat tomorrow. I promise."

The next morning, the bird (whom Emmet was trying to think of as Ann) was stirring something in a pot on the stove. When he walked in, she said, "Have a seat. Porridge is ready."

Despite his wariness, he was curious about what her porridge might taste like. And he was hungry. She placed a steaming bowl in front of him with a spoon. He put just a little on the spoon and took a taste.

Satisfied, he took a bigger amount especially drawn to the part laced with sweet syrup. He became so involved in the process that it stunned him to look up and see an expression of disgust on her face. He held the spoon in mid-air.

She caught herself, the disgust replaced by a neutral look. She pointed at the side of his face. "Your hair is caught in the porridge and is sticking to your face."

Emmet immediately reached over to work the porridge from the hair but it was not an easy effort. He never paid his hair much mind. Thick with a curl to it and cascading down his back in a mess of tangle, it had been left to grow unchecked for all of his born days. Which was about nine years and some change as best he knew.

When he was cared for out at Coopers, Malinda Cooper set him a birthdate of 10 February 1850 on account of the fact that his father had not been able to recall it. She made him a small cake on that date when he was there. He remembered her telling him one time, "In this house we celebrate the birth of our loved ones---just as we commemorate the deaths of them also."

Since being at Coopers, he couldn't count how many Februarys had passed by. But he thought he was about nine or so. Doc Robinson told him that he looked to be that age given his bones and teeth.

"After breakfast you are coming with me for some supplies." He looked up at her with surprise.

"Yes, that's right. It's too much to carry Mary Ann and the bags so..." He looked down and plowed back into the porridge bowl. At least the porridge was tasty.

Walking through town, the bird guided him toward Levee Street and took hold of his arm. He tried to shrug her off but she held firm as they got closer to Chinatown. They passed the small shops that the Chinamen had set up, meager as compared to the other side of town, but nonetheless just as busy. A few men were out on the street tending to their storefronts, sweeping the walks in front or moving about in some other way. Always in the constant motion of doing. Emmet puzzled over the fact that these men didn't have much and yet worked so hard. He wondered if the bird had ever seen people from China in the flesh before.

Emmet felt anxiety mounting up. Did the bird know about the tunnels somehow? Did she know about Old Man Chung helping him? Did she know about his place of refuge?

A line of cowboys five or so deep stood away from the Chinamen's box stand on Levee Street parallel to the river where something was written in strange lettering. Emmet figured it said hair or barber since that is what the men were waiting for. A couple of the Chinese men set up a wooden box stand on Tuesday of every week. Emmet noticed an uptick on those days of cowboys coming to town wanting a clean shave with a straight edge razor and trimmed hair. Later, the brothels and saloons would get busier than usual for a week night.

The bird stopped towards the back of the line still holding his arm tightly. He didn't quite know why she wanted to stand and watch but he looked at the men in front of him with sheer adoration and a slightly open mouth. Both Ann and Emmet and even Mary Ann now at Ann's feet watched with riveted attention as the cowboys from the range fully placed their trust in a Chinaman holding a razor with a steady grip so close to their gullets.

Emmet never watched the process this close up before and he became so engaged he didn't realize until too late that Ann pushed him forward and said to the Chinese barber, "He needs a real close cut." The barber looked at Ann and was silent, his hands still.

The cowboy in line behind them spoke up. "He don't have English, ma'am. Just show him with your hands."

The bird let an "Oh for goodness..." slip out and then stopped herself. She touched Emmet's curls and ran a line with her finger to the point where it needed to be chopped and then made a cutting gesture. It was the first time Emmet had let her close enough to touch him again and he quickly shrugged her hand away.

"Now, Emmet. I want you to obey this man and do as he says. We will be finished in no time."

So enamored with the cowboys, it had not quite dawned on him that he would be getting work done as well. Now it was too late. He could not embarrass himself in front of all the cowboys and ranchers.

The Chinaman took his first snip. The ground below slowly filled up with Emmet's locks, matted and different lengths. The Chinaman held a cracked handheld looking glass in front of Emmet's face and grunted.

Emmet stared into the mirror with a stunned expression and said, "Why?"

"It's much better now, Emmet. You look like a proper boy. Like the boys I used to see on the streets of Liverpool. Proper like."

"I ain't..."

"Don't say 'ain't.'"

Emmet pushed the words out with effort. "Ain't...proper boy. Ain't Liverpuddle."

The cowboy behind them in line gave a loud guffaw but sobered enough to say, "Boy, you mind your mama."

"She ain't," Emmet said, his voice shaky. "She ain't my mama."

Chapter Seven

Emmet sat next to his father on the wagon seat as John Campbell cracked the whip to send the oxen on their way. The wagon held the last load of goods needed to complete the move from the rooms above the store on Main Street to the newly built ranch house three miles due south of town. Behind them was a haphazard pile that included a four-poster bed frame, a wash tub and board, chairs and a rolled-up rug among other sundries.

Emmet cast a glance at his father, his profile as inscrutable as ever. The time spent with the bird and her baby in the rooms had gotten to be a muddle. The baby grew bigger day by day, walking and talking. Taking up too much space.

The only good part about the bird and her baby in their lives was the regular meals in Emmet's mind. He eyed his father again and noted that his girth seemed less lean from her cooking. Emmet looked down at his own belly but it appeared flat as usual.

The edge of town quickly opened up to wide expanses as they traveled the route from town to the ranch. Emmet took in the vast stretch of mixed land in front of him, some fields and some wetlands, only marked by the geese that took over the skies during late fall in Colusa when a nip came into the air.

He knew his father had pushed himself to get the ranch built and move-in ready before the coldest weather set in. His father said to him over the loud creaking of the wagon wheels and the wind, "Now that we are out here, you'll have plenty of space to keep you occupied. You hear, boy?"

Emmet slid a sideways glance his way but did not answer. Campbell repeated in a louder tone, "You hear?"

Emmet only grunted in response. He planned on beating a path back to town at every opportunity. Sampson needed tending to...when

Emmet could find him at the river's edge. Besides, he couldn't fathom being holed up in the new ranch house out here with her all day long. She would probably try to harness him to a chair and go over those letters and numbers again which his mind could not absorb on any level. Just like in that classroom, it did not come to him and maybe it never would. He couldn't be bothered by it.

He recalled the conversation overheard between the bird and his father, not that she was trying to keep her voice down. Maybe she even wanted him to hear it.

"I don't know that he has the wits to learn this, Campbell."

"Oh, come now," his father answered.

"You give it a try, why don't you?" she replied tartly back.

"Are you saying he's a...a...dolt?"

"That's exactly what I am saying! Did you drop him on his noggin when he was babe?"

Getting no response from Campbell, she made a noise of frustration and rounded the corner almost bumping right into Emmet. She stopped and they stared at each other. She finally broke the stare and pushed past him.

Emmet shook the memory off as he saw the new ranch home rise up ahead with the majestic buttes right behind as backdrop. A small curling of smoke spiraled up from the chimney, a sort of welcome. He breathed in the tang of sharp, cold air wondering what awaited him inside.

When they were almost to the ranch, his father turned towards him. "Being out here in the open space will do you good. Do us all good." Emmet figured he was trying to reassure himself of that more than Emmet.

Emmet twirled the spoon in the porridge making curvy furrows in the crock. Time at the ranch house was still brand-new but, just as he suspected, the bird forced him to sit with a primer, slab of slate and a slate pencil after breakfast in the mornings. This usually led to some upset or the other when he didn't "cooperate" as she put it. Sometimes she would force him to go into his small, window-less chamber room if she deemed it necessary. He usually managed to sneak out and escape into town after things had cooled off for a bit.

As he let out a big sigh of resignation, he looked up to see Mary Ann staring at him with those big gray eyes. He saw that she had finished, her bowl empty. A stab of irritation went through him how she just sat and waited for her mama's next instruction. Maybe he could get a laugh or two out of her.

He flicked some of his porridge in her direction just to shake that stare up. Instead of laughing though, she let out a sudden and ear-piercing scream, the likes of which he had never heard from her. A scream like she was being branded with the hot iron they used on the cattle.

Ann whipped around from the cook stove. Emmet watched in fascination as a wave of red color came up from her neck and over her entire face. The look turned into words of fury that she let out in a torrent. He caught them in pieces in his ears. "You are an idiot, an ingrate, an imbecile..." He didn't know what most of them meant but he could figure out their intent.

He skittled back from the table, porridge abandoned, as she descended on him like a storm. Her hands reached him around the neck and hoisted him into his small chamber room with a strength she didn't know she had. He had always gone in on his own when she told him to. Never like this.

He stood in the center of the tiny room, stunned. He only meant it as a little prank. It was nowhere near the stunts that the town bullies pulled on him. Nothing like that. It was just to get some reaction out of her. Some attention.

He heard the hammering first then saw the closed door begin to shake. Was she nailing him in? He slumped to the floor, unmoored at the idea of being trapped in this space. No window and only an iron bed frame and straw tick mattress. Nothing else.

He couldn't do it. He couldn't stay in the room like an animal in a trap. He leapt up and pounded on the door. He worked his fingers into the edges of the doorframe trying to find any purchase to rip it away. He kept at it, adding his teeth even. Then he slammed himself against it over and over again. In between poundings, he listened. Only the sound of Mary Ann's babbling and the movements of the bird walking to and fro were on the other side.

He didn't know how many hours had passed by when he heard the creak of the wagon wheels on his father's rig. Sprawled on the floor, his fingers bloody, his mouth raw and his body bruised from working to get out, he had no energy to yell out anything else.

Lying there, he heard her chirp at his father on the other side. Then just silence. Finally, the noise of the door being pried open came loud and jagged in his ears. The door flung open and John Campbell looked down on him on the floor, shock visible on his face. His gaze took in Emmet before moving around the room where Emmet had thrown the bed frame against the walls and the floor. The room was as battered as he was. His father's eyes ended up at the bite marks along the door frame edges.

Campbell whirled around where the bird stood right behind him. He backhanded her once and she gasped, putting her hand to where she had been struck. His voice came out like a low growl. "Never again."

Casting his exhaustion aside, Emmet did not hesitate. He scurried out on hands and knees fleeing into the night. He heard his father coming out of the house calling for him but he kept going. He took in gulps of the crisp night air, feeling the cold hit the parts of his body that hurt.

With this second wind, he ran the entire three miles to Chinatown. Moving his body began to lessen the jangling of his nerves and the upset inside him. When he got to town, he slowed down to a trot and then a walk, eventually stumbling down the stairs into the tunnels.

He sagged like a bag of potatoes dropped onto the floor. The men at the table looked over in surprise. Old Man Chung gazed at him with an astute eye. It felt like his old friend read something on Emmet's face before gesturing to a seat next to him and saying, "Sit."

Emmet sat down in a daze. He had never been invited to a seat at the card table before. "I teach. You learn," said Old Man Chung.

Despite the gruesomeness of the day, Emmet felt a spark of something. A spark of delight. After all the months of spying on this game from the shadows and the sidelines, he was being offered something. A chance to learn the game the men called Fan-Tan.

The card game dominated the tables down in the tunnels and captivated most of the men who spent time down there when they were not otherwise occupied with the pipe and its smoke. Emmet had watched it being played many times over trying to understand it. Now he stared at the cards as they fluttered quickly with Old Man Chung's shuffling. He lost himself in the action and let it take him away from the ranch and everything there.

Old Man Chung half stood up and pulled out a purse from his pocket. "How many?" he asked each man around the table. He threw down their "chips." Emmet had snuck peeks before at the chips which were really a combination of buttons, dried beans and pebbles.

The elderly man followed that by tossing cards out to each player. Sitting back in his seat with his cards in hand, he gestured with a finger for Emmet to move closer. They stared at the cards together and then Chung pointed at two of them and nodded. Emmet screwed up his face trying to count up what the card numbers meant. It was right there----he just needed it to come in a little clearer.

The elderly man handed his bet of several chips to Emmet who threw them into the battered metal bowl in the center of the table as he knew from watching other times. Emmet looked at the other men from the corners of his eyes to see what they would do. After scrunched up facial expressions and some snorts, they eventually all threw their chips into the bowl also.

With a grunt, Old Man Chung dumped the bowl out. Grabbing the bamboo stick that sat next to him, he waited for each player to play out a round. Then, with the stick, he pulled away a mysterious number of chips that somehow tied into the hand that lost.

After all rounds were played out, there was one card left, one number left. It was Old Man Chung's card. He held it up. He was the winner. The number on the card rippled in front of Emmet's eyes. It came to him finally, popping into his mind, that the number was two. He said it aloud and Old Man Chung let out a cackle and patted Emmet's shoulder. "You bring good luck!"

Chapter Eight

Emmet sat and waited upon a hummock, rare amongst the flat lands of the ranch. A year and some months had passed since that horrible day, maybe the worst day ever in his life, when the bird's anger rose to a level he had never seen prior. And didn't want to see again. He made sure to never be alone with her---ever.

The new grass growing in felt soft under his hands. The wind whistled around his ears as the sun set down behind the buttes. His buttes, he liked to think of them. He could stare at them for hours, and sometimes he did just that, never tiring of their mystery. Especially to avoid being around her.

In the distance, he could hear a wagon moving closer. His father, back from the store or maybe the Mount Hood Saloon. Emmet stepped off from the hummock and stretched, breathing in the smells of the ranch and of spring. As Campbell made his way from the stable to the house, Emmet hastened over towards him.

He could smell something good cooking as he headed in behind his father. She would never refuse him food she cooked. At least there was that. Once, in an unusual moment of confidence, she told him some story about the place where she was from having no food to go around. She broke off talking about it and stared off into space before finishing with, "It was a terrible thing. I'll never stand by and see anyone go hungry like that again. Never." He figured that was why there was always enough food to go around whenever he came back to the ranch.

At the noise of Emmet behind him, Campbell looked over and said, "How do boy?"

"Right as rain I am."

Campbell's mouth corners lifted up at the turn of the phrase Emmet used. "Straight from a cowboy's mouth..."

The late spring days meant plowing at the ranch so Emmet spent days outside there with less time in town and in the tunnels. Campbell hired enough cowboys to help out but Emmet joined in the fray. The prepping of the land involved hoeing the rows and readying them for the seeds to come in behind them. Some hand-held machines were borrowed from their neighbor, Jerry Powell, when possible, to hurry things along.

The noonday meal included the cowboys and sometimes Jerry Powell making for a livelier than usual affair in Ann's kitchen. Emmet tuned into every word uttered from the mouths of the cowboys, every turn and phrase. He was going to be a cowboy someday. There was no finer job around in his mind. He particularly liked the way they cussed right in front of her. She had to hold her tongue because they needed those cowboys to get the ranch up and running and she knew it.

His father opened the door and walked in, Emmet right behind him. The space was filled in with possessions since their moving in. The most recent possession was a grandfather clock that sat against the wall opposite the chimney, ticking slow and steady. Emmet looked at it, staring at its shiny hands. Its newness. The bird was feathering her nest, just like he noticed real birds did out on the plains and in the woods.

He recalled one night when his father protested an expense and she scolded him, but in a light tone. "We Campbells are becoming a family of wealth and prominence in the community and our household needs to look the part!"

Mary Ann was propped up at the new pine farm table with slate pencil in hand, her little brow furrowed with concentration deep into the mysteries of letters and numbers. Already figuring it out at her young age of four. Emmet felt a rush of anger that she could and he could not. But he had tried...

Mary Ann looked up at their arrival and hurriedly gathered it all up as though fearful it would be taken away. She tended to be leery of both Emmet and Campbell. Emmet couldn't really fault her for that.

Emmet cast his gaze over the main living area with the hearth at one end. An iron kettle hung low over the fire and was filled with a stew for supper. The pine table with its one end close to the hearth was the place the bird and Mary Ann spent most of their hours. An oil lamp near the table threw out a rosy glow providing light as day waned into night.

Beyond the hearth and kitchen area, Ann had set up a seating area with a large horsehair-stuffed settee and some hard-backed chairs. A bearskin rug procured in trade at Campbell's store lay in front of the seats. She always seemed to carry her goose feather duster around touching up all the surfaces and ogling her possessions as she did so.

Another oil lamp was situated on top of his father's desk in the far corner where he worked on his figures and books in the evenings. A ledger always sat atop open for all to see. Whenever Emmet passed by it, the numbers were still only a jumble to him.

Now Ann greeted the both of them with the barest of nods and headed over to the hearth. The chill from the outside hung about both Emmet and his father as they pulled their seats to the pine table. Ann bustled between the cook stove and the table, setting things just so. Steam rose from the large crockery that held meat stew redolent with gamey odors. Emmet felt his stomach stir in response.

He looked around the table as Ann parceled out the stew in each bowl. Mary Ann gazed up at Ann with the adoration she always showed her, her face shiny as though just freshly scrubbed. His father, eyes heavy and hooded from the day's toils, picked up the bowl with fingers stained from tobacco as the smell of it glided off his person. Ann herself stood over them all, handing out a piece of corn pone to each before sitting down.

Ann, as always, said the meal blessing, her and Mary Ann with folded prayer hands, while Emmet and Campbell sat ramrod straight waiting for it to be over. Only then did they all dig into the meal in front of them.

After a few bites, Emmet looked up and noticed that Ann's expression was odd as though she tasted something wrong. He gave a furtive look his father's way to see if he noticed but he was too engaged in eating what was in front of him.

Campbell finally took a pause at plowing through the meal and started up with his new favorite topic of discussion, Southern states breaking off from the North. The political cause of the South had struck a chord with his father and had him more stirred up than Emmet had ever seen before. Emmet quickly lost the thread of it and let his mind wander to other places. He realized too late that Campbell asked him a question that Emmet hadn't answered. "Answer me, boy!" his father barked out.

"What?"

"I asked if you liked the stew."

Emmet bobbed his head in response.

Ann put her spoon down in an abrupt manner and Emmet jerked in her direction, not knowing if she was annoyed at his lack of response. Instead, she said, "So...we have an event soon to happen."

Campbell stopped mid-bite with his spoon in hand while Emmet put both hands on the edge of the table as if readying himself. Mary Ann just smiled at her mother in that same adoring way. Ann continued to speak. "Yes...in the fall sometime, I think. It will happen in the fall."

"What will happen?" Campbell asked.

"A new family member will be coming."

Campbell dropped his spoon and his eyes opened wide.

"You don't say? Well, how about that?"

His face crinkled into a grin. He looked over at Emmet. "You hear that boy? A new sister...or brother...soon."

"A brother," Ann said with a decisive tone.

"How do you...well, either way that is some grand news. Yes, indeed."

Mary Ann began to chatter with excitement about babies this and babies that.

"What month do you think?" Campbell asked over Mary Ann's chatter.

"In the fall...maybe after harvest time. But babies can be on their own time, you know," Ann said.

Emmet tuned all of it out as he let the idea settle in. He didn't quite know what to make of it...good or bad. Maybe a little of both.

Chapter Nine

Emmet fanned his cards out close to his face, eyes peeking above the tops. He tried to read the expressions of the men around him. A man named Dong sat directly across from him. His right eye, scarred above, tended to wander off to the side. Another man, Feng, with the bad knee, sat to the right of him. Old Man Chung was to his left.

He had perfected his skills at the game catching on despite not having a knack with numbers. In fact, he often bested Dong and the better players. But not Old Man Chung. He never knew why the elderly man let him into the fold that night. Maybe it was because he was just a kid. Or maybe it was something else.

In the last round, he placed his card down and won. He watched as Old Man Chung scraped the pebbles his way. He did it. He finally beat Old Man Chung.

"Bah!" Dong said and got up quickly, leaving the table. Feng shrugged, got up and limped away. Old Man Chung lifted his head back and laughed in that rapid-fire cackle he had. The noise reminded Emmet of the woodpeckers with the bright red stripes he studied out on the plains.

As Old Man Chung lifted his head up and down, his mouth gaped open and revealed the gold-capped teeth inside. The gold teeth fascinated Emmet and he pondered where the metal came from. Had it come from the mines out in the Sierras that everybody talked about? Ghost mines they were called now.

Emmet felt a giggle begin to tickle his throat and he joined in, without really knowing why they were laughing. The two of them laughed together to a beat only they connected to while the other men in the room looked on in curiosity.

Eventually, Old Man Chung sat back in his chair with a bemused expression on his face as he lit his pipe. He eyed Emmet up. "What you use money for?"

Emmet looked at him with confusion. He wondered if the elderly man was angry that he had won. The man pressed him further and said, "You have house. You have foods. What you need money for?"

Emmet looked down at the floor and scuffed his boots from side to side. He looked up and said, "I can give it back if you want."

Old Man Chung lifted a hand and said, "Nah, nah. Don't want your money. You earned it. Just want to know what you do with it."

It occurred to Emmet that his friend might think he was using it for bad things. He needed to set him straight. He took a breath in. "I'm stocking up...." He paused and then continued, "One day she'll kick me out and I won't have a house or food."

Old Man Chung narrowed one eye and studied Emmet's face. Emmet tried to explain further as best he could. "Dunno when that day will be. But she's got another baby coming soon... so it could be tomorrow or the next day or maybe later. I just dunno..."

Old Man Chung nodded. "You be a'right, boy. You be a'right."

Several nights later, Campbell flung the door open to Emmet's chamber, his silhouette outlined by the light from a full harvest moon.

Emmet sat halfway up saying, "Whaa?"

"It's time, boy. I need you to get the midwife. Widow Talbot on Jay Street. You know the place."

Wiping sleep out of his eyes, Emmet sat upright and leapt from his rope bed. His half-brother was coming soon. He knew it would be a brother. Not because she thought so but because sometimes, he just knew things.

The cold frost in the November air wrapped around him tightly as he ran to the stable. He put a set of bridle and reins over the head of the Spanish horse he liked the best, the one he had a spark with. With no time for a saddle, he flung himself in one swift motion over the horse's back and dug in his heels. The horse took off underneath him towards town with only the light of the moon to guide them. But Emmet knew every blade of grass from there to town anyway.

Someone told him that babies liked to make their arrival based on the moon cycles. He glanced up at the perfectly shaped moon and thought this baby had picked a good one. He didn't know what the baby would be called. He heard her say she would name him John after his father. Emmet questioned why his own mother had not named him that. Why had she named him Emmet? It churned around in his mind. His name. His father's name. The new baby's name.

The dark hulks of buildings filled in the landscape as he made his approach into town. The town slept all quiet with the exception of the occasional soft whinny of a horse and a few other animal sounds in a yard. He almost forgot to guide the Spanish horse onto Jay Street.

As he came up to the Widow Talbot's house, he quickly slung the reins over her horse post and sprinted up to the porch, wincing at the noise of it loud and grating in the night. He lifted his hand to raise the door knocker but stopped just before banging it down. But she would be used to these interrupted slumbers in the night, he thought, and banged it down hard.

After a few moments, he heard rumblings from the upper story and he stepped off the porch looking upwards. A window screeched open on the second floor and a voice bellowed. "Who's down there?"

"Emmet Campbell, Miz Talbot."

"Is it her time then?"

"Yes, ma'am."

The window shut and Emmet scratched his head. He guessed that meant she would come down. He strode back and forth in front of the house until the front door was flung open and the rotund form in black garb came out, looking wide awake as if it were broad daylight.

"Help me hitch my wagon, boy," she ordered while heading to her carriage house.

Once the wagon was set, Emmet led off with his mount, the Widow following behind in her wagon. He felt as though he had been gone for days when they approached the ranch and he could see his father outside, pacing.

Helping the Widow down from her seat, Campbell handed the reins over to Emmet. As he did so, Emmet could see the visible sign of relief on his father's face. He was not alone in this any longer in whatever "this" was going to be. Emmet had seen farm animals give birth before but not humans. He guessed it might be similar but he did not rightly know for sure. He took his time in the ranch stable, afraid of what he might be walking back into.

Emmet sat next to his father as the long siege wore on through the night. Mostly because the noises from the birthing room did not allow for much sleep even though Mary Ann seemed to do so. As the spidery streams of light came through the window from the breaking dawn, he realized the godawful sounds had petered out. He nudged his father whose head was slumped onto his shoulder.

"Huh?" Campbell sat straight up and looked around the room with bleary eyes.

"She ain't screaming no more."

Campbell looked toward the door to the bedroom. "Widow Talbot would tell us if something happened."

Emmet did not know if it was a statement or a question so he said nothing. He itched to get outdoors now that it was light but was obligated to his father on this for reasons he didn't even really understand. He wanted to get up and walk away from all of it. As though she sensed his restlessness, the Widow came out from the bedroom.

"You need to get Doc Robinson. She's run out of steam for this I'm afraid to say." Her brow furrowed with worry. "The baby is too big I suppose." She looked at Campbell in an accusatory way. Campbell lowered his eyes which Emmet found puzzling. Why would it be his fault that the baby was too big?

Shrugging it all off, Emmet was glad for the opportunity to leap up from his chair. "I'll go get Doc now."

Outside, he took in a gulp of fresh air shaking his head to cast the tired away. The Spanish horse galloped all the way to town with the sun rising as they made their progress into town. They skirted east where Doc's house sat on Main Street almost to the bridge across the Sacramento River.

Knowing Doc's late-night habits down at the saloons, Emmet went right to the door of the house. He pounded on it and then pounded some more. In time, he could hear Doc cussing on the other side. When the door flew open, Doc, bleary-eyed with spectacles at a tilt, took in Emmet. "What in the blazes, Emmet Campbell? You know what time it is?"

"I know it, Doc, but Widow Talbot sent me for you..." He hesitated, searching for the word he needed to describe her. "My...she...my father's wife is in a bad way. Having the baby."

Comprehension passed over the doctor's face at the same time that he rubbed over his whiskers with one hand. "All right, all right. Give me a few."

He turned on foot and Emmet followed him in. The usual evidence of the previous night sat on his table just like Emmet had seen other times. Butts of smokes smashed into a plate, empty glass bottles and a half-eaten loaf of bread.

Pulling on his overcoat, he grabbed his scarred leather satchel and walked past Emmet out the door, unsteady on his feet. Emmet's nose picked up the scent of alcohol emanating from the man's skin and hoped it was all out for Ann's sake.

Emmet followed after Doc Robinson to the ranch with the sun fully rising to the east. Once there, he hung back from going inside letting the door close behind Doc. Instead, he stood and looked over to the buttes, not knowing what to do with himself. But knowing that he did not want to stay there. He jumped back onto the Spanish horse and galloped back to town, all of the landscape passing by him in a blurred vision.

At the end of Main Street, he took his horse near the river and tied her off on a strong sapling. He moved with a heaviness in his tread to the tunnels, the fatigue like a weight around his neck. He was too tired to run errands for his usual customers, too tired to check in at the saloon to see if his father's barkeep, Florian, needed help, too tired to do anything other than stumble down into the hidden niche where he could be alone. He snuggled into his safe space giving in to the weight of the fatigue and letting it take over.

When he woke, he heard the sound of shuffling cards and looked over at the table. Old Man Chung sat there alone. "You go back now, yes?"

Emmet lifted himself up and stretched. "All right."

He plopped himself down on the floor nearby and said, "She's having the baby." The elderly man nodded and continued shuffling.

Once out of the tunnels, Emmet blinked his eyes in the late afternoon sunlight letting them adjust to the difference from the tunnels. After collecting his horse, he walked it down Market towards the store to see if his father was there. Along the way, Dudley Shepardson stood out in front of his office holding a cigarillo aloft and looking straight at Emmet.

"Heard Doc Robinson is at the ranch. Any news yet?"

Emmet shrugged as a response.

"Give your daddy my best. And your mama too."

"She ain't my mama," he said under his breath.

Shepardson said to Emmet's departing back, "Boy, you need show some respect for that woman." The words hung in the air behind Emmet.

Not finding his father at the store, Emmet made his way back to the ranch, this time letting the horse take a slow, leisurely-paced walk. As he got closer, he could see that Doc's horse was gone but the Widow's wagon was still hitched. He sighed. When was this ever going to end?

Walking inside, Emmet saw his father's back turned as he faced the fire in the hearth. He was hunched over and holding something. As Emmet approached closer, he saw it was a bundle. Looking up, Campbell gave a half smile. "This is your brother. Come closer, take a look."

Emmet stared down into the mushed-up face of the baby. "He looks like a dried-up fig."

Campbell let out a bark of laughter. "Well, he had a helluva time getting here so no wonder."

"What's his name?"

"John." He added, "John William Campbell."

Emmet felt a hard knot begin to form in his gut. This baby getting the name he should have gotten. Then he thought he should ask, "Did she..."

"Yes, she'll be all right Doc thinks."

"Oh," Emmet said, knowing that was good since this little prune-faced thing needed a mother. He knew too well about needing a mother.

The Widow Talbot bustled out of the bedroom, closing the door behind her. Shaking her head and talking to herself, she looked up and saw the Campbell males looking at her, baby included.

She said with some vehemence in her tone, "Campbell, don't get her in the family way again. She won't make it through another."

Emmet looked at his father to see what he would say but he just looked down at the baby saying nothing.

Chapter Ten

Emmet watched from the end of the counter as Baby John's chubby little legs moved up and down. His father held the scale's weight as Ann placed a hand on the baby's belly to steady him enough for a reading. Mary Ann peered around the side of the scale, always eager to be right next to the baby she considered "hers."

"Looks to be eighteen pounds and some ounces," Campbell announced.

Ann smiled broadly. "Ah...my bonnie prince. A stone and then some. A right good weight for getting on three months old now."

Campbell pointed at the baby's toes and reached down tentatively to touch them. "Look there. Why are his toes like that?"

Emmet moved closer to see what his father was pointing to. He could feel Ann bristle as he leaned in. Since the baby's birth, she didn't much like Emmet being near him.

"Celtic toes, they are. They come from my people. Others in my family have them—all of my brothers. It's a good sign." All of them looked down at the tiny little digits connected with webbed skin at the second and third toe of each little foot. Ann often shared strange beliefs from her homeland that Emmet really didn't know were true or not.

She lifted Baby John off the scale, dusting some flour off his bottom. The baby gave her a toothless grin and reached for her ear. She chomped down on his little fingers and laughed as they all looked on. "We can give Doc Robinson a good report about the baby's weight...he'll be well pleased," she said. Emmet doubted that Doc would care a whit.

The bell clanging on the door diverted attention away from the scale, the baby and the toes. Mrs. Brown stood in the doorway, taking measure of the little family. Emmet recalled hearing Dudley Shepardson talk about her once saying, "She's a gossipmonger if there ever was one. You'd be well advised to keep a distance if you like your business to be your own."

Campbell walked over and bade her good morning, asking how he could help her. "I'll take three yards of that calico cloth I was looking at the other day, Mr. Campbell," she said in an imperious tone.

As Campbell headed to the shelf that held the big rolls of cloth, Mrs. Brown sauntered over to the others. "Well, good day to you, Mrs. Campbell. Your baby looks quite well." She cast a discerning eye towards Baby John as though looking for imperfections.

"Yes, indeed he is that."

Campbell at the other end of the counter worked silently cutting the cloth off the roll but kept a careful watch on the women. Mrs. Brown turned her gaze from the baby and over to Emmet, staring. "Can we say the same for young Emmet here?"

"Pardon me?" Ann asked. Mary Ann left the buttons she was playing with and circled around her mother and brother. Mrs. Brown repeated what she said with some irritation in her voice.

Hearing the discussion, Campbell bustled towards the two women and interjected with a forced chuckle. "Emmet makes his way around town, Mrs. Brown. You know that."

Mrs. Brown gathered herself up like a hen ruffling her feathers. "Of course I know that, Mr. Campbell. Everyone in town knows that. Haven't we all practically raised the poor little devil in the early days with you at the store or saloon most nights? And now…"

She looked pointedly at Ann. "Are you aware young Emmet has been keeping time in the Blue House of late?" Emmet shrank back towards his old hiding place, the storeroom, where he felt safe from whatever life was trying to throw at him.

He tugged the door shut behind him, closing off all of them. He sniffed in the familiar smell of the place. A mix of various grains with a bit of rotten overlay of some item spoiling. He thought about Mrs. Brown's sneer when she referred to the Blue House, one of the most popular spots on Main Street, filled with ladies in frilly dresses and painted-on faces.

His first adventure at the Blue House was Florian's fault. Florian had been rooting around for something in the Mount Hood storeroom and came out with a cross expression and a couple of cuss words flying out of his mouth. He spotted Emmet in front of him and said in his thick German accent, "I need you to run over to da Blue Haus for me."

Emmet shook his head no. He did run errands for the ladies that hung about some nights on the streets but his father made it clear that he was not to enter the Blue House and the other establishments like it in Colusa---houses of ill repoot, he called them. Emmet didn't much understand what that meant but he knew he would catch heat if he went inside them. "My father..."

Florian put a finger to his mouth and cut him off by saying, "It will be a little secret. Dat's okay."

Florian pulled out paper and ink and made quick work of writing out a note. After waving it in the air for the ink to dry, he folded it in half. "Sneak in the back just like you do here. Find the big German man with the bald head. Not handsome like me."

When Emmet hesitated to take the note from Florian's outthrust fingers, Florian pressed it on him and said, "It is fine." Florian was his friend. He had never done him a bad turn before. So, Emmet would do it. He would go inside the Blue House. He nodded to Florian.

Sneaking out into the night, Emmet crossed Fifth Street and entered the alley that ran between Main and Market. A block further in the direction of the Blue House, his ears started to fill with the sounds of loud voices, raucous laughter and clanking glass.

The back entry was not too unlike his father's place and he pushed the door in slowly, making his way into the tight dark hall. He came out into a brightly lit space that revealed a full pageant of humanity. His mouth hung open slightly as he took it all in. The ladies like bright, darting birds, flitting here and there. The cowboys loudly one upping each other. The piano man pounding on the ivory keys of the large baby grand piano in the middle of the room.

Wrapped up in their own doings, no one cast a glance his way. He caught himself and quickly shuffled off to behind the bar where a large, bald-headed man stood drying out glasses with a towel.

"Ach...you too young for dis place. Out you go!"

"Here," Emmet said in response. "From Florian."

The man took the note and read its contents. He laughed out loud.

"Okay, okay. I owe him more than this, I s'pose." He reached under the counter and pulled out a bottle of liquor. "Take this back to him and mind you don't drop it."

Emmet felt a whisper of cloth touch his arm and looked up to see a woman with beautiful, light-colored eyes gazing at him. "Who's your little friend, Scheibman?"

"What is your name?" the big man asked.

"Emmet Campbell."

The lady lifted her eyebrows. "Is your father, John Campbell?" Emmet nodded.

"He's starting you out pretty young, ain't he?" she asked.

Emmet stayed still, not knowing what to say as the man and the woman broke into laughter.

"Well, we can at least give you a tour now that you are here, can't we, Scheibman? Come with me, little fellow." The lady hooked her arm over his and her sweet perfume flowed over him.

"Lookee here fellas..." She paraded around the room with Emmet on her arm like a house pet. He got a lot of back clapping and grins and felt a warmth come over him. Feeling at home in this place but not at home at the same time.

As they made their way to the corner of the room, Emmet saw Dudley Shepardson seated with a young lady pulled onto his lap. He looked at Emmet with bleary eyes, almost to the point of crossed. "Why, Emmet Campbell. Why you here?" he slurred out.

The lady patted Dudley with her free hand and said, "Now, now. We are showing him a grand time. Just keep it under your hat, Dudley." She gave him a big wink with one of those beautiful eyes.

Once back by the end of the bar, the lady took Emmet by both shoulders and said, "You come back most any time to visit, you hear, little man?" She planted a big kiss on his cheek. Emmet left with one hand on his cheek and the other hand holding the liquor bottle.

Since that first time, the Blue House was added to the list of customers for whom he ran errands. Especially Miss Charlotte, the lady with the big eyes. She was partial to paying him for his errands with very nice chocolate bon-bons.

Sitting on the floor of the storeroom, he picked at a scab thinking about this Mrs. Brown trying to ruin the whole thing for him. The piercing wail of Baby John suddenly cut through the murmurings of conversation on the other side of the door, as if he knew they all needed the reprieve. Emmet heard Ann say, "Ah...the baby needs feeding. I'll be off."

The door jangled and Emmet knew that Ann, with the baby slung to her chest and with Mary Ann at her heels, fled, leaving his father to tend to Mrs. Brown's request for calico cloth and more. He pushed the door a crack and saw Mrs. Brown pointing a forefinger at his father and talking on and on. He snuck out to the back hallway, making his escape too.

Once in the alley, he frowned at the aggravation of Mrs. Brown's hectoring and walked towards Market. Dudley Shepardson had been right. The woman had gotten into his business.

Several days later, Emmet waited at his usual hummock until Campbell made his way home. His eyes started to close as all the varied birdsong trilled out around him. Different notes, sharp and short, high and low. He tried to count how many he heard. He could do that now at least--- count upwards.

Concentrating so hard on the bird's music, his father's rig sounded like a thunderbolt when it passed by him. Emmet stood up like a shot and stretched his arms wide into the California sky before following his father to the ranch house door.

Once inside, he picked up something in the air between his father and stepmother, something cracking between them. He became still and observant. Like he did when he went out hunting for white-tailed jackrabbits with Major Cooper and Sarshel. They taught Emmet that stillness was everything. Observation was more.

Ann said to no one in particular, "Supper will be on shortly." When she half turned from the cook stove to tell them this, he saw the flush on her face from the heat of the stove and also a wince as she turned back. Something still pained her after the birth of the baby. He didn't know what that could be but, just like he could tell when an animal was in pain, he knew his stepmother was in pain too.

So much so, in fact, that she took secretive sips from a bottle propped on a shelf above the stove. She said it was "cough syrup" when he asked once adding, "Not that it is any business of yours at'll." He wondered about that syrup and what was in it just as he wondered about that pain.

Once seated, his father rambled on about the latest news of the war and boasted about the South's victories. Emmet really didn't give a fig about the war or its sides and focused on the crocks that Ann was passing around. They held boiled potatoes and mincemeats with some beans that Malinda Cooper canned and sent home with Emmet.

Ann sat heavily in her seat, pulling the basket that held the baby between her and Emmet. Emmet looked down at the baby who had come out all prune-faced months earlier. The baby had changed up with his jowly cheeks, saucer blue-gray eyes and constant gurgling sounds. Whenever Emmet looked at him, it seemed the baby focused right at him. But that couldn't be right since he was just a baby. Mary Ann did the same across the table, staring at him with the same shaped gray eyes, always watching him.

He ignored all of it and let his mind wander until his father stopped talking and said sharply, "Emmet! Are you listening?" He looked at his father and shrugged.

"I said...the town is building a brand-new schoolhouse." Too late, Emmet realized his father must have stopped the war talk and moved on to something else.

John Campbell paused and looked at each of them before continuing. "Mr. Satterfield came into the store and asked me to pay a subscription. I paid more than our fair share. You know why?" He directed the question to Emmet who just shrugged again in return.

"Because you will have a fine new brick building for a school instead of a warehouse basement. So now, Emmet, you will have no reason not to attend school on a regular basis."

Emmet's eyes shifted back to the meat and potatoes in front of him. Campbell continued. "Do you hear what I'm saying? I have paid money for this, Emmet..." As his father droned on, Emmet reached forward for a fresh yeasty roll and his sleeve slipped back.

"What is that?" Ann's sharp tone cut through his father's talk. She stared at the most recent huge welt on his arm where the Gunderson brothers and their fellows grabbed and stuck him with a lit smoke. Emmet quickly drew back his arm into the sleeve, giving no response.

Several days earlier, he left the tunnels at dusk. They had lain in wait for him. The boys knew Emmet went down into the tunnels on the regular. They guessed he gambled with the Chinamen and it spurred their anger towards him. Yet they were too yellow-bellied to venture down themselves not having someone like Old Man Chung in their corner. The tunnel entrance being hidden between two buildings was convenient for their purposes.

They pushed Emmet onto the ground with a thud after he exited that night. Holding him down, they stuck him with one smoke on one arm and were about to do the same on the other. Major Cooper just happened down the street at that moment and heard Emmet's strangled cries.

The Major's meaty arms grabbed several boys off Emmet in one go, hoisting them aside by the scruff of their necks. He slapped them away easily like no-see-em bugs and they all scampered away into the night. Emmet wished he could have the Major by his side all the time. A weapon against his tormentors...for the other times he knew would come.

Ann repeated, "What is that?" After Emmet still did not respond, she turned to Campbell and said, "Did you see that? What is going on with all kinds of bruises and scabs and marks on this boy? Is he clumsy or is something else afoot here?"

Emmet could hear the alarm in her voice and was surprised by it. What did she care what he got up to and who was hassling him? His father took a draught of his ale and then cleared his throat.

"Cooper did mention to me something about the boys getting on Emmet." He turned and asked Emmet, "Is it true, boy?"

Emmet did not understand what he was supposed to say. It had been going on for so long and no one seemed to notice or call it out before. Why now? He just shrugged again.

Ann threw up her hands and pushed her chair back, rising too fast which made her wince again. "Well, how can you get any help if you won't help yourself?"

He did not know what she meant but he finally spoke and said, "Don't send me to no school is how to help."

"But that is exactly what will help you!" she shouted.

He stared down into his half-brother's eyes. They had no idea about the life he led.

His father repeated what had already been stated. "I paid the money. You'll go to that school. You'll learn to read and you'll learn to write. You hear, boy?"

Emmet left unsaid that he had no intention of ever setting foot into anything with the label "school" on it again. He was figuring out there was not much either his father or stepmother could do about it.

Chapter Eleven

Walking back from town on an early spring evening, Emmet kept his fingers warm by rubbing the greenback bills together in his pocket. His night's winnings. Once within sight of the ranch, he could see a bonfire burning bright out to the side with huddled figures around it. As he crept closer, he made out his father, Dudley Shepardson and maybe their nearest neighbor, Jerry Powell. He stopped well before they would be able to see him.

He also saw the tip of Shepardson's lit cigar with its red embers. He was fond of his cigars and Ann had made it clear on more than one occasion that she wouldn't put up with cigar fug inside her house.

His father's voice rose as he railed on about "the damned Yankees" and "Old Abe thinking he can do that." The war talk again. Emmet was sick of it. It was all his father ever thought or talked about it these days it seemed.

He moved a few feet closer and suddenly Shepardson's voice boomed out over Campbell's saying, "Boy, I know you are out there. Now, come on out and make your presence known."

Shepardson had a good ear...and a good nose. Before leaving Kentucky, he worked as a tracker finding runaway slaves for bounty money. Emmet never had been able to pull much over on the man, not that he hadn't tried. He sauntered close enough to the bonfire to be made out in its light. He could see them better too. They were a study.

His father, his hair still a thick mat that sprung up to its ends but tinged now with more salt than pepper. Craggy lines like trenches were embedded in his face. It was ironic he hated on Lincoln so much because, by Emmet's recollection of a photograph, Campbell resembled 'Old Abe' more than a little.

Shepardson, by contrast, retained a more youthful persona. He still donned the thick mutton chops that so fascinated Emmet when he was just a little tike. And his moustache was still meticulously groomed and detailed.

Jerry Powell was his own man and didn't necessarily follow the ways of the other two. A maverick, he had not come up with the contingency from Kentucky like the majority of Colusans. He stood tall, taller than Abe Lincoln probably as best Emmet knew, and he was built wide to go with the tallness. His head was without hair and about as shiny as the billiard balls in Mount Hood Saloon but his face was covered by a thick thatch that grew down to his belly to a point. He housed Indian orphans at his ranch and, by all accounts, did right by them. He kept them under close scrutiny so it was rare for any of the townspeople to have interactions with them.

Now he spoke up to make his sentiments known. "Come on, Campbell... Lincoln ain't all that bad and change needs to happen down in the southern states. You know that's true. Plantations like they got aren't right to be run like they do."

The two men began to spar, voices rising higher and higher. Emmet cut through the noise as it became overwhelming and said, "What's that?" in a loud enough voice for them to hear. He pointed to the large copper circle pinned on Shepardson's waistcoat and his father's as well.

Shepardson thrust the badge forward for Emmet to look at. With pride in his tone, he said, "This here is my Copperhead badge. We cut 'em out of the cent coin. Represents what we stand for." He added, "We'll get you fixed up with one, Emmet. Don't you worry."

Powell gave an audible sniff and Shepardson looked over at him. "You too, Powell."

Emmet kept it to himself that he would not be wearing any badge. He didn't buy into any of their malarkey as his stepmother called it. It was maybe the only thing she and he agreed upon.

Leaning against the end of the bar, Emmet studied the cards in front of him. One face down, unknown; the other, the number six. He looked up at Florian and said, "Hit me."

Florian slapped another card facedown.

"Okay. Stay."

In slow hours at the saloon, Florian trained Emmet in 21 or Vingt et Un as he called it, adding to Emmet's card playing repertoire. Between Fan-Tan, 21 and some other tricks picked up along the way, numbers were now friendlier to Emmet, making sense after all the early years when they were just a jumble. He couldn't actually recall the exact moment in time when it all fit together---he was just glad it did.

Emmet flipped over his cards and Florian threw his down saying, "Bah! You did it again!"

Emmet let out a low chuckle and replied, "You always told me 'use makes perfect'."

Florian's attention was suddenly drawn to the plate glass window at the front of the saloon. "What is dis, today? All these people have been up and down da street. Too many people..."

Emmet halfway noticed the build-up of activity out on the streets, idly assuming it was more war doings. News reaching the West was generally delayed but, by this early May day, Colusa was all caught up. For Emmet, current events came through the filter of Campbell with his particular slant on it. Campbell took the war's end and the Southern defeat hard. His was a sour and grim mood at the change in victor, a change he had not reckoned for. That was followed by President Lincoln's assassination which had stirred up the Copperheads, as they still called themselves, all over again. Campbell's mood shifted then to a giddiness that didn't sit easy in Emmet's mind.

"I'll go see..." he told Florian. Florian nodded as he deftly swiped up the discarded playing cards.

Once outside, Emmet followed the direction of the crowd as they headed down Fifth to the Courthouse Square. The Colusa Courthouse, completed years earlier on a grand scale, took up the better part of two Colusa town blocks. It stood majestically in the central part of the commercial district overlooking Market Street with green space surrounding it. Emmet recalled Dudley Shepardson proudly declaring that the Southern families in town held the majority and therefore the style of courthouse needed to be in keeping with their people.

The green space was what caught Emmet's view at the moment. It jarred him to see it filling up with people. Sometimes at night, it was a space he had all to himself, lounging on the wooden seats installed for the casual visitor. Now, it was being overrun by too many bodies.

Emmet was behind Mrs. Morton and Mrs. Cheney who walked side by side as though attached, their wide girths connecting each other and blocking his view. He heard one of the women say, "Oh for shame it is!"

The other replied, "Yes, celebrating an assassination. Rejoicing over the death of Lincoln. Who ever heard the likes of it?"

Emmet pushed past the women where the crowd opened up enough for him to see the small group of men gathered around the biggest tree in the square. The small group included his father and Dudley Shepardson along with a few other cohorts that Emmet recognized as local ranchers.

Emmet paused at the sight, realizing right away that the Copperheads were the ones celebrating. He took in these grown men, all with obligations, hanging about the park on a May afternoon, taking pleasure in the death of another. His gaze moved away from the small group and scanned the crowd. His eyes locked onto the sight of Ann with Little John at her side, half holding onto her skirts, sturdy on his legs now and talking up a storm.

Staying out of his father's direct view, he edged in closer and caught snippets of two wranglers talking. "I heard they were here making merry all night about it. And they have been arrested. Timmy Sullivan over there is keeping watch over them for now," said one man.

The other man shook his head. "Whether you are for or against, this is taking it too far."

A flash of movement from across the crowd was Ann as she marched over to the tree with Little John hanging onto her. He sidled closer to where Ann was headed and where the Copperheads, all laughing and whooping it up, donned their badges with pride.

The guard, a local man named Sullivan, stopped Ann from getting nearer saying, "Mrs. Campbell, step back from the prisoners."

"Timmy Sullivan, I need to find out what Campbell thinks he's on about." Timmy stepped back at her sharp tone with a frown on his face.

"Campbell!" Emmet heard her hiss to his father. His father raised his chin and stumbled over towards her. Emmet could hear Ann say in that low hiss, "What do you think you're doing? Have you lost your mind entirely?"

Slurring his words, he said, "Jus' having a little party is all."

Ann stepped away with a wrinkled nose. Emmet too stepped back pondering what would happen if they threw his father in jail. Who would mind the store, the saloon and take care of the ranch?

As his thoughts buzzed, a man in a Union uniform rode up on horseback. Noise in the crowd of spectators and in the small group of men under the tree dissipated until there was silence.

The man spoke up loudly. "Ladies and Gentlemen! I am Captain Augustus Starr of the Second California Calvary. These men here at the tree have shown treacherous and treasonous conduct. They will be taken to Alcatraz forthwith."

A collective gasp went through the crowd that had swelled in size before the arrival of the officer. Emmet nudged a man next to him and asked, "What is this Alcatraz?"

The man spit out some chewing tobacco onto the ground. "Prison up in San Francisco. Right on the bay. Horrible place I hear."

Emmet turned his gaze towards Campbell and studied him in his current condition. Campbell never took it this far before even after bonfires riled up about the Southern cause, and Emmet didn't quite know what to make of it. He felt a tug on his hand and looked down into Little John's big gray eyes. "Emmet?" he asked.

Emmet pressed his hand into that of his brother's and said, "Don't worry."

Ann swung through, grabbing the little boy from Emmet and taking leave of the courthouse scene. Emmet could almost see sparks of fury flashing off of her. Angry at his father beyond measure, she probably did not want Little John to see their father being hauled away. But

Emmet would wait right there to see if it really was going to happen. His father taken to jail.

Many hours later, Emmet returned to the ranch house and wordlessly handed Ann a note. Before reading it, she asked him, "Did they take him away then?"

He nodded, looming over her where she sat at the table. At age fifteen and some change, he had shot up in height and his narrow frame became even lankier. In fact, he grew almost a head taller in the years that matched the timeline of the war.

She stared at him longer than she usually ever did and he wondered what she saw when she looked at him. He was no longer a child even if he still felt like one at times. Was she still seeing that boy she had met seven years earlier?

She turned her gaze downwards and said gruffly, "He'll be all right. Don't fret none."

He stood and waited. She looked up at him. "What?"

He pointed at the note. He could do numbers now but not letters. The letters had never come together for him. "Oh...yes." She took a deep breath and opened it.

Emmet could see the strong lines that his father had made. He wished he could read them for himself. Her eyes went from word to word. She pushed the note forward and let out a big sigh. "He must have sobered up when he wrote this," she said in a bitter tone.

"What does it say?"

"Huh? Oh...he lays out what needs doing. Lists some men to help here and there when needed. That sort of thing..."

She let out a strangled laugh and said, "He ends it by saying..." she picked it up and read aloud. "'I apologize for the extra burdens placed upon the household but I hold true to my convictions while we wait for the South to rise again.'"

She slapped the paper back down and shook her head. Picking up the cup of tea that had been cooling in front of her, she took a sip.

Emmet turned and left her like that with the grandfather clock ticking
away.

,

Chapter Twelve

Emmet rode his horse the mile that took him to Coopers' ranch west out of town. The horse's hoofs stirred up the dust caused by the long dry spell that was not unusual but always distressing to the farmers. Especially since sometimes getting too dry was countered by getting too wet.

His father had been imprisoned for a couple of months with nary a word sent back about him. Before he was hauled away, Campbell pulled Emmet by the sleeve and whispered, "You take care of things. I know you don't cotton to her much but stay nearby. You hear?"

Emmet had no other choice but to nod. Then he had handed Emmet the note for Ann. Emmet stayed since then, keeping watch until his father's return whenever that would be. But it was not an easy time...and he was venturing away from all that just for a bit.

Malinda Cooper got word to Emmet that her granddaughter, Mary Benicia, was down for a visit. It had been some time since her last trip and Emmet felt excitement stir at the thought of her but also a hesitation. He hoped it would still be the same between the two of them.

As he got closer to the Coopers' ranch, he could see all of them congregated on the porch as one body, just as they usually were. He held back for a moment, feeling shyness overcome him. Always feeling the odd one out. But picking out the figures of Sarshel and Mary Benicia in the cluster buoyed his spirits and set him right.

Mary Benicia's eagle eye caught sight of him and she rushed off the porch towards where he stood. About ten feet away or so, she stopped in a sudden jerk and the two of them squared off and took each other in.

Emmet felt the rush of heat to his face at the girl in front of him who had blossomed into a fine-looking young lady. "What do you say, stranger?" she asked, not missing a beat.

He immediately relaxed and fell into their old pattern. She was still Mary Benicia and he was still Emmet.

"Sure is a hot one today," he said.

She nodded and started regaling him right away with tales of her life at Pulsifer's place in Spring Valley as they walked back to the porch.

The others hailed greetings to Emmet and made a spot for him to fit in just as they always did. Bashfully pulling his hat off and holding it to his chest, he greeted all in kind before making his way to the end of the porch. There, Sarshel sat off by himself in his rocker looking straight ahead where all the fruit trees were blossoming.

Emmet waited. Finally, Sarshel shifted his eyes sideways and said, "You got taller."

"Yeah, still not as tall as Mary Benicia."

"You'll catch up. Girls stop growing before boys."

Emmet took a seat next to Sarshel with Mary Benicia on his other side. She continued to chatter about this and that while Emmet and Sarshel sat silent.

The porch door screeched open and Malinda Cooper came out with arms on hips.

"Well, there he is. Hello there, young man. I hope you're hungry for some of my cornpone and bison stew."

Emmet ducked his head and said, "Yes'm."

She looked at him with affection and not a small amount of worry. Emmet knew Malinda Cooper felt bad turning him back over to Campbell when she did. She also could guess how his days were since Ann's arrival and now with his father at Alcatraz.

He looked over at Mary Benicia, gesticulating with her hands to make her points, her eyes sparkling. He didn't really listen to the words as much as take in her person and her nearness. He hoped one day to always be by her side.

He left Coopers' with enough light left in the summer sky to see the vast California plains around him and the buttes beyond. Late summer in the valley was a thing of beauty, a work of art.

Upon approaching his father's ranch, he found that all was still, too still. Sharp pinpricks started up along the nape of his neck. His other sense was triggered---his stepmother called it that. The other sense.

His stepmother's voice suddenly cut into the silence as she shouted out a strangled cry. Emmet quickly tied his horse off and grabbed his rifle. Moving silently to the side of the house where the cry came from, he came to an abrupt stop.

A man loomed over the sturdy porch swing behind where Ann sat, pressing her down with hands on her breasts. He was the goose herder who had been hired and then fired a month or so back, no good at keeping the geese out of the fields so that the plants could have a chance to grow in properly. Ann mentioned off-handedly that the man also unnerved her, staring at her chest every time she had to talk to him.

As the man pawed at her, his eyes glazed over, Emmet watched his stepmother squirm out from underneath and leap up from the swing. The goose herder was quicker, grabbing her with arms acting like taut bands of steel. She grimaced as he reached for the front of her bodice, ripping it in half in one go.

In that split second, all of Emmet's frustration and anger at her came barreling up. It would be so easy to just walk away and let her be punished like this. By this man, this goose herder. But he could not do that.

Instead, he stepped forward, rifle in hand. "Stop." His voice came out as a command. The stench of the man unused to bathing at regular intervals blew all the way over to where Emmet stood.

The goose herder looked at the boy, first with surprise, then with a sulky glance that registered the rifle that Emmet held onto.

"Let her go."

The man slowly released his grip, running a dirt encrusted finger on top of her nipple. Ann swatted at the hand, rage infusing her movement, and spit at him right in the eye.

"Bitch," he yelled out, wiping at his eye. He moved towards her again saying, "I oughta…"

Emmet fired up into the air. "Leave now." His voice cracked partway through. A give away that he had not completely found his manhood yet. But he was close, very close.

The goose herder looked balefully at him and took his time loping his way back into the fields. He and his stepmother stood and watched until he was off the ranchland and on the road to town.

"I'll go tell Deputy Marshall about him," Emmet said.

Ann swallowed as though she had not done so for a while and said, "Yes, do that." Clearing her throat, she asked, "How did you know…why were you here?"

"I'm usually around this time of day. Checking on things." Pausing, he added, "I told Pa I would do that."

"Ah," Ann said. "Well, I'm…I'm…it's good you were here." Her dark eyes stared at his light ones, and he wondered if she had figured out his inner turmoil. Her lips parted as though she wanted to say something more, but she didn't. Emmet averted his gaze, embarrassed by the interaction, and headed back to the stable.

A month later, Emmet walked into the Mount Hood Saloon and Florian rushed over to him. "Sullivan was jus' here. They will let them go at Alcatraz. All six of them he says."

His father's imprisonment had gone on for more than three months now, his return date always unknown. Florian grabbed his hand and shook it. "The news is good, yah?"

Emmet nodded and stumbled over his words. "Yes…what…why?"

Florian gave a shrug saying, "Sullivan says they need to fill up that prison with others they think are traitors. Clear the space."

Several days later, on an ordinary evening, Emmet waited on his old hummock for his father's return. He heard talk earlier in town that the prisoners were sighted out at the nearby town of Williams and their arrival was due soon. He headed to the ranch and waited with a feeling of relief that he would soon unhand his duties.

It was suppertime when the military marshal delivered Campbell and he stepped into the ranch house. Emmet followed closely behind him. If he sensed Emmet behind him, he didn't show it.

Ann, Mary Ann and Little John were seated at the pine table and all looked over to see who had entered. Emmet watched the scene unfold as all of them were stunned silent at the sight of Campbell, bedraggled and unkempt with ragged attire. Campbell coughed before speaking and said in a sheepish voice, "Can a man get a spot of supper around here?"

Ann stood up wordlessly and went over to fill a plate for him. They watched as he took slow, careful bites of his food. Almost painful bites. Emmet took a hard look at him. The toll of Alcatraz was on him in his lean countenance, in the grey pallor of his skin, in the scars on his face, and especially in that raspy cough.

He broke off from chewing to cough again. It was a deep sounding cough. Word around town was that there was a sickness the men at Alcatraz all picked up. This must be it.

When he finished the meal, he stood up abruptly pushing his plate forward. "Thank you, Mrs. Campbell. Indeed, it is good to be back in Colusa." His father walked out of the house with Emmet following behind.

"You want me to take you..." Emmet said but stopped at the look on his father's face, one he didn't recognize. It was a lost look. Emmet tried again. "Do you want to go to town and check the store and saloon?"

"Well...I...yes. We'll go to town." Campbell's voice trailed off as he stared across the way at the buttes.

Emmet made a noise in his throat and said, "I'll saddle up one of the horses for you."

Once Emmet readied both horses, they rode into town side by side. Emmet snuck half glances over his father's way trying to puzzle out the changes in him. How could someone be so different after just a couple of months? He took in the bits and pieces again, the scabs on his forehead that maybe were from insect bites or worse, rodent bites, the thinness that was almost skeletal on a man who had always been rail thin but wiry with muscle. And that cough.

It was not the time to ask all the questions he wanted to ask. His father was not a man who answered questions anyway. Especially the one uppermost in Emmet's mind...did he wish he acted differently that day at the courthouse square? His father never took back a word or a deed done and Emmet did not expect that he would now either.

Emmet pulled out the big brass key once they arrived at the store, locked-up tight and empty. When opened, his father stood at the threshold, his gaze wandering around the space. He cleared his throat noisily and said, "Looks fine. It all looks fine."

Emmet was taken aback. He thought for certain the man, as particular as he was, would have a litany of complaints on how it was kept in his absence. Campbell coughed again, bending over with it. It came from somewhere deep within. Not like the coughs in the tunnels from the smoked pipes and not like the coughs in the saloons from the tobacco. This cough...this cough was something different altogether. Painful to listen to and painful to endure.

"Can...can I get you something to drink? For the cough?"

His father waved a hand indicating no as tears came to his eyes from the coughing fit. He worked his way to standing, clutching his ribcage as he did so. "It's all right...let's get down to Mount Hood."

His father took mincing steps on the block-long walk from the store to the saloon on Fifth Street. Emmet scaled back his own pace wondering what had happened at Alcatraz. By the time Campbell came to a full stop outside of the saloon where noises from inside drifted out into the night, a grimace was plastered on his face from the effort. His hand found the nearest hitching post and he leaned against it heavily, struggling to regain his breath.

He finally said, "You know...I think...maybe it'd be better to come back tomorrow." He paused and sucked some air in through his teeth. "Bring the horse over here, boy."

Emmet hastened to collect the horses and walk them back to where his father stood. As he did so, he wrapped his mind around the fact that his father was sick. He had never seen him sick before. This must be the difference. He was just sick, that was it. He would get better and all would go back to how it was.

Chapter Thirteen

Under the light of a lantern, Emmet worked in the stable oiling down the scythes now that the summer harvest had wound down. The stable doors cracked halfway open revealed a view of the fire pit where his father sat with Shepardson and his stepmother.

Emmet watched when they came out, his stepmother draping a wool blanket over his father's lap to ward off the chill that set in the air, a portent of the winter to come. The last of the summer bugs danced around the beeswax candle that she placed between them.

A year after coming back from Alcatraz, his father still had the cough. The new doctor in town who replaced Doc Robinson, Doctor Calhoun, handed out the same blue pills to all six of the Alcatraz prisoners. Campbell was the only one who the pills didn't work for. His stepmother was quick to remind his father over and over again that Alcatraz left a calling card. The cough was now an ever-present guest they were accustomed to.

Shepardson brought a Cuban for Campbell and some honey mead wine for Ann. The two men swilled some whiskey to go along with their cigars while Ann sipped the wine and sat back with her knitting work. Emmet could tell his father was just pretending to puff on the cigar. He wasn't fooled by it nor was he fooled by the grey pallor on the man's face that never really went away.

Shepardson, raising his southern drawl an octave, said, "Think I saw our young Emmet at the Blue House the other night..."

Ann gave an audible sniff.

Shepardson continued. "Yep. That could be where he sneaks off to in the evenings." He let out a loud guffaw for emphasis.

Emmet's hand clenched the scythe he was holding. Shepardson wanted to get a rise out of him. Not too unlike the Gunderson boys when he thought about it.

Campbell began to sputter. "I'll tan his hide if..." His ire peaked out with another ragged cough, the rest of his thoughts left unsaid.

As if, Emmet thought. As if his father ever minded Emmet being wherever he was as long as he was out of sight. Even now it was only because Shepardson raised it up that Campbell felt compelled to take a stance. Emmet remembered his first time at the Blue House when Shepardson sat in a corner diddling with a young girl, barely out of nappies, on his lap. The gall of a man never called out for his own doings.

After the cough ended, they all sat out there in silence until his father spoke up again. Speaking as if to himself, he said, "You know, when I married Amanda, she was a widow with a small son. And he really turned out like those brothers of hers. Difficult as can be..."

Emmet dropped the blade he held, making a clanging noise. Who was his father talking about? Amanda was his mother, that much he knew, but had she birthed another son before him?

Out by the fire, he heard Ann ask the question that was bobbing up in his own mind. "Do you...do you mean Emmet? Are you saying Emmet is not your natural born son?" The tone of her voice held surprise and something else. Something that was new to Emmet's ears.

"What?" Campbell said, his voice wavering.

Shepardson interjected with a chuckle and said, "Too much whiskey for you, Campbell! Of course, Emmet is Campbell's boy. Haven't I known him since he was just knee-high to a grasshopper?"

Emmet shook off any doubts. Just like Shepardson said, of course, he was Campbell's son. Who else would he be otherwise? It must be too much liquor or...could it be his illness had affected his mind? He felt a frisson of fear at the thought. The thought of his father losing all his marbles would not do anybody good. Especially him.

He became aware that the conversation by the fire came to a standstill. He peered out the half open stable doors and saw Ann staring into the space where Emmet was, her eyes glittering in the firelight.

Several months later, Emmet swept the floor behind the bar while Florian tended to the patrons at the Mount Hood Saloon. Saturday night was big doings in town with the cowboys getting paid. They came to town ready for liquid refreshment to go along with other pursuits like gambling and time with the "upstairs girls."

With Campbell now bedridden, Florian ran the bar almost single handedly. But Emmet had been filling in, now in a legitimate capacity given the height on him.

One of the cowboys well into his cups cast a glance Emmet's way and said, "Boy! How's your daddy doing anyway?"

The mention of Campbell seemed to have snagged all attention and conversation diminished to a stop. Emmet felt all eyes on him. The truth was his daddy was on his last days on earth and there was no easy or gentle way to put that. He looked around him at the crowd who had all seen their fair share of misery, poor luck and death and figured they would want the straight story.

Putting a hand on top of his broom, he said aloud to one and all, "Not good, Frankie. Not good." An uncomfortable hush hung in the air.

"Aaah. He'll pull out of it all right," Frankie said, trying to put a positive light to what Emmet said.

"No...I reckon any night might be his last."

Emmet's mind took him back to the dimly lit room out at the ranch that now served as the deathbed for John Campbell. Where Doc Calhoun came in on the daily and Ann bustled around while the younger two kids made themselves small and scarce. The smell of sick permeated the house and even beyond to outside as well. No, he could not see it lasting much longer at all.

"Well, you best be staying there these nights then."

"Huh?" Emmet came back to the room.

"Floor sweeping and tending bar can hold off when a pappy is at death's door. Everyone knows that."

Emmet looked up at the speaker blankly. A cowboy he didn't know well continued on the topic. "It's tradition. Oldest sons sit it out with their fathers 'til the end."

Emmet looked around the room and saw others in the room were nodding and murmuring as though confirming this to be fact.

"You the oldest, ain't you boy?" Frankie asked.

Emmet thought about this and slowly took off the apron around his waist, stained with the work of that day. He could do this, he thought. He could sit with his father to the end. If that indeed was the job of an oldest son. He looked over to Florian who shrugged and Emmet made his way out into the cold January night.

At the ranch, all was still when he gently pushed the door open and entered the house. The lamplight glowed and revealed the open door of the room where his father lay.

Moving into the room, he took in his father motionless on the bed and his mask-like face. Then his gaze turned to Ann sitting on the bedside chair, her chin slumped onto her chest. He could hear a slight snoring noise from her open mouth. The room surrounding them was orderly but dingy and needed a thorough cleaning after Campbell's bedridden months. Some sunshine is what it needed he figured.

Emmet cleared his throat to wake her up but she did not budge. He didn't want to touch her but finally pushed her on the arm. She jerked, eyes opening wide. "Oh, you gave me a startle creeping up like that!" she said with a flash in her eyes. She looked over to the clock and, in a confused tone, asked, "Why are you back so early?"

He stared down at the knots on the wood floor, gathering his thoughts. Looking back up, he said, "Oldest sons sit with fathers...near the end."

Her face scrunched up and she said, "What are you talking about then?"

He didn't answer so she finally stood up and dusted off her skirts. "Fine. You want to sit with him. Please do. Gives me a chance to sleep in my own bed for a change."

She was too exhausted to wage much of a protest against Emmet spending time with his father---unlike days gone by. He watched her departing back, her usual neat hairdo all mussed up and her clothing disheveled. He felt a stab of sympathy that came from somewhere inside him. He realized it must not be easy to sit here night after night. And, if nothing else, she had done that.

His father rolled side to side murmuring unintelligible words as Emmet took Ann's place on the chair. He had heard the doctor say to keep him calm but Emmet was at a loss on how exactly to do that. How to soothe a man writhing and coiling in pain?

He looked into the abandoned teacup on the side table stained with a ring at the bottom. The rest of the table was lined up with the detritus of the sick; the blue glass syrup bottle filled with Emmet didn't know what, a face cloth to wipe off the sweat and other fluids, the Bible with a tassel hanging out of one of its pages.

It must be what Ann was reading aloud to his father last. He opened it to the marked page, staring at the words. He still couldn't read, the print rising up and blurry to his eyes. He could only make out a word here or there but not all of them together.

He sat with his chin in his hands and watched the figure on the bed. Watched and watched until eventually there came a settling when the pain seemed to lift. His father's eyes blinked open, big and wide, and he started talking. Emmet could just about make out the low gravel that now served as his father's voice thanks to the Alcatraz disease that ravaged his lungs, chest and throat.

Leaning closer, Emmet picked up on the thread of a story that Campbell was at some point in the telling. "...floors were stone. Hard stone. Like granite. Cold as hell. Who knew the city on the bay could be so cold in May, in June, in July. So cold..."

After a raspy cough and a sputter, he continued, "Cold, hard slab. They made us lay out on it lined up. Pushing us together." A grimace crossed over his face at the remembrance of it, maybe thinking of the bodies he touched.

Emmet leaned closer as the rest of the household slept on, undisturbed. His father's voice got a little stronger. "They would start in on us. Kicking us with their square-toed boots. Mad 'cause we were Southern. 'Sympathizers', they heckled at us. Then later—in the middle of the night when they were long gone—one of us would start the hum and the rest of us would take it up."

Campbell began to hum off-key. "Hurrah for the Bonnie Blue Flag that bears a single star...."

Emmet knew it well as the rally cry that his father and his cohorts had often sung around the bonfires at night where they worked themselves up over the war. Worked themselves up to the point that they had felt the need to "celebrate" Lincoln's death and hence ended up in Alcatraz.

Campbell stopped the hum and said in the clearest voice yet, "They couldn't keep us down. They tried with all the sickness and the bugs crawling over our bodies. You'd think they won. You'd think that. But they didn't win. They'll never win."

The outburst suddenly left him deflated and he slumped back into the gray tinged bedding. Emmet stared at the husk of the man in front of him and there was little room for doubt in his own mind: They had won.

The sickness from Alcatraz fermented and took root throughout his father's entire body and now, at just under the age of fifty years, it would take his life. Emmet didn't know if it would be this night but he did know it was a night coming soon.

His mind then rolled back over the conversation he had happened upon when his father first took to the sickbed around the clock.... the conversation Emmet could not get out of his head...

He had come back to the ranch on a brisk day in late November, sitting on Ann's porch swing gazing up at the clouds, mind adrift. Inside, he knew his father lay in bed again. More days in bed then up and about. He needed to collect himself before going in.

Overhead, a gaggle of geese flew off to someplace more accommodating. As they got closer and swooped lower, it seemed he could almost touch them if he reached high enough. Their wings moved strongly in unison making a noise like a poorly oiled ancient hinge. As they soared back high, he felt envious of their escape.

Sighing, he rose from the swing and opened the door slowly. Once inside, the pervasive sick smell hanging about in the air all the time filled his nostrils. He edged nearer to the room where his father lay, the door half open. Peering in, he saw his stepmother sitting by his side and heard his father babbling.

From his vantage, Emmet could see the glazed sheen on his father's skin and the bones in his face even more pronounced so that they stood out as though in a relief. He bore an even closer resemblance to Abraham Lincoln.

Ann was leaning in closer to catch what his father said and Emmet too approached closer. His speech had become less and less intelligible and a lot of his talk was about Emmet's mother, Amanda. One time, Emmet heard him talking about "all the babies" which he took to mean babies never born.

Another time he yelled out, "Don't go! Don't go!" which Emmet assumed to be reliving Amanda's death on the trail. Enough stories around town from other settlers about enduring hunger, thirst, Indian raids and devastating illnesses made that assumption likely.

He tuned in to what his father was saying now. "The baby, the baby...I told you I would get you a baby."

A perplexed look came over his stepmother's face and she nudged him on his shoulder saying, "Campbell, Campbell..."

"Huh?" His eyes opened into half slits.

"Who is the baby?"

"Whaa..."

"You were talking about a baby."

He shook his head a little, eyes still half slits.

Emmet figured whatever had been on his mind was lost but he spoke up. "Every man wants a son, you know."

His stepmother agreed with a nod.

"...after Amanda lost so many, we met the young girl who was heavy with child. It was like a gift for Lilah to show up so heavy with child like that."

"Lilah?" Ann asked.

"Lilah. She was from the farm over a piece. We took good care of her because those brothers of hers were not going to....a terrible lot, fighting all the time, never taking care of their farm. Not much sense between the three of them."

Emmet stayed still as a statue waiting for what was to come. His father coughed and the spell was broken. But Ann held a glass of water by his lips and, after a sip, Campbell spoke again. "We took her in and then she had the baby, showing no interest in him at'll. Amanda named him, cared for him night and day and then...the girl took off a few months after the birth. And he was ours."

His eyes opened wider and he stared off in the middle of the room, not seeing Emmet at the edge of the door. "But I should have known. I knew his uncles the way they were. I should have known he'd be just like them."

His face reflected in the afternoon light like a mask. "All's we can do is do right by him. Get him schooled and when he turns eighteen give him some money and send him on his way."

"Does Emmet know any of this?"

"Any of what?"

"Well, that's he's...he's adopted...not your natural born son."

"What do you mean?"

"Campbell, you just told me that Emmet is the child of a girl named Lilah and you adopted him into your home with your first wife."

"I didn't ...why would I tell you that?"

Ann puffed air out of her mouth and made a frustrated noise.

Emmet hung back and, with silent footfall, made his way back outside not knowing what the straight story was anymore at all. Were there any kernels of truth in his father's wild ramblings? If so, what was that truth?

Now, watching his father move restlessly in front of him, Emmet's head eventually drooped down onto his chest. Slumber took over and images filtered through his brain. Memories came back in pieces from other times. Times when it was just him and his father....

The pictures all rolled together of how it was then...positives and negatives blended into a whole. Coopers' ranch, Chinatown, the saloon, the store...their ranch. Before...before she had shown up.

The smell of Colusa in those early days was the smell of pine shavings, all the buildings around them new or just going up. He remembered feeling the dust on his bare feet in the street and deciding that Colusa would always be his. His town. He decided that right away, hanging onto it because it was the only foothold he had.

Then, later riding out to Coopers' every day. Sitting in front of his father on the horse, the odor of horse sweat ever present no matter the weather, hot or cold. And the sight of Coopers' as the horse got closer that always brought a warm glow to his insides.

And Chinatown and the tunnels. The scent of mold rising up as he approached the hidden stairs that took him down deep underground where it was a world unto itself. Old Man Chung and all the other Chinamen finding respite from life above ground with Fan-Tan gambling, the pipes they smoked and always the teas concocting and brewing with their strange earthy smells, grabbing what pleasures they had left.

Was it all just a dream or did it all really happen to him?

He opened his eyes suddenly and the light from daybreak struck through a slit in the blinds. He took it all in, his father in his sickbed on yet another new day.

Leaning closer to his father's face, he listened to a brand-new noise coming up from inside, a rattle. Scarier maybe than all the other sounds his father's chest had been churning out. He frowned knowing it could not be a good sign. Knowing it might, in fact, be a final sort of sound.

PART TWO: The Middle
Chapter Fourteen

The morning after Campbell's funeral, Emmet stood with one elbow propped on the fireplace mantel and a brown leather satchel bulging at the seams at his feet. As he waited for Ann to come out from her chamber, he stared into the framed photograph on the mantel as though it might have answers for him.

The photograph, taken years earlier at Wolfson's Photography Studio in town, immediately brought to Emmet's mind Mr. Wolfson himself with his scraggly yellow moustache and wet eyes. His shop was a block down from Campbell's store with very fancy lettering painted precisely on the glass front.

The two children positioned on a bear skin rug were Mary Ann holding Little John on her lap, both dressed in their finest with faces scrubbed clean. Mary Ann's doting devotion was caught for posterity in the photograph as she gazed down on her little brother, two peas of a same pod. Between Mary Ann and Ann, the baby never wanted for a thing.

Ann sat behind them with her dress skirt billowing and flowing over her middle, thickened after Little John's birth. Emmet guessed she sat atop a stool. Her hair was pulled back severely and her eyes were squinty. Just like the very first time he had laid eyes on her.

Emmet remembered his father viewing the framed photograph on the mantel upon its display and saying, "Where was Emmet that day?"

She bristled and said the photograph was for her mother in England to finally see her grandbabies. His father didn't press the point. The photograph just affirmed what he must be aware of. Ann had worked on wiping Emmet out of the picture from the moment she set foot in Colusa.

Now, Emmet turned at the sound of her chamber door opening. She walked into the kitchen attired in the black garb purchased well before Campbell's passing. Her widow's weeds he had heard it called before. Now she was a widow twice over.

Emmet sometimes mused over that. The true details of her life before Colusa and her life with her first husband, a man named Ginty. She didn't seem like a widow then nor did she seem like one now, despite wearing the black.

She looked at him and then down at the bag, one that Campbell had taken on business trips to other towns in California. Not that big of a bag but then Emmet's possessions were few. "What do you think you are doing?" she asked.

He stood tall and upright, towering over her five feet stance. He looked at her directly in the eyes but did not speak.

"Well?" she said when he did not answer.

"Not staying here no longer."

Taking in a deep inhale, she sat down with a thud at the pine table. She ran her forefinger over a scar on the wood where one of the little ones had done some damage, Emmet didn't remember exactly what. Without looking up at him, she said, "Where are you off to then?"

"Jerry Powell's."

Emmet lined an arrangement up with Powell a while back. Located one ranch over, he housed a number of Indian orphans in a ranch building and had room for one more.

She nodded as if that made sense. "You know, on the day your father passed, I figured I was thirty-three and ninety-three days old. Now ninety-eight days. Campbell was seventeen years my senior. Did you know that?"

She glanced up at him and, getting no response, continued on. "I didn't give that age difference a second thought when I married him. Why would I? That sort of difference among men and women was typical at home in Ireland. And here also..."

She sat back in her chair and nodded as if to herself. "So...married for a total of eight years, give or take. If nothing else, we were good together in business..."

Emmet continued to stand where he was, satchel in hand, not knowing where she was going with all of her talk.

Ann hesitated as though collecting her words and then spoke, this time looking at him straight on. "Emmet, you are welcome to stay here until you are eighteen. And continue your schooling."

She looked askance at that and he let a smirk slip over his face. They both knew that Emmet's "schooling" was nevermore having ended years earlier. It was a façade they both kept going for Campbell's sake. But now that Campbell was dead...

She cleared her throat and continued. "After that...when you come of age, I mean...I will give you five hundred gold coins."

It was clear to Emmet that Ann had prepared this "offer" and determined it was the time to deliver it. He looked at her and then smiled a thin, grim line. He answered with one word, "No."

Emmet stood outside the ranch door that he had just slammed. He looked off into the fields where the sun rose up in the sky. His hands shook from squaring off with her. He wished it would be the last exchange but knew it probably wasn't.

He would come back once he was eighteen in a couple of years' time and it would all be his. He was the oldest after all. It was only just and right that he get what was his. Her paltry offer of five hundred gold coins would not stand up to anyone's scrutiny.

As he walked away from the ranch one step at a time, he focused on the land all around him instead---all its beauty mixed with its rawness. His father's land. It had meant everything to his father. Now...it meant everything to him too.

It was a mile walk over the harsh winter landscape of dead weeds and frozen ground to Powell's and, as he walked, Emmet shook off any tattered ties to Ann, his stepsister and his half-brother.

Powell's ranch came into view: a motley collection of various farm buildings and a low-slung residence not unlike Campbell's ranch. A couple of hound dogs barked announcing his arrival. He made chucking noises as he got closer until they recognized him. Their tails wagged as they came up to him looking for treats.

The front door of the ranch swung open and Jerry Powell filled up the space of the opening. His bald head gleamed on top of his tall body, beard long and flowing. Rubbing his belly after hiking up his suspenders, he eyed up Emmet.

Emmet raised a hand in greeting, here to take Powell up on the offer he made one night at the saloon. The man nodded his head saying, "Well then...let's get you a bunk 'round back."

Powell walked around the house towards the rear. Emmet trailed behind with the dogs intertwining themselves between both of them. A shed-like building with a tin roof sat within several yards of the main house.

Powell opened the door to the one room space that held multiple bunks, neat and orderly. "Ayah...everybody up now," he said to the small group inside. "This here's Emmet. Some of you know him; some of you don't. He'll be staying here with us for a while."

Emmet looked at the boys inside. All Indians but dressed in Western clothes. A subdued bunch, they seemed cowed by Powell but then Powell did cut an imposing figure.

Powell pointed to an empty top bunk. "That's you there, Emmet. Get settled and then come on over for chow time."

As he watched Powell's departing back, Emmet felt anything but settled. He took a breath and looked around at the cold, barren bunk house and the inquiring eyes of the Indians. He would figure it out...

Chapter Fifteen

"Your daddy can't cover your ass anymore. You're on your own out here."

From his seat on top of his mount, Emmet ignored the cowboy's words and the snarl on his face. Instead, he stared out into the open expanse of the range. What the cowboy and all the rest of them didn't realize was that he had always been on his own.

Jerry Powell set him up with some rangers out in the north quadrant and it was still early days fitting in with them. They were testing him and even hazing him at times. Just like they did with the Indian boys from Powell's. But those boys got it worse. Much worse.

It reminded him of the town bullies. His mind flashed through the scenes of the boys who abused him: Each scene flitted by fast like that spooling ticker tape from the Western Union office on Market and Tenth. The times they tried to chase him into the tunnels. The times they grabbed him when no one was around and tortured him with their smokes. The times they mocked his way of speaking. The times they mercilessly ridiculed him for not knowing how to read and write, calling him name after name after name. Coot, ninny, idiot, simpleton and all the rest.

It made him think of the pecking order with the yard hens that Ann kept at the ranch house. One hen was the boss while the others fell into a laddered order of their own devising. It was also in the saloon. It was also in the tunnels. It was really everywhere.

He figured it would always be this way in life: bullies in one form or another everywhere he went. Maybe everybody dealt with them in their lives or maybe it was just him. There was nothing to do for it but pick back up and dust off. Start up again. Every time. This much he knew.

Looking over at the man hassling him now, Emmet let loose with his distinctive, high-pitched giggle. The cowboy's mouth dropped open. "What the hell is wrong with you?" he said.

Emmet cracked the crop on the backside of his mount and rode away from the cowboy, dust kicking up behind. If Emmet made himself the one off-kilter, the one off-center, the bullies were thrown off the game. It changed the mix.

The day was done and he headed in the direction of Coopers', a place where he always had a seat at the table. As he got closer to the ranch house, he could see the dark clothed figure seated where he always was, Sarshel on his rocker. Sarshel always wore black; Emmet didn't know why but he always did.

Tying his horse off, he lit off from the saddle and felt the soreness from the long day on the range. A long day of riding and a long day of dealing with cowboy politics. He gave his legs a chance to get their bearings before stepping onto the creaking porch steps.

He walked over to the end of the porch and sat down in the rocker next to Sarshel. After a bit of silence with the two of them rocking and staring out on the horizon, Emmet began to talk. He told Sarshel about his day. He described the animals seen out in the wild. He told him about the different colors of the sky that had passed above him. He told him about plants newly blooming. Their colors too.

If Sarshel was paying attention to his words, it was hard to tell. It didn't matter whether he was or not. It was Emmet's opportunity to be the talker rather than the listener. And Sarshel was a good listener.

The porch door opened with a whining noise and Malinda Cooper came out onto the porch. "Supper time!" she announced. "Oh, hey there Emmet. I didn't know you two were out here having a gabfest. Well, of course, you will eat with us..."

No sooner did Emmet take in her words, when a figure appeared at the corner of the porch in front of the railing. She propped her forearms on the top rail and gazed over at Emmet and Sarshel. "There she is! Look who's back, Emmet," Malinda said.

At the sight of her, Emmet felt as though his breath was sucked out of his chest. As she leaned closer, he took in the deep violet color of her eyes that were offset by the lilac bush in bloom bordering the porch. With the last bits of sunlight, Emmet's gaze swung from the blooms to the girl and then back to the girl. A girl no longer though.

Mary Benicia smiled widely at him with her beautiful smile and it took him right back to all those days spent together right where they were now.

"Emmet, I declare. You are a full-fledged cowboy looks like."

He looked down, embarrassed by her gaze and whatever it might be seeing. His arm had mended after falling out of the tree, only sometimes paining him on a rainy day. What never mended was the wrenching of Mary Benicia from his life...

"Well, time's a wastin'. Come on and git inside, all of you." Malinda hustled them into the ranch house for the meal she had prepared.

That evening, breaking bread again with Mary Benicia and her family at the long refectory style table filled up by family members and assorted others, Emmet couldn't help but resurrect his dream of weaving his life into hers. Sitting directly across from her, Emmet was mesmerized by her rosebud lips, her raven hair that gleamed in the candlelight and those violet eyes. She was a vision. Everything about her meant home to him.

His eighteenth birthday was coming soon. That would be the day all of it would come to him and he would take over what was rightfully his---his father's ranch. Then he would make it all happen, the home he never truly had before.

Later, after supper, Emmet sprawled out on the field to the west of Coopers' homestead, letting the last of the early evening sun seep into his body. He soaked in all the smells and sights of the season now in play. His eyelids drifted shut after his full day of riding hard with the cattle out on the range. He let it all go until he felt a tickle under his chin.

His eyes popped open and his body jerked as he took in the face above his. Heavily lashed bright eyes, plump rosy cheeks and those

106

rosebud lips...she held a weed in one hand used to tickle with. She laughed and said, "You should see the look on your face..."

She lay back next to him taking in the big open sky and all the spring things with him. When she reached her hand over to his, their fingers intertwined. He listened to the sound of her voice as she talked, soaking up the tone of the voice rather than paying attention to the words. He eventually rolled over and gazed down at her as she continued to chat away. He wanted to lean forward and kiss her. Wanted it like he never wanted anything else in his life.

Finally, she stopped the flow of her chatter and observed him. "What? You don't think I should ask Mama to do that?" He said nothing. She continued, "Or you do?"

Still, he said nothing, willing his body to move. But it wouldn't. He couldn't. He knew how to kiss girls. He kissed plenty in the various brothels. In fact, he had been told more than one time that he was a good kisser. But Mary Benicia was different...

They eventually made their way back to the ranch house side by side. Him thinking about the next chance he would get to kiss her. Her still chatting away.

Chapter Sixteen

Emmet walked into Blue House and lifted the brim of his hat back. He scratched at the edge of his hairline where the hair was matted down with sweat after riding out on the range all day. Sunup to sundown was the general policy.

He needed a haircut in Chinatown soon. His mind flashed back briefly on that first time when Ann hauled him down there. The loss he felt seeing his curls fall around him onto the ground beneath and her attitude of triumph at accomplishing that. He shook the thought off. He tried his damnedest to keep thoughts of her out of his head. Sometimes they crept in anyhow.

He took in his surroundings and tried to get a bead on the mood of the place. No longer the errand boy here, instead he stood on his own two feet and held his own at the bar for a drink. The bartender set up a whiskey and he slugged it down in one go waiting for the warmth in his belly to reach up to his head.

He didn't venture into the Mount Hood much anymore. It had been sold at auction by Ann to an out of towner who made changes. One of the changes was Florian no longer behind the bar. He moved onto San Francisco leaving Emmet with a few parting words that tied into his love of sausages. Or as he called them, "wursts." He grabbed Emmet by his shoulders and said: "...in my country, we say everything has an end, only the sausage has two."

Emmet felt a hard clap on his back and looked up to see Smitty, one of the cowboys he rode with. He gazed at the hand that circled around his shoulder, missing two fingers. Older than the others, Smitty gave Emmet a fair shake or two out on the range.

"You going to get in over there?" Smitty gestured to the poker game unfolding in the corner of the room where a tense silence hung over the table indicating how serious the round had become.

108

"Nah. Not tonight."

Smitty shrugged. "High stakes tonight. I'm waiting for an in."

The two watched until the table opened up one space. Smitty stepped forward. Emmet walked over and stood off to the side, looking at the expressions on the faces from his guarded view. Poker faces, he heard it called. But he could read each of them for what they were.

Smitty, to start with, was too nice for his own good. His face could not hide that he just got a good hand in front of him.

Jack Rafferty, an Irishman, talked too much. Unlike Emmet's Irish stepmother who maybe did not talk enough. His face showed a mediocre hand but he was trying to bluff and fake them out. That was the kind of person he was. Maybe not unlike his stepmother in that regard.

Lolly, another new cowboy, who was in line with Emmet for lowest on the rung, showed his greenness in his facial tics. Too eager, it was clear he had nothing.

A dark-haired man named Sam had an air of casual. But really it covered up a mean spirit. Emmet could sense those ones a mile away and avoided them whenever possible.

As the rounds set in, Smitty was winning and the drinks were flowing until Sam stood up suddenly. He dumped the table up and down, no longer hiding his mean-spirited ways or number of drinks imbibed. The small group took an ugly turn as a crowd gathered round.

Smitty stumbled up and got ready with fisticuffs. But, before doing so, he handed over the purse with his winnings to Emmet. "Go," he said.

Emmet dodged the others and headed out into the Colusa night. Sneaking out the back door just like when he was a kid, he exited onto the alley moving straight towards the tunnels to wait it out there.

Once in the tunnels, the familiar sights, smells and sounds made him feel grounded, like he had a place in his new life after all. The smoke drifting up the ceiling of the tunnel room now comforted rather than baffled. The scratchy sound of the dealer scraping the stones back after each round was familiar instead annoying.

Settling down for a Fan-Tan game, he tossed the pebbles from one hand to the other, feeling their coolness as he waited his turn. Only half in the game, the other half of him was thinking about all the things above the tunnels. Despite the color of his skin, he fit in so much better down below than up there.

Old Man Chung poked at him to place his bet. He absentmindedly placed it down, his mind still other places, until when one of the Fan-Tan players gave a loud exclamation. "Bah!"

Emmet looked down at the square cloth in the center of the table and saw he had won again. Old Man Chung shook his head in amazement and said, "How you do it every time?"

Emmet shrugged and said, "You taught me how."

The elderly man shook his head again. The others left the table and it was just the two of them. He picked at a tooth with a small pocket knife. "So how it goes for you?"

Emmet assumed he meant since his father's passing. "I do all right. Out on the range learning how to wrangle the livestock. Take care of the fences. That kind of thing..."

"Not easy, this life."

Emmet nodded in agreement.

"But...you come here you need help. Yes?" Emmet felt a pang at the man's concern. He managed to nod again.

The next morning, he rallied himself out of the niche in the tunnels where he used to sleep as a young boy. Sunday was a day of rest for almost everyone. He headed out to the town of Williams where Smitty lived above the mercantile store, with his woman, an Indian gal according to another cowboy.

He followed the wagon trail that connected Williams the four miles to Colusa. Riding along the trail, he tried to imagine how it would look when the railroad tracks were laid down. His piece of the world was going be connected soon with what was out there, everywhere else. A world where he had not ventured too far other than Sacramento a few times with his father. He had no recollection of coming out on the trail when little from the middle of the States.

After finding the mercantile store in the center of Williams, he climbed up a wobbly outside staircase and knocked at the door. A slip of a girl with a tawny complexion opened it and stood there. "Smitty here?" Emmet asked.

Maybe even younger than Emmet, the girl stared off to the right of him and closed the door. A minute passed before the door reopened and Smitty stood with his hair on end and a raw cut on one side of his face. Confusion passed over his face.

"What...why you here?"

Emmet thrust the money forward wrapped with some piggin string, a bit of leather used on the range to wrap cow legs together. Smitty's expression was one of astonishment as he reached for it.

"Ah...good man. I thought it was lost in the fray. Wouldn't half blame you if you ran off with it."

Emmet bristled. "Why would you think that?"

"Now, now...don't get on your high horse. It's just that most wouldn't take such good care of another man's purse is all."

"That's not my way," Emmet replied.

The man in front of him nodded slowly. "I can see what's right in front of me...an honorable man is what. Don't let anyone tell you different." He held up the money fastened by the piggin string and said, "I owe you one."

Emmet rode out of Williams thinking about the young girl and Smitty and how that came to be. Even though numbers were coming to him easier, puzzles like this involving people still baffled him. He also thought about being called "an honorable man." He said it out loud and liked the way it sounded.

Chapter Seventeen

The sun was setting in the distance as Emmet used every last bit of strength to work the wire around the fence, securing it for the cattle pen. Sweat dripped down into his eyes making the exercise all the harder. The others left him to it, calling it his just due since some of the cattle had been lost on his watch. It hadn't been his fault. It was just more of taking his licks as the newest cowboy. That didn't mean it galled any less.

Looking up, he saw a rider coming towards him shadowed by the lowering sun. With the sweat in his eyes and the glare of the sun, he shook his head not quite believing what he saw. It looked like John Campbell, his father. How could that be? He grabbed a hold of the nearest post and swayed, trying to make sense of it.

As the rider got closer, then even closer, he shook the vision off realizing it was Sarshel Cooper. A rare event to be sure for Sarshel to be off the Coopers' front porch and on his mount. Sarshel pulled his horse to a stop with a tug on the reins. The two looked at each other and Emmet tipped his hat back. The planes of Sarshel's face stood out strongly in the harsh fading light revealing the life he led. He was tall and thin like John Campbell had been. And he was not much for words, also like John Campbell. Emmet thought not for the first time ever that his father and Sarshel were reminiscent of one another...

Still not saying anything, Sarshel got down from his horse and stepped over to the fence and held the piece taut so Emmet could finish the work. In the years that had passed, Sarshel's oddness did not diminish. In fact, it became more pronounced. Most stayed away from him including some of his own family members. But not Emmet.

During Emmet's visits to the front porch that spanned the Cooper ranch house, the two would sit together sometimes not saying more than a word between them, other times Emmet doing most of the talking. Both though would gaze out at the wide open California land, trying to let go of whatever demons plagued them.

When the fence work was done, Sarshel went over to the rucksack on the back of his horse and pulled out a flask and some biscuits. "From Mama," he said, handing the biscuits to Emmet.

Emmet wiped his brow and said, "Mighty big of you Sarshel. Coming out here."

Sarshel wordlessly handed him the flask. Emmet took a gulp and the fiery liquid lit up his throat giving him an immediate bolt of energy.

Sarshel suddenly stood at attention. "Listen. You hear it?"

Emmet went still and listened. "What bird is that?"

"It's a thrasher."

They listened some more to the loud, brash song of the bird. "Haven't heard one in a long while....but then I haven't been out here in a while," Sarshel said.

Emmet thought about that. He wondered why Sarshel had come out now. Maybe it was the change in the weather. Maybe it was something else. Sarshel looked over at him and said, "Pack it up. We're riding out a ways. Want to show you something."

It was the week's end and Emmet gladly took up the opportunity to ride out with Sarshel. It reminded him of when he was younger and finished his chores up on the ranch. His father would tell him to go out for a ride on one of the Spanish horses and he would do just that. Riding with the wind at his back and the clear blue skies in front of him as he rode bareback going as fast as he could get the horse to move.

Now he followed behind Sarshel riding at the same all-out clip heading into the direction of the sunset. Sarshel had not lost his way with horses. Some called him the horse doctor because he seemed to have a special line of communication with the ones at Coopers'.

Sarshel eventually began to slow down and Emmet did the same. They reached a plateau where there was a rocky outcropping. Once there, Sarshel lit down from his horse. Turning towards the east, Emmet looked to see what he was staring at.

A different view of the buttes, a new view. After all these years, the buttes could still surprise him. Sarshel knew his love for them and brought him here to see this. But why? Why did Sarshel want Emmet to see it now? Emmet puzzled over it while sneaking a look at Sarshel as he did so.

No words passed between them as they stood and watched the show of the sun setting over this facet of the buttes. When it was done, Sarshel said, "I got provisions to camp out for the night." Emmet nodded but was taken aback. Again, Sarshel surprised him.

They set up camp with the rocky outcropping as a protective backdrop. Sarshel skinned some freshly killed game that hung from his saddle and Emmet got the fire readied up. The two men watched the sparks of the fire as the game cooked over it, spitting and hissing.

Emmet devoured the gamey meats as the juices oozed over his taste buds. He looked up to see Sarshel just staring into the fire. Finishing up the meal, they passed Sarshel's flask between the two of them until it was emptied. Lulled by the liquor and the night noises, they heard the rustlings too late.

The low growl from the cat's mouth was close to the worst sound that Emmet had ever heard. The mountain lion was poised and ready on the rock ledge above them, the ledge that was supposed to provide cover. His rifle was too far out of reach and all he could do was fix his eyes on the animal and wait for its next move. He knew Sarshel was doing the same but could not see him in his view.

With the tail twitching, the gleaming eyes and that growl, Emmet knew it was going to leap at him and there wasn't too much he could do about it. It seemed like a million minutes before the cat finally flung its body towards Emmet with claws out. He grabbed the animal's neck to strangle it for all he was worth. As the cat clawed at his arms and bit him wherever it could, Emmet's arms started to lose the battle and he was close, so close, to letting go. But he got a final burst of almost unnatural strength and life began to seep away from the mountain lion.

When the animal finally went slack, he threw it down on the ground and staggered back. Sarshel pushed him aside and fired off three quick shots making sure it was finished. Then Sarshel stood with a loose hold on the rifle and closed his eyes. It struck Emmet that he just killed a mountain lion with his bare hands. He had just done that.

Then they heard it: mewing noises, like a baby's cries. Sarshel lit a stick for a torch and swung up to the rock ledge. Emmet scrambled after him, becoming aware of the blood seeping through his shirt where it had shredded. Shredded skin mixed in with shredded fabric.

There, behind the ledge, lay two little cubs, eyes still closed and mewing into the night. Their small heads moved around in search of their mother. Side by side, the two men stared down at the motherless animals.

"She was only doing what comes natural, I guess," said Sarshel. He gave a heavy sigh. Emmet turned his eyes away as Sarshel lifted the rifle and shot one cub at a time.

Emmet thought about what Sarshel said. Mothers doing what comes natural....his stepmother did that for her two young-uns. But not for him. Maybe she viewed him as what they needed protecting from.

They headed back to Coopers' ranch before the sun began rising, neither one of them getting much in the way of rest. Once there, they walked up onto the old creaking porch boards and Malinda Cooper came out of the door. She sized them up in one glance and said, "Get in here so I can tend those wounds."

After getting Emmet seated at the big, long dining table that the Coopers used for everything, she left to gather what she needed. Sarshel looked at Emmet as though he needed to say something. But he left the room instead heading into one of the back chambers.

Coming back in, Malinda said, "We need to get that shirt off you...what did you get in the way of?"

"Mountain lion," Emmet answered. He added, "Just defending her cubs was all..."

Malinda made a tsk-tsk noise and carefully peeled off the shirt pieces that stuck to Emmet's skin. He winced. She said, "I know, I know. You boys ought to have come straight home last night."

Emmet grunted. Once she was able to get warm water into the scratches, the pain subsided some and he gave in to her gentle touch, closing his eyes.

"Almost done now. Just need to get some of this liniment into the open places..." she hummed a bit as she worked through.

"All finished. Let's put this fresh shirt on you. Thomas Benton doesn't need this one so just keep it. Don't worry none about getting it back."

Emmet bobbed his head. "Thank you, missus."

She looked at him and smiled with some affection. "The things that you boys get up to..."

Emmet thought that she was deceiving herself in a way. It was not often Sarshel got out and up to anything but he nodded just the same.

She sat back as she wiped her hands off on a towel. "So...did Sarshel tell you our news?"

Emmet looked at her blankly.

"Oh...maybe he didn't get around to it. Well, we got word that our Mary Benicia got engaged."

Emmet's heart beat kicked in hard but he kept the same blank look on his face. Now the night before made sense. Sarshel tried to help him with this news...in his way.

"Yes, that's right. To a man who just bought a dairy farm. How about that? Our little Mary Benicia..."

Emmet stood up all of a sudden and the chair made a screeching noise. She looked up at him with surprise.

"I...I have to go, missus."

"Oh, all right then. Now take good care with those wounds so you don't get infection in them, you hear? Sad to say but it probably is going to scar up some on you."

He nodded, thinking that the scars on the outside nowhere near matched those on the inside. He strode off resolutely through the back door with a sting in his heart. Mary Benicia would not be his. Maybe she never was...

Out back, he saddled up his horse with quick, jerky movements and rode hard into town. He got to the Blue House in record time.

Inside the brothel, Miss Charlotte, now known as Madam Charlotte, sat at her usual spot at the corner table, shuffling cards and laying out a game of solitaire. Charlotte had taken over as brothel keeper a few years earlier, keeping the place in good order. No one actually knew who the owner of the brothel was and Charlotte kept mum on the subject.

During the day, business was scant and she was the only one seated. She wagged a finger at him and he headed over to her table which served as her office. Once he was in front of her, she gave a low, shrill whistle at the sight of him. "What did you get in a tangle with, Emmet Campbell?"

He plopped himself down with a grunt. Touching a scratch on his face, he said, "Just a kitty. Wasn't too happy with me."

"I'll say....where you been at these days? I haven't seen you in a coon's age." She studied him with those same light-colored big eyes heavily decorated with makeup.

"You know, here and there." He glanced at his arms, sealed up with bandages underneath his shirt, and held back a wince.

"I hear you're out at Powell's now. I know Jerry Powell is no fan of our wonderful establishment. Is that why I haven't seen you lately?"

Emmet shrugged.

"What's vexing you so? Where's that easy smile on your face?"

He shrugged again and she said, "Aww, come on. Tell auntie all about it. I got time."

She snapped her fingers and one of her girls brought a couple of whiskeys to the table. After downing his in one shot, Emmet found himself telling her that Mary Benicia had gotten engaged.

"That's real nice for her...isn't it?" Looking at him hard, she said, "Oh I get it. You're sweet on her, ain't you? Cooper isn't going to marry off his grandbabies to just anybody. You know that."

"Is that who I am, then? Just anybody?"

"'Course not. You're one of us. You got a heart of gold on you, boy. And listen to auntie here and listen good. Don't you ever let the scent of a woman get in your way. Just ain't worth it.

"She already has done. Too late for that—"

"Ahh...pshaw! None of that now. Drink up and let's have some fun."

Later, much later, Emmet found himself seated back at Charlotte's table no worse for wear after a romp with one of the upstairs girls. He watched as Charlotte laid out one card after the next, lining them up just so. She had plumped up from the early days and her bountiful bosom spilled over onto the lineup. Studying them, she asked without looking up, "Do you ever think about getting out of here for a while, Emmet?"

He looked at her with surprise and said, "Where would I go?"

"Change of scenery always does a body good I say. Maybe it's time for your change of scenery."

When their eyes met, he saw concern and care. He knew she was only thinking about the best for him.

"Do you mean leave Colusa for good?"

"Oh heck no. Just like a...like a sightseeing trip."

He never ever imagined leaving Colusa even on the worst of days with his stepmother. This was his world: the only world that made sense to him.

He answered her firmly. "I'll be eighteen come the February after next."

She looked at him and said, "So? I'll be twenty-one myself then." Her laughter came out in peals and she had to wipe tears from her eyes.

He frowned and continued. "I'll be getting my father's ranch then."

She narrowed her eyes and stared at him. "Huh. Is that right?"

He nodded.

"What about that stepmother of yours? Where's she going when that happens?"

"I dunno...won't be my problem, will it?" But he felt the worm of doubt start to wiggle its way in. He never thought too far ahead. He only focused on getting back to the ranch and having it be his...

"Hmmm," she drew out the sound as she shuffled the deck of cards in her hands.

Chapter Eighteen

Emmet sat behind the pew of Indians. As the preacher droned on and on about Jesus and other things, Emmet became mesmerized by the dark sheen of their hair that made a wave from one to the next across the whole row. Slicked and polished, their appearances were in accordance with what Jerry Powell expected from all who resided in his bunkhouse. It was almost as though Powell had gone through every strand of hair on each head, that precise.

Emmet was edgy under Powell's domain. His rules were many and one of the primary ones was attendance at the Sunday services. Emmet chafed more and more at being at the Christian service. Ignoring as best he could the nonsense that spewed from the preacher's throat.

His head throbbed from the previous night at Blue House and the whiskeys he imbibed, though he was building up his tolerance to match those of the other cowboys. He had to---if he wanted to fit in. He shifted his neck side to side under the tight collar. Again, his shirt pressed to the specifications of Powell.

Being in a church on Sundays took him back to the times Ann had force marched him into her style of church, a Catholic one, established by a group of Papists, mostly Irish folk like her. They met at a farm on the occasional Sunday when a priest could come out from his established parish fifty miles away. Not too often but often enough to be a burr in Emmet's side.

His father had not been under the same requirement which made it all the more vexing. In Emmet's mind, he was the one who married her so why did Emmet have to go to the blasted services? The only upside was that he could move up and down a lot. The Papists did a lot of kneeling and standing and then sitting. For reasons he didn't quite understand.

The two-hour long service was wrapping up and Emmet stood as the voices around him all chimed in to the song that ended it all: "Nearer My God, to Thee." He hated the song.

As their motley group collected outside the church, Powell tugged on him and moved off to the side. "Need to talk to you after supper. Come on up to the house then."

Emmet nodded and immediately wondered what his infraction was. Sighing inwardly, he made his way to his horse and headed back to the bunkhouse.

On Sundays after services, Powell's wife, Priscilla, pulled together a noon day meal to rival any other meal being placed on tables throughout Colusa. Hailing from the great state of Virginia and letting all know that fact, she took great pride in her efforts which resulted in a heavily laden table filled with dishes from the top to bottom.

The meal was usually a loud affair due to the oversized personalities of both Powells who were quite a match in temperament and almost in size. Like Jerry, Priscilla had a robust physique and her chest almost overpowered the rest of her body. The two of them generally tried to outtalk each other if in the same space. Despite the Powells' ways, Emmet did not turn his head when their table was on offer: freshly baked yeasty rolls, creamy butter beans, venison hanging off the bone...and much more.

After the meal, Emmet went back to the bunkhouse waiting for a discreet amount of time before returning to knock on the ranch door. He could see through the windows that Priscilla bustled about here and there, her mouth moving a mile a minute with her physical actions.

Jerry lumbered towards the door upon seeing Emmet and came out to the porch into the early evening air. As Emmet stood with arms awkward at his sides, Powell struck a match on his boot and lit a smoke. Then he offered one to Emmet. Emmet shook his head no, waiting to hear what the man would say and trying to gauge the man's mood at the same time.

"Your stepmother has been at the courthouse a lot this past year or so...since your pappy died."

"Why's that?" Emmet asked.

"Well, I took it upon myself to figure that out seeing how you're living here and whatnot."

Emmet waited for what was to come.

"She set herself up as the executrix of the estate. That was fair enough. So she's had the auctions and so on...newspaper's made mention of them. You read the paper, son?" Powell said as an aside.

Emmet gave a shake of his head.

"Well, you oughta. Anyway, she got Cheney as her lawyer and he's been running things. I think it's time you got involved...we'll go down to the courthouse together to see what all has been set up here."

Emmet hesitated and then said, "All right, Mr. Powell. If you think that's best. The thing about it is, I'm not real good with letters."

"Huh? Letters?"

Emmet ran his tongue over dry lips and came out with it. "I can't read."

Understanding flashed in Powell's eyes and he said, "Ah...don't worry none. I'll stand for you."

The sun shone bright on the granite steps up to the courthouse entrance. Emmet followed behind Powell as he puffed his large girth up them. Reaching the top stair, Powell pulled on the shiny brass handle to open the door and held it for Emmet. Inside Emmet took in the clerk's office with the walls filled from top to bottom with books and who knew what all. Framed paintings filled in spaces between the bookcases with scenes of the plains.

The clerk at the open booth eyed the two of them up: Powell with his tall bulk and bald head and Emmet showing up as the cowboy he now was. He wondered briefly what the clerk saw when he looked at him. He knew his time on the range now visibly marked him with skin dark like tanned hide and lines riveting into his face from all the days outside. His face, just like anybody else's, carried his experiences.

"Help you with something, Jerry?"

"Yeah, Martin. We got young Emmet here. Emmet Campbell."

Powell put a beefy hand on Emmet's shoulder prodding him forward. The clerk again gave Emmet the once over.

"He'll be eighteen soon enough and ready to get his fair share of his daddy's estate. John Campbell's estate. What paperwork does he file for that?"

The clerk frowned and said, "Didn't you know?"

"Know what?"

"Mrs. Campbell has been in and out of here for months now. Almost on the daily seems like..."

"And?"

"Well, she's got it all set pretty much."

Losing his patience, Powell let out a big sigh. "Martin, speak English, man. What's she set up?"

"Well, she's the executrix..."

Powell interrupted and said, "Yes, yes...we know that."

Martin continued over Powell's words, "...and young John Campbell, their son, is the heir to the entire estate. She's his guardian, of course, until he comes of age."

"What?"

The clerk threw his hands up then he went on to explain. "It's all above board, Jerry. She came in here right after the death. He died without a will so she had to put five legal notices in the paper. Then some more paperwork to become executrix. Then more to get money to live on. She got Cheney lined up to do all the legal work for her..." his voice drifted off.

Powell scratched his head and asked the clerk, "Wait a minute, Martin. How can the young boy be the heir when Emmet here is the oldest son?"

The clerk looked down and shuffled some papers. Then he cleared his throat and said, "Well, someone did ask that question and Cheney said she claims the other son was adopted and therefore not entitled to it. Any of it."

Emmet watched Powell's expression change in a similar way to how storms came in and covered clouds, dark and threatening. "What does this mean?" he asked Powell.

Emmet went back to those bedridden days where his father had spouted off various ramblings that in no way could have been the truth. With that memory came the smells, the sensations, the overall feeling of gloom. Is this what she was saying was the truth?

Powell's face focused in on him. "It means...it means you've been hoodwinked. Come on...we'll figure this out."

A line had formed behind them and, as they passed by the curious onlookers, Emmet took in the sight of his stepmother at the end of the line. Powell did too, coming to an abrupt stop in his tracks. His large looming figure stood over her whole five feet. She looked straight up at him and Emmet knew she did not back down for any man.

Powell pointed a finger at her saying, "You!"

Others in the line shrank back so that space was created for just the two of them to face off, Emmet too. His eyes wandered to the paintings on the wall depicting Western scenes, studying the details of one, to get out of where he was.

In a loud voice Powell said, "Did you really mean to cut Emmet out of inheriting any of Campbell's estate?"

The others in the room were silent, shifting their gazes from looking at her directly but yet looking at her nonetheless. Emmet turned from the painting and watched her mouth form a grim line as she said, "This is none of your affair, Mr. Powell."

"I beg to differ, Mrs. Campbell. I done take that boy in so that he had a roof over his head and food in his belly for almost a year now. It has become my affair."

His stepmother's sharp tongue had never failed her before and it did not now when she said, "So is it you looking for Campbell's money now then?"

"Ma'am, I have taken young'uns in all my adult days. Young'uns whose folks did them wrong. Like Emmet. If you think this town is going to stand for you treating him like this, you are dead wrong."

124

Powell jammed his hat on his head and headed out the door. Emmet caught her thunderous expression before following Powell out.

Chapter Nineteen

Emmet woke with the sunrise beaming down hard. He blinked his eyes and felt the hammer beating in his head. Looking around through slit eyes, he saw that he was lying in a bed of crushed chaparral. Hearing chomping noises, he looked over to see his horse jawing on some of it.

He had no memory of how he had ended up in the clump of chaparral apparently all night. He realized his right hand was stiff, the fingers clenched around something. He lifted it up and saw it was money wrapped tight with piggin string. It started to come back in bits and pieces. It was the McCausland brothers' purse. One of them--- Breck maybe? ---had won big the night before at the Blue House. But how had Emmet ended up with it?

He righted himself up slowly to stand, feeling the ground shift and swirl underneath him. Once up, he stumbled towards the thin rivulet of stream near him. He marveled that he had the forethought the previous night to end up near water for the horse.

Leaning over, he sucked in through his teeth some water flowing over a smooth stone and splashed it all over his face. Climbing up on a slight plateau, he looked around to get his bearings. Even with bleary eyes, he made out the nearest landmark that all cowboys in the region of Sand Creek knew, an oak tree that forked out in two directions at its base, making a huge V.

The McCausland brothers' cabin was along the creek further to the west and he figured he might as well get their purse to them. He searched his mind again for why and how he had ended up here....

After he and Powell had seen his stepmother at the courthouse, he remembered a driving need to block it all out. He had made his way to the Blue House and pounded down whiskeys like he never had before. In quick order, the room and all the people in it had become blurry and he stumbled around as the faces, lights, and sounds all blended into one. Two faces, in particular, loomed in front of him, the McCausland brothers, John and Breck.

He knew them from encounters out on the range where the chaparral became deep and dense. They ran a herd of sheep out that way and lived in the cabin on the creek. Hailing from out east, they had arrived a year or two prior and, with their pug noses and flat faces, might as well have been foreigners from another country in Emmet's view.

When they appeared in his vision, Emmet stared from side to side at the two noses that were identical until one of them clapped him hard on the back. "Come on over and play poker with us."

From there, the night took on more spins with the spirits flowing and the high stakes at the poker table rolling. But memory failed at that point and now Emmet could only assume that he had tried to get their purse to them on the moonlit night prior.

Once on top of his horse, it didn't take long to follow alongside the creek bed and reach their cabin. As he got closer, he saw the front door hanging half open and no smoke coming from the chimney. Although they could still be abed after the raucous night in town, the hairs on the nape of his neck began to prickle.

All was still and quiet with the exception of the morning birdsong as Emmet made his way to the door. He pushed it open all the way and stood at the threshold. The sight in front of him kept him stuck and frozen.

One brother was sprawled out on his back and the other prone on his front. The sparse furnishings in the room were tossed around like a storm had come through. He moved closer to see if there were any signs of life. But the bullet hole that blasted through the one brother's chest had put a hard stop to that. He turned over the other brother to see the same.

He half stumbled and half crawled out of the cabin to the outside, vomiting up bile and acid until he didn't have any left. As soon as he could stand up, Emmet jumped on his horse and galloped all the way back into town with the scenes at the cabin etching onto his mind permanently.

Emmet turned the whole mess over into the hands of Jerry Powell and then the local magistrates who grilled him about his recollections of those last hours with the brothers. A wisp of a memory came back to him about one of the brothers angry at a sheepherder, Van Dyke, who had done them wrong after being paid for his services.

Others from that night verified that Van Dyke was the most probable suspect and a hunt for him commenced. But it was discovered that Van Dyke was long gone.

The events came back to Emmet in pieces when he sifted and sorted them out in his head. He could not tie it together as a story, a real story. There were so many questions about what he had seen and done that night....

Several days later in the bunkhouse, he sat on his bunk and tossed the wrapped money between his hands. He kept the fact from Powell and the other authorities that he hung on to the purse winnings. Not because he thought the money was his but because he wanted to hand the money off to someone deserving of it.

The most important bit of memory from that night, the girl, finally surfaced. Breck had gone upstairs for a while leaving John and him at the poker table. When Breck came back down, one arm was heavily flung over a petite little thing, a new face in the house. The girl with creamy colored skin was named Bonita. Emmet heard she hailed from Tennessee. Her bright green eyes gazed calmly into the room, eyes that seemed to be waiting for something.

Even though he was drunk, Emmet could see something was amiss. She shrugged out of Breck's heavy hold and those bright green eyes flashed with anger. When she stalked off, Breck lurched after her and Emmet felt worried that he was going to hit her.

Emmet headed out behind them, skulking behind some paces not unlike how he used to as a young'un in the nights. He remembered feeling the fresh air hit his face, a break from the smoke-filled saloon.

Down one block, they stopped and the girl yelled out loud, "This baby is yours! You said...."

Breck interrupted and muttered something at her, jerking her arm. She flung away from him, her voice now an octave higher. "You made promises. An honorable man keeps his promises." She ran fast and hard away from Breck who did not follow her.

As drunk as he was, Emmet now recalled thinking that the girl thought Breck would make an honest woman of her, take her away from the Blue House.

With that memory now uppermost in his mind, he stood up resolutely and headed out to the Blue House. Once there, he asked the bartender where Bonita was. The man looked at him as though evaluating his intentions. Knowing Emmet well enough, he said, "Down by the river."

Emmet walked the straight line from the back alley of the Blue House to the Sacramento River. He could see the back of the girl, her shoulders slumped over. Once near enough, he cleared his throat to get her attention. She turned slowly to look at him with red rimmed eyes. He was struck again by what a striking figure she cut despite her obvious despair.

"I guess you heard about...about the McCausland brothers," he said.

"Yeah, I heard."

"Maybe this might make it easier." He set the money down next to her. She ran a finger over the leather strap and then looked at him with a question mark on her face.

"Why?"

"They won it that night. I don't remember which brother. But I had it on me for safekeeping..."

She continued to stare at him so he added, "I tried to go out that night to get it them...but didn't make it as far as the cabin...in time."

She narrowed her eyes and said, "Maybe that was a lucky thing...for you. Why are you giving it to me?"

He shrugged. "Thought it might help you out...I heard you and Breck talking some that night..."

She said nothing and turned back to face the water. He worried about what she was thinking of doing. When he stood up to leave, she said, without looking at him, "It's kind of you. Most would keep it. So...thank you."

Walking away from the girl, he mused over how she had ended up at the Blue House as he often did about the other girls there. Maybe in time he would learn Bonita's story.

Several days later, Powell summoned Emmet into his ranch house. It was rare to be invited into Powell's side room that served as his office. Emmet took in the surroundings as they entered the room, pine sided walls, stacks of paperwork, account ledgers and a brass spittoon on the floor within striking distance from his work desk.

The two sat down and Powell pushed some paperwork forward. Emmet could see the elaborate flowing cursive of the dried ink and recognized the names but asked Powell, "What does it say?"

"It says: 'Emmet Campbell vs. Ann Campbell, with Jerry Powell serving as Emmet's legal guardian.' You are suing her for your God given rights and since you are still underage, I am your guardian now." He added, "Wouldn't you like to be a fly on the wall when the messenger rides out and hands her this? I sure would."

Chapter Twenty

The showdown between him and his stepmother became the talk of the town. Emmet couldn't walk two feet without someone hailing him over to ask about the trial. It happened almost without any action or thought on his part. He had Jerry Powell to thank for it---or to not thank. He was uneasy in his skin over it. Nervous about facing it full on in the public arena.

In the days leading up to the trial, he stayed busy on the range but limited his nights at the saloons. Figuring it wouldn't do any good if he got caught up in any other trouble. He did, however, remain curious about Bonita.

One early evening, he headed into the Blue House and found himself at Madam Charlotte's table once again. Placing his hands on the back of the chair, he looked over at the woman.

"Emmet, what's on your mind?" she asked, without looking up as she laid the cards out for her solitaire game. The woman didn't miss anything in her establishment even if it seemed as though she wasn't looking.

He came out with it. "Is Bonita all right?"

She looked up at him with a knowing glance and said, "She could use some cheering up, I think. "

She paused and then added, "She's a good girl but if she can't start earning her keep here..." She let the rest of the thought hang and Emmet knew that Bonita could lose her standing at the Blue House. Madam Charlotte was good to her girls and everyone in Colusa knew that but business was business after all.

She nodded her chin up towards the staircase and said, "Go on up there and talk to her. Second room on the right."

He kept a light tread as he made his way up the thick carpeted stairs into the upper hall. He stopped in front of the door and listened. Only silence. He wiped his hands, suddenly sweaty, on his pant legs before knocking softly. Hearing nothing back in return, he knocked louder. After some more moments, her voice finally came out low as she said, "Come in."

She sat on a bed made up tightly with a white quilted coverlet. The room was without a speck of dust, all things tidied and put away. Attired in a plain homespun dress with her hair neatly plaited down her back, she looked like a young farm girl. Her face was devoid of expression. He stood at the doorway not having any idea of what to say to her.

His eyes cast their way around the small room until they lit on a guitar propped up near the window. He gestured towards it and said, "You play?" She looked over to it and nodded.

"Wish I could learn how to play guitar..."

She shrugged and said, "I could teach you. Ain't that hard."

She got up from the bed carefully as though something was hurting her. Picking up the guitar, she leaned against the window and strummed her fingers along the strings. Eventually, her strumming became a familiar tune, a song Emmet had heard his whole life called the Riddle Song.

When she came to a finish, he asked, "Where'd you get your guitar from?"

Her gaze wandered over towards the window. He worried the fragile thread to her was lost but she finally answered. "My uncle. Back in Tennessee. He...he was a good guitar player."

A cloud passed over her face. Emmet could tell there was a story there but she was nowhere near ready for the telling. She spoke again. "It's a Martin. Finest ever made. According to my uncle anyway."

So now he knew a little more about her: she was from Tennessee and her uncle was a guitar player. But he didn't know yet how she ended up in her line of work. He didn't know what misstep, false move, or wrong turn made her veer off path and into place like the Blue House.

She looked up at him as though she had made a decision. "I'll show you the basics and you can figure out the rest."

"Why? Why would I want to learn to play the guitar?"

"'Cause it'll take your mind off your problems. It does mine so it could do the same for you. Come over and sit."

She gestured for him to sit next to her on the made-up bed. She propped the guitar on his lap and he stared down at it...nice finish to the wood, strings taut and some mother of pearl underneath the fret. When he didn't move to touch it, Bonita took his hands and positioned them as though he were a lifeless doll. He wanted to humor her but his heart wasn't in it. "I don't know about this...maybe later..."

He could see disappointment cross over her expression so he quickly added, "I'll try it tomorrow. I'll try."

He saw a faint lift at the corners of her mouth and knew that the muster of energy needed to pay attention to the indecipherable lines and strings and other parts of the instrument in front of him would be worthwhile.

Several days later, Madam Charlotte flagged him down as he was walking down Market. "Well, I guess you have a way with the ladies, young Emmet."

"How's that, ma'am?"

"Our Bonita is back on the job. Whatever you said to her seems to have done the trick."

Emmet shook his head and said, "I don't think that..."

"Aww pshaaw."

She gave him a squeeze on his upper arm. "Take credit where you can, sweetheart." Blowing him a kiss, she sauntered her way along Market with her skirts billowing wide.

Emmet frowned, not understanding women folk and their mysteries much at all. He didn't know if it was necessarily a good thing that he was the one to get Bonita back to work...he also was still confused about her baby. If there had been a baby even? He gave himself a shake and continued on his own way.

Chapter Twenty-one

On a bright May day, Emmet stood and stared at the courthouse in front of him. So many times he had walked by it, just part of the background of his life. In the early days, when it was being constructed, he searched around for treasures in the upturned earth on the site. Later, he stood and watched his father being hauled away by the Union soldiers to Alcatraz. Now, he would be inside it, facing the bird down.

Emmet was not alone though. On his right, he was flanked by Jerry Powell. He decided he was grateful to Powell for figuring out what his stepmother contrived to do. Shutting Emmet out of any inheritance from his father and, in fact, claiming that his father had never been his father. The man could be harsh---very harsh as Emmet had experienced---but Powell's sense of justice would not stand for his stepmother's actions. After getting himself declared as guardian, Powell fully took on Emmet's cause as his own.

To Emmet's left was another supporter, Major Cooper. The Major had joined Powell in an official capacity, cited on the petition as "friend to Emmet Campbell." Of course, he was much more than just a friend. He was Mary Benicia's granddaddy, Sarshel's daddy. He, along with all the Coopers, had never let Emmet down.

Powell and the Major made sure there was another man standing with Emmet. Colonel C.D. Semple, a town elder, took on Emmet's case pro bono as his counsel. Colonel Semple, with his thick thatch of pearly white hair and long scraggly beard draping off his chin, was looked up to by one and all in Colusa, maybe the most important man they had.

The Colonel pulled out the gold timepiece hanging out of a pocket on his colorful green vest and glanced at it. "'Bout time we go in," he said in the booming, melodious voice that he was known for.

People gathered in anticipation in the courthouse square festooned by early spring blossoms on the trees. News of the trial had been fanned for some time. All were eager for the face-off to finally be ignited on this day between him and his stepmother. As the four men walked side by side up the front courthouse stairs, someone yelled out, "Go get her, Emmet!" Emmet didn't turn to see who it was but felt the power of those words nonetheless.

Emmet's footsteps felt clunky on the marble floors as they walked into the main galley. Powell reached first for the door handle to the courtroom where trials were held. They entered the packed room with all eyes turned to look at Emmet. In the room, he saw townspeople he had known his whole life, townspeople he had done odd jobs for, townspeople he had helped in one way or another, townspeople he had never let down. And, in those eyes, he saw sympathy and good will. Maybe that was enough right there. Maybe that was winning right there.

Semple pulled on his elbow directing him to the left front of the room. The other side was still empty. She had not arrived yet.

He sat while the low whispers from those seated buzzed around him. He looked around the grandiose space and thought about what it meant for him to be in it, getting maybe more focus and attention than he ever had in his entire life. He never wanted for this to happen, never asked for this to happen. It felt like he was being scratched from the inside out.

The room went silent as the doors opened again in the rear. He knew she was walking in. He felt Powell and Cooper stir behind him. Semple paid no mind and continued to study the papers that lay in front of him.

Emmet couldn't stop his neck from craning for a look-see. She walked down the aisle in her widow's garb with a little hat tilted on her head, holding her own to the hisses and low voices that were clearly about her. Next to her was Richard Cheney, her counsel, his heavy gut hanging over his tight suit pants. She stared straight, not looking at anyone as she and Cheney made their way to the right side.

Emmet took in the paler than usual visage and her pursed thin lips. He had forgotten how thin her lips were but he knew that look well. She was mad but there was not much she could do about it here.

The bailiff called, "All rise," and all stood to attention. Judge Frank Spalding entered the room, his black robes flowing behind him.

The Judge situated himself behind the bench and shifted some papers around. When he finally spoke, his voice came out in a low timbre. "Plaintiff and Defendant approach the bench."

Semple nudged Emmet and they walked towards the Judge as Ann and her lawyer did the same. Spalding pushed paperwork forward for each party to sign. Emmet signed off first: an X for his name. He ducked his head, embarrassed at the sight of it but not able to do much more than that.

When he looked back up, he saw where she signed next to the X with a flourish in her perfect cursive, *Mrs. Ann Campbell.* He could make out what each of those words meant.

Once all were seated, the Judge said, "Colonel Semple, call your first witness."

"The plaintiff's side calls up Mrs. Catherine Sisk to the stand."

Mrs. Sisk stood up and came forward with mincing steps. Her white hair, pulled back in an old style plait behind her head, had the look of being blonde at a younger age. After being sworn in, she gazed resolutely out into the room with pince-nez resting on her nose.

"Mrs. Sisk, tell us how you know Emmet Campbell."

After her eyes flitted in Emmet's direction briefly, she spoke with a strong and steady voice. "I was on the wagon trail with my husband, Mr. Sisk. Campbell, John Campbell I mean, desired to trail with us along with his wife, Amanda, and the babe, Emmet. We camped together every night."

"And did you get to know Amanda, Campbell's first wife, well?"

"Indeed, I did. I got to know her whole life story. A pious woman who kept the Sabbath."

Emmet's eyes were riveted on this woman who had known his mother better than he ever had.

"What did Amanda tell you about Emmet's parentage?"

"Why, there was never anything to tell. He was their son. Son of the both of them. She named him after her Baptist preacher back home in Illinois when he was born, she told me. And after he was born, she became with child again but fell from a horse. She was told she wouldn't be able to carry any more children."

Semple stroked his wispy, white beard and stared off into a corner of the room. Then he continued. "So you never heard her even hint at such a thing as Emmet being any other than her own child?"

"On the contrary, Colonel. We had many conversations when she spoke of Emmet as being her first child and the particulars of his childhood. I never had a suspicion that he was the child of anyone else but Amanda and John Campbell!" Her voice carried some indignation.

Semple placed his thumbs in his vest pockets. "Now, did you ever have any conversations with John Campbell, later here in Colusa about Emmet being his son?"

"I did. It was a few years past out at Sulphur Springs that I ran into Mr. Campbell."

"And what did he have to say at that time?"

"We talked about our time on the trail and he happened to mention that the very horse his first wife fell from was sold when he came out here and he used that money to buy his store."

"Anything else?"

"Yes." She looked over towards Ann with an uneasy glance and said, "He said that Emmet did not get along very well with his stepmother when he was away and he worried about that."

Emmet sat back in his seat, struck by the idea of his father worried about him. He snuck a peek at his stepmother. Her mouth was pursed as though she had tasted something sour. He could tell she was working hard to keep her face immobile but she must be ruffled at this observation. As far as Emmet could remember, she only knew Mrs. Sisk in passing, as was the case with most of the other matrons in town. Too late Ann must be realizing she should have been more of a friendly sort.

Some Cooper family members were called up next to the stand, one by one. The Major, his son, Thomas Benton Cooper, his daughter, Mrs. Susan Calmes---they had all known Emmet from his earliest days in Colusa, a time he could barely recall. All testified that there had never been any hint that Campbell did not recognize Emmet as being his son. Missing was Sarshel, but Emmet did not fault him for that. He knew Sarshel would have been there if he could. But...he was Sarshel.

Semple called up his next witness: Stephen Smith. Smith, a large man, lumbered up to the stand, taking his time. Once he was finally situated, Semple said, "Mr. Smith, please state your relationship to the deceased, John Campbell."

Smith sat back in the chair, comfortable in his weight, and said, "I knew him from the time he came to Colusa until his death. We had numerous business dealings together."

"Did you ever hear John Campbell say that Emmet was his own child or whether he was an adopted child?"

"I never heard it hinted that Emmet was not his son...until after his death."

A murmur rose in the galley and the Judge hit the gavel on the bench.

"Mr. Smith, did you hear him say anything to the fact that he **was** his son?"

"I did. He generally called him 'my boy' or 'my boy Emmet'. He did often speak of the trouble he had with his little boy. I went with him to the southern part of the state to buy cattle and, while we were gone, he often expressed uneasiness that his boy would not be treated well in his absence."

Again, Emmet felt dazed that his father had been concerned for him. He had never known it, never felt it...or had he? Was he not remembering it right?

"Anything else Campbell said about 'his boy'?"

"Well...he told me he wanted to purchase a ranch on the plains for his boy when he was grown."

Semple stroked his beard and then said, "To clarify that point...in your mind, when Campbell said 'his boy', he was talking about Emmet Campbell. Correct?"

Smith gave a nod saying, "Absolutely."

Even though he directed his next words to Smith, the entire galley knew that Semple spoke to one and all when he said, "So, in other words, Emmet was Campbell's boy..."

Chapter Twenty-two

After a full day of the proceedings, the court recessed and Emmet found himself crowded into Colonel Semple's one room office with Jerry Powell and Major Cooper. A one-story frame building, it stood between other more grandiose ones off the courthouse square but served its purpose just fine. Semple reached into a cabinet behind his desk and pulled out a decanter of whiskey, pouring each man a drink.

"Not too shabby for a day's work, gents," Semple said, raising the finger of whiskey to his lips.

Jerry Powell gave a harrumph and said, "Yes, indeedy. She never realized we all had the boy's back like we do."

The others nodded, turning their gazes to Emmet who shifted uncomfortably in the stiff chair. All day long, Semple called up townsperson after townsperson to testify on Emmet's behalf. Without fail, they testified that Campbell never alluded to Emmet not being his natural born son. As the procession of characters came up to the stand for him, he felt, with some measure of embarrassment, like the entire town might have his back.

"Not only that but tomorrow she'll be in for another surprise," Semple said.

"How's that?" Emmet asked.

"Our friend, Shepardson."

"Thought he was her friend on this count? Didn't see him there today come to think of it," said the Major.

"Funny that, given it's the biggest trial probably in the history of Colusa. Seemed like the whole town was there. Not like Shepardson to not be out, front and center," Powell said.

Semple looked into the glass and then sucked down the last sip. "Yep. It's like this. He's testifying tomorrow. For Emmet."

Emmet sucked in his breath and said, "What?"

"You heard me. I cornered him a while ago and asked him to stand for you. Things being what they are...well, I think it's our best move to try to head off any closed-door politicking between Shepardson, Mrs. Campbell and Judge Spalding." He stared down into his empty glass and said, under his breath, "It's worth a shot anyway."

Emmet heard about town that Shepardson's bride-to-be, a distant Irish relative of Ann Campbell, was due to arrive in Colusa for a late December wedding. A Christmas wedding in fact. Emmet assumed Shepardson would fully back Ann at the trial due to the bride, Winifred May, and due to the vague sense that Shepardson and he never had good feelings about each other. He didn't envy Shepardson facing his stepmother's wrath over this.

"If nothing else," Semple added, "Dudley has taken an oath under the law to do the right thing. We don't know what was on your father's mind in the end. By all accounts, he was not himself. Not himself at all."

Emmet nodded but felt some nerves jangling at what was left unsaid by Semple about Shepardson, Ann and Spalding.

The Major chimed in. "It shouldn't sit right with anyone that Emmet's left with nothing. Not even his name since birth." The men around the table all nodded in agreement and Emmet again felt the weight of their support, their backing.

A voice hissed in his head at the same time. His stepmother's voice. He imagined her filling Shepardson's ears with thoughts like, 'Do you really think Campbell would have gone on with all of this being wasted on a lad like Emmet? He's a wastrel is what he is.' Or maybe, 'All the labor Campbell put into building this up just to have it knocked down? I can tell he would not like it one bit and it was not what he wanted.' It rang in his own ears, the thoughts she must spew about him.

The second day, all were seated and waiting on the Judge. When the rear doors opened, Emmet looked back to see Dudley Shepardson saunter down the aisle. His was a presence that all noted whether they liked him or not. He nodded and patted shoulders as he walked through, knowing more than his fair share of people seated there. Finding a seat, he settled himself and removed his hat, automatically reaching back to smooth a coif that tended towards the longish side.

Emmet turned resolutely back to the front waiting for whatever was to come. After the call to order, the buzz of conversation stopped and the Judge came out.

"Colonel Semple, do you have any more witnesses for us today?"

The Colonel rose to a standing position. "I do your honor. The plaintiff's side calls the honorable District Attorney, Mr. Dudley Shepardson, to the stand."

Shepardson walked up to the front, holding his hat in both hands. After he was sworn in and seated behind the stand, he gave Semple a big grin and a nod. Emmet cringed at the man's theatrics.

Semple ignored it and said, "Mr. Shepardson, please tell the court how long you knew the deceased, John Campbell."

"Happy to oblige, Colonel. I knew John Campbell from the first day he arrived here in Colusa. So that would have been in 1853. I guess we are talking fourteen years thereabouts."

"Hmm, hmm. And, in that time, what was your understanding of Emmet's parentage?"

Shepardson paused and then said, "Well, when Emmet was a small boy and being badly treated by other boys, Campbell seemed less careful of him than a parent ought to be. So I asked him flat out if Emmet was his son."

"His response?"

"He merely looked at me with astonishment and asked why I would ask such a question."

"So there was never a question in your mind that Emmet was his son?"

Shepardson seemed to weigh each word as he said, "Emmet was reputed to be his son throughout the community."

Semple stood still in front of Shepardson as though internally debating whether to pursue this. Thinking better of it, he announced, "No further questions of this witness, Judge." Semple took his seat while Emmet breathed a sigh of relief. Shepardson seemed to have left little room for any debate.

The Judge directed the proceedings to the other side. "Mr. Cheney, cross-examine?"

"Yes indeed, your honor."

Shepardson again smoothed his hair back, seemingly unperturbed at being cross-examined by Cheney. Walking his girth closer to the witness stand, Mr. Cheney paused as though in deep reflection. Then he said, "Mr. Shepardson, can you tell us about a conversation you had with John Campbell in the summer of 1866?"

Shepardson squinted and said, "Can you pin down a night for me there, Cheney? That's a broad expanse of time, ain't it?" Some chuckles came from the room.

"Yes, I can. It was a night that you brought a special Cuban cigar for Mr. Campbell and a bottle of honey mead wine for his wife, Ann. Do you remember that night now?"

Shepardson shifted a bit, showing he was jarred, and Emmet felt his stomach clench. He remembered that night too well. The night his father had spewed off a bunch of nonsense. The first time that Emmet had ever heard anything like that about who he was.

"All right. I know the night in question. What about it?"

"What did John Campbell tell you about Emmet that night?"

Shepardson looked up over the room and pinned Ann with his eyes. "He told me Emmet was not his child." There were gasps in the crowd.

"Anything else?" Cheney prodded.

"My recollection is that he said the boy was the son of his first wife who had been a widow when he married her. He mentioned the boy was like that woman's brothers. Said they had been hard to manage. But Campbell was already in bad health at this time."

"No further questions," Mr. Cheney puffed out his chest and sat back down.

Amidst murmurings in the crowd, Shepardson made his way back to a seat. The Judge again banged the gavel. When the court became silent again, he spoke to Semple. "Any further witnesses for the plaintiff?"

Semple rose to a stand again and said, "Indeed, Judge, indeed. I call DA Shepardson back up to the stand."

Shepardson stood back up and twirled around as though making jest of coming and going, getting some laughs from the room.

After Shepardson got back to the stand, Semple walked up, taking measured steps. "Now, Mr. Shepardson, you testified a bit back that you knew Emmet to be John Campbell's son all these years, isn't that right?"

"Correct."

"You also mentioned that John Campbell was in ill health at the time you heard him say otherwise. Did I get that right?"

"Yes sir."

"So, in your summation, with all things considered, do you discount what John Campbell said as not being true that night?"

Cheney stood up and sputtered out. "Objection! Conjecture."

The Judge nodded and said, "Objection sustained."

Semple crossed his arms over his chest and paused. Then he started again. "All right, DA Shepardson. I am going to ask you the same question I did earlier. Was there ever a question in your mind that Emmet Campbell was not the son of John Campbell?"

"And I'm going to give you the same answer. Emmet was reputed to be his son throughout the community."

Semple studied the man behind the stand for a beat and then said, "No further questions, your honor."

The Judge pounded his gavel and said, "Court is recessed until afternoon."

Chapter Twenty-three

When court reconvened that afternoon, the room took on too much of the unseasonable humidity from outdoors. Gazing back behind him, Emmet could see folks fanning themselves, already overheated and probably becoming just as weary as he was of the court doings.

The only two witnesses that Cheney called up for Ann's side were no surprise to Emmet. Both women were mealy mouthed and annoying like gnats, standing by Ann when no other townsfolk had.

The first one was Mrs. May. A slight, bird-like woman, she had great difficulties with her husband and Emmet remembered she sought Ann's advice on the matter whenever they crossed paths. Sometimes she just showed up at the ranch seeking guidance. His stepmother always complained about it afterwards saying she had to listen to the woman and give her plain speak about what to do out of Christian charity. Even though the woman just paid her lip service and never really followed the advice. But now here she was, loyal to Ann's cause.

"Mrs. May, did you ever hear John Campbell discuss the parentage of Emmet Campbell?" Cheney asked.

"I did."

"When did that occur?"

"It occurred in either the fall or winter of 1866, thereabouts."

"And what did he say?"

"He said Emmet was the illegitimate child of a girl in the States."

"Where did he say it?"

"It was in his own house at the ranch. Emmet and Ann Campbell were both there when he said it." Somebody in the galley gave a guffaw that all could hear. The Judge let it pass.

Cheney then called up Mrs. Frieze, the second witness for the defendant's side. Mrs. Frieze made weekly trips out to the ranch to teach Mary Ann the pianoforte ever since Ann had purchased it. After receiving weekly payments for the lessons, Emmet supposed it may be some sort of odd payback for her to be up on the stand now.

"Mrs. Frieze, can you tell us what you know of Emmet Campbell's parentage?"

"Yes, I can. Sometime in December 1866, about a month or so before his death, I heard John Campbell say that Emmet was not his own child."

"Did he say who he was the child of?"

"Yes. He said he was the child of a girl in the States and that he took him at six weeks of age to raise up."

After Mrs. Frieze stepped off the stand, Emmet digested the paltry testimony on offer from Ann's side. It boiled down to the twisting of Shepardson's testimony on the part of Cheney earlier in the day and, now, the two women who looked up to his stepmother for advice or money and were lying for her. It couldn't possibly overturn all the testimony from the first day on his behalf. Or could it?

There was just one last witness to be heard: Ann herself. Semple told him that she intended to defend herself by testifying. Semple wanted Emmet to take the stand to tell his truth but he had said no, the idea of it making him go frozen inside.

Emmet's palms began to sweat as he watched her walk up to the stand, seemingly unaffected by the battering of the testimonies that had gone on around her and against her. The Cooper family members and Jerry Powell still sat right behind him as they had both days of the trial. Their presence made him sit a little taller. Their support meant everything.

As she was sworn in, Emmet bit down hard on his lower lip tasting iron and realized he bit too hard. Ann seemed impervious to all the stares her way. Especially Emmet's stare. All eyes in the courtroom drilled into her as Cheney asked the first question that let her begin her tale.

"Mrs. Campbell, would you kindly tell the court what you recall about Emmet's parentage?"

"I certainly can. John Campbell told me in 1858 before we were married---when we were making arrangements to marry---that he did not have any children. He said his first wife was sickly and never had children."

"So how did he explain who Emmet was?"

"He said Emmet was the illegitimate child of a girl---Lilah was her name---who lived in his neighborhood in the States..."

Stirrings and mumblings grew to a higher pitch in the room. The Judge spoke out saying, "Quiet in my court!"

Once it settled, Cheney prodded Ann. "What else did he say about Emmet?"

Ann cleared her throat and then continued. "He said that he and his first wife had taken the girl and the baby. They kept them for about three months and then sent the girl off, adopting Emmet as they had none of their own."

As the words spilled forth from her mouth, Emmet shut them out and, instead, sat back in his chair to avoid having a direct view of her. His mind went back to one of the many springtime days walking the fields with his father...

The warm sun beaming down took the edge off the bitter spring wind. Early cottonwood blooms floated by in the air. Winter wheat was beginning to grow in tall and lush. Later, at harvest time, it would be cut to the quick, shorn off like stubble on cowboys' faces. It was the one thing, maybe the only thing, that he and his father had between them: the land.

He thought about his father telling him, "Someday, this will all be yours." Emmet repeated it to himself now as she sat on the witness stand, her mouth moving and forming words to the contrary. She was saying that Campbell frequently told her this same information in the presence of Emmet during their marriage. She claimed that Campbell said the boy was just like his uncles, Lilah's brothers, at home back in Illinois where Emmet had been born. Unruly and hard to manage.

Emmet kept repeating what his father had told him again and again, "Someday, this will all be yours", because if he didn't, he might burst out of his seat and cover her mouth to stop what came out of it. It was like she was denying his very existence. She had changed the story to fit how she needed it to go.

His stepmother's words finally wound down as she said, "Campbell said that if the boy stayed with him, he intended to give him an education and do a good part by him. So, after Campbell's death, I told the boy if he would stay with me until he was of age, I would educate him and give him five hundred dollars. But he preferred to leave."

The Judge spoke up again. "Order in the court. I will not have my court be disrespected like this. You have a problem with these proceedings, take it elsewhere."

Emmet tuned back into the room wondering if the Judge was talking about him but then realized that people were hissing and booing. They supported him. They knew the real truth no matter what she said up there.

When she used the word, "adopted", he heard Powell bristle behind him. He was a man who knew what adopted meant to a boy's life, having been adopted himself. But Emmet had not been adopted which was why this whole thing had an ugly stench about it. His father would have told him at some point along the way especially as he got close to death. He may not have been the best father around but he was truthful. He would have told Emmet the truth of the matter.

His stepmother, on the other hand, was not being truthful. She had not added the much needed details to her tale. Like how John Campbell had slurred his words as he went soft in his head without his wits about him.

He thought back to one of those nights sitting by his father's sick bed. His father opened his eyes and asked him for a sip of water. He had been fully aware and present so Emmet took a leap. He asked him straight out, "Pa, is there anything you want to tell me?" His father gazed at him, eyes open wide and innocent as a newborn baby. He did not utter one word in response.

After Ann finished her last words, Cheney, with a smug grin on his face, tossed out a "Your witness, counselor," to Semple as he swaggered back to his side of the courtroom.

Semple stood up and sniffed out loud. "Thank you, Mr. Cheney."

With careful paces, he walked up until he was a few feet from Ann, closer than he had approached any of the other witnesses. "Mrs. Campbell...there are a number of contradictions with what you have said compared to what numerous others have testified over the past two days, aren't there?"

She gazed at him without saying anything.

Semple repeated himself when she didn't respond. "Aren't there?"

"Isn't that your job to figure out, Colonel Semple?" At her sharp retort, someone inhaled sharply directly behind Emmet. But he knew this woman. He knew she didn't take well to be called out on anything.

"Well, yes, Mrs. Campbell. Yes, it is. So here is the question...was Emmet the son of John Campbell's first wife because she was a widow when he married her? Or...was he the son of a girl back in Illinois? And who exactly were these uncles that you claim he is like? Were they the brothers of the first wife...or of the girl? You can see why I've become a little confused, can't you? And I'm thinking if I'm confused, everybody else is too."

Her Irish accent came out more pronounced when she answered. "I can only tell you what the man himself told me. That's all I can tell you."

"Hmm...well, I don't know that you got a straight story out of that man, that's the problem."

"Is that a question?" Cheney sputtered out. "Judge, can the counselor please get to the point here?"

"Yes, Semple, please stop the rambling," the Judge said.

"Okay, yes, here it is so we can get you off the stand. Here is my question. Do you think when your husband spoke to you on these matters he was in any state of mind that he knew what he was talking about?"

Ann thrust her chin up and looked at Semple with daggers shooting from her eyes.

Enunciating each word, she answered. "Yes. I do."

Semple shook his head at her in response. Walking back to Emmet's side, Semple did not hold back from rolling his eyes as he said aloud, "No further questions for this witness, your honor."

The next morning in the courtroom, Judge Spalding's fingertips tented together and the expression on his face was somber. He took a moment before moving his hands apart to speak to all assembled. "This has not been an easy couple days in my court. We have heard testimonies from numerous folks but those testimonies, taken as a whole, have been conflicting."

He paused and his gaze took in the entire room. "In situations like these, weight must be given to what we call the preponderance of evidence. In this case, I deem that to be what was shared in marital confidence. John Campbell told the wife he lived with for over eight years that Emmet was the child of a neighbor girl who had found herself in a family way. And that, according to her, the boy was adopted by Campbell and his first wife."

Rumblings stirred up in the crowd as the Judge spit out the last part of his statement. "After careful deliberation of both sides of this unfortunate situation, the preponderance of evidence lies heavily on the side of the...the...defendant."

There was an immediate audible reaction to his statement: a range of emotions being expressed from disgust to surprise to anger. There were all these sounds around him but Emmet had none from his own self. Not one sound.

"Ain't have nothing to do with you being best mates with Shepardson, does it?" Jerry Powell said loud enough for all to hear. Emmet could feel Powell's anger at the injustice beaming out into the room, out from his large form.

"Powell, I'll see you held for contempt, you keep that up!" the Judge called out into the room in his Kentucky twang.

Collecting himself, he followed with, "The decision of this court is that Ann Campbell is the executrix of the Campbell Estate with John W. Campbell, her son by John Campbell, as its rightful heir."

Semple encouraged Emmet to a stand as the bailiff said, "All rise." Placing a fatherly arm around Emmet's broad shoulders, he said softly, "Son, we are going to appeal this, don't you worry."

The crowd worked its way out of the courthouse with Emmet and Ann both reaching the aisle at the same time. Emmet stared into her stone cold eyes and said, "You will regret this." Her eyes flickered as he repeated it. "You will regret this."

The four men again gathered in Semple's office. Semple poured shots for each man which they all swallowed down at once. Emmet barely felt the heat burn down his throat. Instead, he just felt numb after listening to all the talk about him as though he had never existed.

Powell was the first to speak. "Well, that was a fine kettle of rotting fish, wasn't it? Spalding and Shepardson under the covers together is what that was. Everybody knows their daddies were thick as thieves back in the States, in Kentucky. Straight up politics is what it is." He sniffed after he finished.

"Now, now, I've known Spalding to be a fair and righteous judge in his days on the court. He made the call as he saw fit. That doesn't mean we have to like it though," the Major said. He threw a glance over towards Emmet. Emmet gave him a weak smile.

Semple took a deep breath in and sat back with hands placed on his belly. "It's not all black and white in a courtroom, gentlemen. Not by a long shot. Instead, there are many variants of grey. Shepardson's testimony brought out some of those greys."

"The question is now what can we do for our boy here," the Major asked.

"Couple of thoughts come to mind. But the main thing is his judgement is not sustained by the evidence. That is what I intend to make the basis of the appeal. And we will ask for a new trial based on it," Semple said.

Emmet filtered out the talk of the other three men as he stared out the window at the courthouse that loomed in front. He never wanted this kind of attention and this is where it had ended up. No one, not even himself, knew who he really was.

Later, after riding his horse hard out towards the buttes, Emmet eventually wore himself and the horse out and made his way back to town. To the Blue House.

He entered the room and a number of men came over to clap him on the back or offer a word of condolence. He shrugged it all off and went back to the Madam's table. She looked at him with a careful eye. "She won?"

"Yeah. She did."

"It'll work out. You'll see."

Emmet looked down at the ornate carpet beneath the table studying its teardrop shaped pattern with deep reds and purples intertwined. He smelled her before he saw her, the scent of lilac that was always just a whiff. Not too much and not too little. When he looked back up, Bonita was sitting next to him with her guitar.

She thrust it forward and said, "Here."

"What?"

"Take it. You need it more than me right now."

"Nah. I can't take it from you."

"Yeah, you can. It's yours now."

She picked up his hand and placed his fingers saying, "This is the E minor chord."

As he sat strumming Bonita's guitar, he focused on that. Just that.

Chapter Twenty-four

A couple of days later, Emmet found himself seated across from Semple again.

"Son, I have laid it all out here...take a look." He pushed the document towards Emmet.

Emmet picked the paper up but, as usual, the words blurred in front of him and he could only make out one or two of them. He kept his eyes on the paper and finally looked up at the Colonel.

"I can't read."

"Oh, that's right. Pardon me for not remembering. I'll read it aloud to you, shall I?"

Semple raised his spectacles to his eyes and cleared his throat. "'We ask the court for a new trial based on the following:

The declaration of John Campbell that Emmet is not his son was given while he was in ill health and under the influence of a second wife.

Ann Campbell's testimony should not have been entered into the proceedings legally.

Dudley Shepardson's testimony was a surprise testimony because he was originally supposed to support the plaintiff.

And then here is the document that affirms that you state that you are the son and heir of John Campbell, deceased, dated 6 July 1868."

He pushed that forward and added, "Sign your X at the bottom there."

After Emmet signed an X, Semple placed the document back into the pile.

"So 'we request the new trial be given based on the following grounds: 1) Error of law which occurred at trial 2) Newly discovered testimony 3) the judgement was not sustained by the evidence.'"

Looking over his spectacles at Emmet, he said, "Did you understand all that? Ask me anything you want about all this. I know it can get confusing."

Emmet looked down at his boots before saying anything. The two men sat together in the silent room except for the ticking of Semple's clock that stood on the mantel over his fireplace.

Eventually, Emmet lifted his head and said, "How is she allowed to do this? I just don't get it. How is she allowed to strip me of my very own identity?"

Semple let out a big sigh and said, "Son, I wish I had an answer for you. The law can work in some mysterious ways and sometimes it comes out not right. This is one of those times. I wish it had gone differently here...I really do."

Emmet took in Semple's words but they really didn't do anything to soothe the raw anguish that he felt inside. The same raw anguish he had been feeling long before the trial. And now he realized this feeling would not be leaving any time soon.

A couple of weeks later, he stood at Semple's office door. He got word that Semple was ready to talk to him again. He hesitated as he lifted his hand to knock but then did so forthrightly.

Semple yelled out for him to come in. Entering, he found Semple sitting behind his desk, heavily loaded down with stacks of papers. He held out one document well in front of his spectacles. Seeing Emmet, he stood up from the desk and greeted him with a "Hello, son. How you faring today?"

After Emmet greeted him in return, Semple said, "Take a seat, take a seat." Sitting back down himself, he said, "Well, the Judge's final ruling came through on our appeal."

Emmet bit his lower lip and waited for more.

"Sad to tell you, it just didn't go in our favor." Semple paused to let it settle in before continuing. "Let me read it to you so you can hear for yourself. Where is it..." he moved his hands over the papers and pulled it out of one of the piles.

"Ahem. It's dated 25 July 1868. And it states: 'While evidence for Plaintiff was only negative as general reputation, four witnesses swore positively for defense---that John Campbell told them directly that Emmet Campbell was not his son. Court dismisses the motion and a new trial is denied.' And it's signed, of course, by Frank Spalding, Probate Judge."

He looked up from the paper and peered at Emmet over his glasses. "Did you understand all that?"

Emmet gave him a slight smile and said, "Colonel, people think 'cause I can't read and write that I'm a dolt. That I'm dumb. But that's not so. Yes, I understand. But I don't like it."

"And you don't have to. I don't like it either. And I have never thought you were dumb, not for a second. But do you have any questions about the letter of the law?"

Emmet looked down at his hands. "Yeah. What does it mean when it says only negative as general reputation? Doesn't general reputation count for something?"

"Well, I would argue that it does and it should, but the law is not a science necessarily. There's some art to it and that means it's open to interpretation. In this case, that's how Judge Spalding interpreted it. If it was my courtroom, all those witnesses we had standing for you would have counted against the three the defendant had. But it's not my courtroom."

Emmet nodded and moved to stand up, saying, "Well I guess that's it then Colonel. I thank you for all..."

"Sit back down for just a sec here, son. Something I want to say to you before you head out."

Semple took his glasses off and laid them down in front of him. "I read one time that some folks have something called 'word blindness.' It means the mind gets the words on a page messed up. It's something that didn't get tuned right maybe when you were coming up. But there may be people out there that can help you figure out a way..."

Emmet put a hand up. "Colonel, I thank you again for looking out for me but it's too late for all that. I'll just carry on as I am."

155

Semple nodded his head and said, "I understand, I understand. But listen. I know you got smarts in there. I've seen it in you since you were a young'un. So don't ever let that or anything else keep you down."

After he stood up and Emmet followed suit, the two men shook hands. When Emmet left and walked down Sixth Street, he could feel Semple's eyes on his back. If Semple guessed that Emmet was heading right on over to the saloons and brothels, he guessed correctly.

That early evening and into the night, Emmet made the rounds a couple times over from saloon to saloon. By mid-evening, he was given a wide berth by all. Everyone in town knew he was on a bender and they knew why.

After the bars shut down for the night, Emmet slumped down against the outside of the Mount Hood Saloon, his father's bar that she had sold to someone else. His vision danced in front of him at the shadows on the street and the pool of vomit lying beside him. In front of this view came a triple image of Old Man Chung. His old friend. Who had never let him down once.

Old Man Chung's skull looked like a shiny globe. Emmet now stared at that globe instead of the man's eyes. He could hear care and concern when the elderly man said, "Up, up. Come."

With an arm slung over his old friend's shoulder, Emmet made slow progress down Market Street until they reached Chinatown. He had not been down in the tunnels for many moons. That had been his childhood. Now he was in the very different realm of manhood.

Somehow Old Man Chung got him down the narrow staircase and through the passage of tunnels without both of them tripping and breaking their necks. Once in the room, Emmet's bleary eyes took in the candlelit space and saw the scene like it had always been, a Fan-Tan game with a few participants, the smoky opium pipe and the big tea kettle brewing its strange concoction.

Chinese words were volleyed around. Emmet had mastered rudimentary aspects of the language years ago at least. In his fogged-up brain, he still managed to understand the interchange between Chung

and the other men: "too much drink, needs special tea, sleeps here."
He knew that Chung and his pals would take care of him for the rest of
the night.

Since there was never any natural light in the tunnels, Emmet had no
idea what the hour was when his eyes popped open. His head
immediately felt as though it was splitting in two pieces and he
reflexively placed a hand on top. He looked over to see Old Man
Chung laying out in stillness on a mat nearby. All the others were gone
and it was just the two of them. It must already be morning, he thought.

He carefully lifted himself up with one arm and the room went
spinning round. He felt the bile rise up in his throat but suppressed it,
taking in a deep breath instead. It was a deep breath of pungent odors
from the teas brewed the previous night. Those odors made it hard to
keep his guts in check.

Once he got settled with the spinning, he rose to standing and
limped over to the chair by the card table, the heart of the room. Upon
hearing Emmet move around, the elderly man rose up himself, shaking
his sleep away. Saying nothing, he sat across from Emmet at the table.

"Feel bad?" he asked eventually.

Emmet nodded.

He picked up a cup filled with something and pressed it to Emmet.
"This work. Made for you last night but you fall sleep."

As the cup got closer to Emmet, that smell was even greater. He
shook his head. "No, no. I can't drink that. It will make me sick again."

"Won't. Take sick away."

Emmet saw in his eyes that Old Man Chung really believed it to be
the case. Bracing himself, he took the cup and slugged its contents back
into his gullet.

"Ugh," he gasped out after he was finished.

When he finally got control of himself, he wiped a hand across his
mouth. He saw the back of it was gouged and blood-stained. It must
have happened along the way but he couldn't remember exactly how.

"Tell me last night. What you do that for?"

"I don't...I don't remember much."

"Why you start like that?"

"Well, there was a trial. You didn't hear about it?"

"I hear some. But not all. No Chinamen allowed there."

Emmet turned the chipped cup this way and that and then stilled it. When he looked up, Old Man Chung stared at him with the question in his eyes. The question of what had happened.

His tongue was heavy in his mouth when he spoke. "She said I wasn't ever his son. And that's what was decided. That is what was put down on paper. Forever. So, who am I then?"

The Chinese man's mouth went into a thin, straight line. "That woman...no good."

Emmet just shook his head. There was nothing that could be said or done to make it any different. To make it any better.

Old Man Chung spoke up again. "You know who Emmet is. Emmet good. Emmet good man."

Emmet felt the start of a smile light upon his face. They were the only words that Old Man Chung had ever said about him in that way. He just had to remember that he had people like Old Man Chung in his life...he had to remember that.

Chapter Twenty-five

Everything boiling around in his mind the whole summer long led him to finally pay her a visit. Catherine Sisk. The woman who had known his mother or at least the person he thought was his first mother. Amanda.

Catherine and Richard Sisk lived in one of the earliest homes built in Colusa. Near the river, it was set off a piece from the houses nearby. After riding in from the range one afternoon, he went straight there. It had been burning more than ever in his thoughts that entire day.

Catherine sat out rocking on her porch, sewing in her hands, pince-nez propped on the bridge of her nose. She looked up at him as he jumped off his horse. Squinting as he approached closer, she finally said, "Emmet Campbell. I wondered if you were ever going to come talk to me." He walked up onto the porch taking it as an invitation.

"Go help yourself to the pitcher of water in the kitchen. My legs give me trouble this time of day or I would get it for you. Bring out a glass for me too, dear."

He walked into the house, taking the moment to collect his thoughts. He was only barely aware of the stark rooms he walked through, filled only with the essentials, which maybe spoke to Catherine Sisk's time on the trail and all it had taught her. He found the pitcher on the butcher's block and poured out two tall glasses and then made his way back to the porch.

She set her work aside and took the glass from him. "Have a seat now. Let me get a look at you."

She eyed him in an appraising manner and said, "You been working hard. I can see that in your face."

"Yes, ma'am."

"What is it you need from me?"

"I guess I want to hear the story all over again. From the start. From when you met them on the trail and then all the rest too."

She nodded. "Alrighty then. I can offer you that."

She took a long draw from her glass first. Then she took up the tale he already heard at the trial. Her talk took him right back to the pain of sitting through the trial with each line hitting him like a punch to the gut.

After expanding on many of the details, she finally reached the end and said, "Fair to say, I never would have guessed that I would be telling it all in a courtroom but life is funny that way. Memory is a fickle mistress. Sometimes, you don't realize what is happening to you at the time is the thing that ends up staying with you the most."

She had wound down and was silent for a pause. "Do you have any questions about any of it?"

"Was I really named after a preacher called Emmet?"

Mrs. Sisk nodded. "She told me that herself."

Emmet shook his head at the idea of it. "What town?"

She looked at him with a curious expression and repeated, "What town? What do you mean?"

"What town did they come from?"

"Oh, you didn't know that...well, if memory serves it was called Downer's Grove. In Illinois."

He nodded.

"Why are you asking about it, son?"

When he didn't answer, she said gently, "Are you thinking about going back to Downer's Grove? Leaving Colusa?"

"Colusa is my home. I would never leave here permanent like. But..."

She looked away from him out somewhere he couldn't see and said, "I wish I could go back sometimes. Not for long. Maybe for just a day."

She turned back to him. "Isn't that silly? An old lady like me thinking she could take such a trip." She gave a sad smile before continuing. "I left a lot of myself back east, you know. We all did..."

He took in the woman in front of him with her white blonde hair, not one strand askew, her tissue-thin facial skin and her neat and tidy house and wondered if this life had been enough for her. He hoped it had been. He hoped that his life too would be enough for him when he reached her age. He had to try and make that happen.

Emmet sat in Powell's bunkhouse and studied the lines on the map in front of him. Red lines, blue lines, green lines. They were hard to figure. His finger moved across to the right towards the center of the country where he found Illinois, dead center of the country. The idea had grown bigger and bigger until now he was pulling pieces together to make it happen. Like the map.

The old Pony Express map had been lying around the bunk house left over from the very brief time that the Pony Express operated. He had never taken a gander at a map before in his life. As he picked it up and examined it, he knew it held the key for what came next. It took him a while to figure out all the lines, imagining it. Imagining America. He got the sense of it now and it would take him there. One of the Indian boys who could read found Illinois on the map and he memorized what the letters looked like and its placement on the piece of paper.

If the pony express boys could do it then, he could do it now. He figured he probably had more experience and hours of riding than those boys ever had. He was not fooling himself that it would be an easy trip though----could be the reason that the mail service only lasted a year and some months. There was a certain beauty in those lines---those lines that really looked to be a straight shot across the country to its middle place. The place where maybe, just maybe, he could figure out how it all started.

The only way he knew to do it was to leave in the middle of the night. He didn't want to hurt Powell and his wife none but he knew it had to be a clean break. The only one he told was Sarshel. And Sarshel kept himself to himself.

He found a floorboard in the corner of the bunkhouse where he squirreled away enough gold coins to last him for a good while. It worked out nicely and he made sure no one ever saw when he put more coin in. Powell would owe him some more pay by his departure so it felt fair enough to take hardtack and pone to fill up his saddle bags from their larder. His horse was his property, one of the Spanish horses that originally been Campbell's. Powell bought it at auction and Emmet worked off the cost. The horse was his only real possession.

On the night he planned on his leave-taking, Sarshel rode over to the bunkhouse. As usual, it was strange to see Sarshel anywhere other than Coopers' front porch. The two stood away from the bunkhouse and Sarshel reached over to hand him something saying, "Here."

In the light of the moon, Emmet could see that it was a locket.

"Open it," Sarshel said.

Inside was a photograph of Mary Benicia. Emmet looked at Sarshel and said, "How did you get this?"

"I took it off Fanny one time she was here. For you."

"Sarshel..."

Sarshel waved a hand. "She and Pulsifer have more money than God. She'll just get another."

Emmet was conflicted inside. He wanted the remembrance of Mary Benicia but it didn't feel right to take it this way.

Sarshel said softly, "It's okay to take sometimes."

Emmet nodded slowly. He stuck his hand out and the other man took it in a shake.

"I'll be back. Soon enough."

"I know you will. I know you will."

Later, the bunkhouse was still, aside from the occasional snores and other slight or big noises a body might make. Emmet made slow careful movements like he did when he was hunting in the tall grasses. Movements that would not wake any being.

A neat tidy pile hidden under his bedding held his scanty belongings. Carefully picking it up, he left the building without a backwards glance. He had readied his horse earlier and now he swung up onto the saddle. Heading down the long drive out from Powell's, Emmet made it to the main road, the one going south to Sacramento. From there, he would follow the old Pony Express route eastwards.

Emmet was leaving Colusa.

PART THREE: Endings
Chapter Twenty-six

Emmet stood back along a stand of cottonwoods watching from a distance. A small group circled around the open grave site that awaited Sarshel Cooper's coffin. He took his hat off and slid a hand over his hair to smooth it, holding hat to chest. A cold, cutting wind whipped around as the preacher droned on with the all too familiar words: ashes to ashes...

Emmet never made it to the middle. Never made it much past the Sierras. One bad luck night at a saloon in a town called Cicero wiped out the majority of his stash of gold coins. He drifted into work on a large ranch and settled into what he did best, riding out on the range. Occasionally, he got news of Colusan folk and Colusa through the loose network of cowboys who flitted in and out of the ranch where he was. The pull to venture further east slowly ebbed away...maybe because the string that tied him to Colusa was always stronger, always in play.

The string pulled him back one day when the news was about Sarshel. Sarshel had been found dead on the road to Marysville in October of 1873. Without too much thought put into it, Emmet detached himself from his place of work and rode hard to get back to Colusa for the funeral. But he was too late for the church doings and barely made it in time to the community cemetery in the center of town.

Emmet took in the family members standing closest to the open grave. Major Cooper with new lines etched hard into his face, Sarshel's two sisters with eyes downcast, his one brother, Thomas Benton, looking like he wore a death mask himself and Mary Benicia, standing next to her husband, her belly swollen with child, her eyes raw and red.

164

At the sight of Mary Benicia, he inadvertently placed a hand on his chest pocket where he kept the locket that Sarshel had given him. Maybe the only possession other than his horse that he never misplaced. But now he could not look at her. They were too far from each other.

He felt the tug of connection but, at the same time, there was also the thin divide, the divide of not being blood. He thought how Malinda Cooper, notably absent now, bridged that divide as much as she possibly could by her kindness to the boy without a mother of his own. But even she could only do so much.

Before the preacher finished his last utterings, Emmet turned and left, not ready to say what needed to be said. He assumed they would all go back to Coopers' and he would go there too but first he needed to let the strangeness of being back settle in.

It had been just a two-day ride from the ranch outside of Lake Tahoe to Colusa to come back home for good. He thought about snakes shedding skins and getting used to new ones. That would be him. He always wondered what that felt like when he saw snakes out on the range. Now he would be finding out.

He headed north from the cemetery to the river. He breathed in its smell---the smell of Colusa. At the sight of its churning waters, memories rushed up at him. Oddly, the one that came to the forefront of his mind was old one-eyed Sampson, his erstwhile pet. He was a good cat, a companion who made the lonely nights above his father's store bearable. Emmet hoped he had done right by Sampson, visiting him at the river's berm when he could until Sampson had not shown up anymore, joining the roll call of other ghosts from Emmet's past.

Turning away from the river, Emmet directed his mount to Market, taking in what was old and what was new as he looked around. Market Street was still Market Street. Changed but yet unchanged.

He drew his horse to a halt at the building that appeared the same other than a different sign that read, M. L. Sussmont's. His father's old store. Opening the door with the familiar jangling twang from the bell, he walked in. It overcame him, the place. The same smell hung in the air, the smell of a store where food and sundries and other supplies were sold. The counter displays were also the same, some slightly altered. His eyes wandered back to the storage closet where he had spent so many hours hiding.

A man stood behind the counter and looked at Emmet. "Good day to you, sir, what do you need?" His accent came out thick and maybe German to Emmet's ear.

"I'm Emmet Campbell."

The man, his broad belly covered with a taut white apron, placed his hands on the countertop. Big hands used to doing all sorts of tasks. "I am Sussmont, the proprietor."

"You don't recognize my name?"

The German shook his head.

Right after the question was out of his mouth, Emmet realized it had been over six years past since his father's death. The store had changed hands at least twice, maybe three times. Why would this man with the German accent recognize his name?

"My father set up this store back in the day when Colusa was just...well, when Colusa was getting on its legs."

"Ah. I see. So, you come to..." the man's gaze took in the entirety of his store, "you come to see."

Emmet felt a sense of relief that the man seemed to understand. "I'm just back here. I've been gone five years now."

It seemed funny that the very first person he talked to in Colusa was a stranger but yet...yet...the man did not feel like a stranger. Maybe because they were standing together in John Campbell's store.

"Five years. Is a long time. What will you do now?"

Emmet nodded more to himself than the man. "That is a good question. Need to find work, I guess."

"Well, if there is any way I can help you, Emmet Campbell, let me know." The two men shook hands and Emmet felt a strange rapport with Sussmont.

He experienced that kind of quick connection with others at times. It now made him think of a man named Dizzy, whom he met at the very first saloon he stopped at in Sacramento. Standing at the threshold of that saloon, he was overwhelmed by the place, huge by Colusa's standards. It had been a full house that night with painted ladies plying their trade, cowboys in chaps and Dizzy, a dwarf, sitting on top of a baby grand piano in the corner.

Emmet was fascinated by the sight, never having seen a dwarf before. His eyes kept turning to the small figure perched on top of the piano. An older gent with a white shirt and a bowtie was playing the piano as Dizzy sang in a high falsetto. It was a tune with a haunting lilt that Emmet didn't know. Dizzy cut quite a picture with his jet black hair, too black to be natural, a large bulbous nose and pouty red lips.

After he finished the song, a smattering of applause recognized his accomplishment and he jumped down with an easy agility from the piano. Picking up a hat, he made the rounds from table to table. At Emmet's table, he plopped down on the chair opposite and pulled the money out from the hat. He counted it aloud, licking a fingertip before picking up each new bill. Emmet stared at the little man more in surprise than anything else.

Finally, the dwarf spoke. "You look like you have a story for me."

"I do?"

"Something in your face...."

They had a stare off until Emmet broke his eyes away and said, "No story. Just a cowboy on the open road."

"Well, cowboy, I know you are hiding something. Some secrets. That's okay. Because we're all hiding secrets in this room."

The barmaid came to the table with Emmet's ale and Emmet gestured to the dwarf to order a drink of his choice.

"Why, thank you, sir. Don't mind if I do. Libby, I'll have the usual."

When Libby returned, she plunked down a glass of water by the man, apparently his usual. He caught Emmet looking at the glass and explained. "I get the kidney stones due to my size, you see. Old Doc Tenney told me to stay off the sauce. So I do. Those kidney stones will tear you up bad. You ever get 'em?"

"Nah...don't reckon I have."

"You don't want to. Anyways, I been here too long now and I need to be heading out. Where you headed?"

"Oh...the middle."

"Where's the middle?"

"The middle of the country, I mean. The middle of the States."

"Huh. What takes you there?"

"Uh...it's a long story."

"I got time. I ain't going to sing until the Piano Pete comes back. What's your name anyway? Mine's Dizzy."

"Dizzy?"

"Yeah, on account I often get head spins---also, 'cause of my size. You might have noticed I'm on the shorter side of the fence." He cracked a smile and Emmet watched those red lips expand into a grin.

Emmet shook his head at the memory wondering where Dizzy was now...

Eventually, he made his way in the direction of Coopers, finding the drive to the ranch littered with fallen weeds and untrodden of late. Getting closer, he could see the ranch house itself appeared wilted around the edges. Almost five years had gone by. Time enough for things to change.

A figure sat on the porch bundled in a tartan blanket. Emmet swung off his horse and walked closer. The face looked over at him and lit up with recognition. The Major. Alone with no sign of his devoted wife and companion, Malinda, nearby...

"Emmet Campbell? That you?"

He climbed up the stairs and the Major reached both hands out for Emmet's. As Emmet took his hands, he could see the Major was not well in his visage and he could feel the shakiness of his grip.

"Ah, you are a sight for sore eyes. I been worried after you the past couple years."

Emmet looked over to Sarshel's rocker. "I heard about Sarshel...and I came back."

Pain flashed over the old man's face and he nodded. "Malinda died back in '72. He took it hard. All of us did, of course, but Sarshel...."

Emmet stared off towards the fruit trees at the edge of the property before answering. He said, "I didn't...I guess I..."

The Major waved at him with a weak hand and said, "Aww, none of that now. You were a good friend to him, Emmet. Maybe the best friend he ever had."

Emmet wiped a hand over his face. "I shoulda come back sooner...it wasn't right, me leaving him here alone."

"He waren't alone, young man. He had his whole big family around him every day. Most don't have that," he said with a huff of his old indignation.

"Well, how did he...I mean..."

"How did he die, you're asking. Just come out with it, son. We've known each other too long for pussyfooting around, haven't we?"

Emmet gave a slight smile and nodded. The Major's way with words was coming back to him. He had forgotten how he was to be around. He had forgotten about a lot.

Stephen Cooper rubbed a hand over bristly whiskers and told Emmet that Sarshel had been found on the road to Marysville just a mile from Colusa, unconscious and lying in the gully by the road. He then said, "Sometimes, I wonder if that is what he sat here on the porch and thought about all those hours before getting up the gumption to do so. Doc thinks he took some kind of poison. No telling what it was though..."

There was bitterness mixed with the sadness in his voice. "Of course, Malinda dying unexpected like that...it was the first day of the year it was. I guess her body had decided it couldn't go on for another year. Hit Sarshel too hard. Hit all of us..."

Emmet turned his head away from Cooper, overwhelmed by all the losses not only for the man sitting next to him but for himself as well. He should have stayed for Sarshel. He berated himself for not staying. For Sarshel.

As if he could read his mind, Cooper said, "Nothing you coulda done about it, Emmet. Nothing any of us coulda done."

Emmet knew that as often as he told himself those words he would never get to the point of actually believing them. Cooper reached over and gave him a weak slap on the knee. "You remember the first word you spoke finally?"

Emmet shook his head.

"It was Sarshel. You said, 'Sarshel, stop it' and it was the first time any of us had heard a peep from you. We all had a good laugh that day...."

Emmet gave the man who had known him all those years back a big smile.

Cooper continued, "So I'd offer you a place to stay but we are closing up the operations here." His gaze travelled over the property which had clearly been left untended. "Things started to get away from me after Malinda....and now Sarshel..." He let it all hang.

"Where are you headed, Major?" Emmet asked, alarmed at the prospect of the older man heading off into the yonder on his own.

"Going up to Winters. Moving in with Martha." He paused and then added, "I'll be all right." The last bit seemed almost more for himself than Emmet.

He then said, "The rest of the family is inside. You go on in and get something to eat, you hear?"

But Emmet did not think he could face Mary Benicia and her husband so he made his excuses. The Major accepted the excuses seeing through them for what they were and then looked at him astutely. "You need work now that you are back?"

Emmet gave a slight grimace and said, "Yeah, I do. But I'll figure out something."

"Head up to Wakefield's place over near Williams. Tell him I sent you. He's got a big operation now."

Emmet nodded but felt wrong leaving the man alone on his porch with his ghosts. All alone now. No family circling around.

Sensing his hesitation, the Major said, "Off with you now. Go find your way out there, young man." Emmet placed a hand on one of the man's shoulders before leaving the porch and riding away.

He headed out to the place that he loved so well with the buttes hanging right behind it, the Campbell ranch. He knew Ann had sold most of the land off to others and moved to town but the ranch house still sat there, now unoccupied. The ranch buildings had not been maintained in a while but he assumed they were being used for storage by nearby farmers. He doubted Powell was using them though. Not after the trial and the bad blood that stirred between her and Powell.

He got off his horse and tied it off. Walking around the place, he took it all in. The land was not being farmed, not being used for livestock. It wasn't right. The ranch needed to come alive again. Like it was when he and his father were just starting out and it was only the two of them.

He ended up back on his old familiar hummock where he used to wait for his father to come in from town. Closing his eyes, he felt the sharpness of the wind on his skin and smelled the winter wheat being shook out by that same wind. It struck him what he needed to do. He needed to get it all back. He would work hard and make it happen

Chapter Twenty-seven

Chinatown was busier than Emmet remembered with more Chinamen walking out and about in the area. He knocked on Old Man Chung's door and felt anticipation at seeing the face of his old friend. But a new Chinaman stood there when the door opened.

"Chung?" Emmet asked as a question.

"He no live here."

"Where is he?"

The other man shrugged and said, "Go see Feng."

Emmet's memory was that Feng ran a small apothecary at the end of the row. Filled with all sorts of oddities. His memory served right when he walked into the small one room building and gazed around the tight space. It now struck him as a bit amazing that Feng was able to procure all of it and somehow get it to Colusa.

Feng did not look a day older than when Emmet had seen him last. He gave Emmet a nod upon recognizing him. "You come back for Chung?"

Emmet looked at him perplexed. "Come back?"

"He sick. Bad lungs."

Emmet felt something shift. Old Man Chung in trouble now too from the sound of it.

"Where is he?"

"No place for him but tunnels. He down there. I take herbs to him." The man waved both hands forward and added, "Go. Go to him."

Emmet wasted no time and found the alley he knew so well that took him underground into the tunnels. The familiar odor rose up as he walked down the stairs and entered into the darkness. Using his hands on the walls and crouching down for his head, he felt his way until the room opened up.

Emmet looked over to see a blanket covered figure in one of the alcoves niched into the earthen walls. The figure was still and Emmet hesitated to go closer. Then, as if sensing Emmet's presence, the elderly man rolled to one side and Emmet could see his face. Mask-like, Emmet knew that Old Man Chung's time had come due. It was a look he recalled too well from sitting at his father's bedside before the final hour.

Approaching closer, he heard a deep, wrenching cough. When the old man pulled the rag back from his mouth, Emmet could see the bright red blood. His voice came out in a gravelly whisper. "I hope to see you again."

"Chung, what happened?"

"Got sick a while back. Nothing to do for it." He gasped for another breath and continued. "All those days working on train tracks, I think. Bad for breathing."

Emmet thought Chung should have ridden out with him on the miles and miles of open range when he headed east. Where he could breathe in all the fresh air and wipe out the bad, getting rid of any rot harming his body. But no chance of that now, Emmet could see without much doubt.

Old Man Chung used one shaky arm to push himself up to a seat. Pausing first, his eyes closed briefly and then he stood up, weakness revealed in his efforts. He made a slow, careful path over to the table littered with the detritus of whatever game had last been played.

"What do you need, Chung? I'll get you anything you need."

He shook his head slowly. "I need nothing. I get down to the shops when I can. But...this..." his finger pointed at Emmet's chest as he slumped down into the chair. "This is good. You are good. I didn't know where..."

Emmet felt the double wave of guilt and shame that he felt on the Major's porch. He hadn't let people like Old Man Chung and Sarshel know his whereabouts. They had worried over him when he was gone. That wasn't right.

"Well, I'm here now. We'll get you fixed up."

Old Man Chung nodded and reached over to pull a mortar and pestle closer to him. A small pile of plant material lay nearby and he picked through some root like pieces that looked strangely human in form. After sorting them, Emmet watched as the elderly man mashed them down under the weight of the pestle. It took Emmet back to being a child and all the hours he had watched this same laborious process to make tea again and again. Somehow, there was always a stash of fresh material on hand.

After it was ground to his satisfaction, Chung poured water over the mixture in a tea cup. Emmet sat next to him, just like in the days of old, not really talking much just sitting next to each other. After it steeped, Chung took a long draw of the hot liquid followed by a contented sigh.

When leaving, he told the old man he would return as often as possible. Old Man Chung just nodded.

Emerging from the tunnels, he came out into the night and knew it was time. He had waited long enough but now it was time to go to the Blue House. On a packed weekend night, the place would be at full tilt and he could blend in.

Anticipation built in each footstep as he walked from Chinatown into the heart of Colusa. At the corner of Fourth and Market, the Blue House pulsated with bright lights and loud noise. Standing at the threshold that led to three steps down, he struggled with a shyness about seeing Charlotte and her girls again. Especially one girl in particular---if she was still there.

Five years earlier when he had said goodbye to Bonita, he handed her guitar back over for safekeeping. They both looked away from each other's eyes and Emmet said finally, "I'll pick it back up soon..."

She shrugged, not really indicating one way or the other how she felt about him leaving. But now...he hoped to see her again.

There had been plenty of women at plenty of whorehouses while he had been gone, of course. He thought back to one especially. One night at a saloon, he stood at the bar downing an ale when he felt a wisp of something at his elbow. He looked over and then downwards to see a petite Asian woman next to him, saying nothing. He studied her and took in her delicate facial features powdered heavily in white. Despite the make-up, he placed her at a younger age than himself. He gestured to the bartender to give the lady a drink and the arrangement was made without any words spoken.

Later, in the room upstairs, he watched as she pulled her dress back on. One side of her body had a deep knot of scarring that began at her shoulder blade and ran down below her thigh. He reached forward to stop her from pulling the rest of her dress down and said, "What happened?"

She looked at him and then down at the scar. "A remember? A remind..."

"A reminder? Did it happen from where you come from?"

She nodded and sat back onto the bed next to him.

"Where is your country?"

"Nippon."

He looked at her with a question on his face so she continued in her stilted English. "You call Japan. Land of rising sun."

"Ah. So, a long way aways."

She nodded. Then she seemed to feel it important that he understand the scar. She touched the fabric that covered it and said, "This like kintsugi. You know kintsugi?"

He shook his head with apology. "No. I don't know Japan words. I do know some Chinese words though."

She looked down as though searching for the words on the floor before continuing. "Broken parts seal up with gold. Get strong there." She pointed to her chest and said, "Like me. Strong."

Emmet smiled at this young girl. She was strong to be here. With her scarred body. To have come east over the seas. He wondered if she was banished from her country because of that scar, changing it around to be a different thing, an okay thing. His smile was tinged with sadness knowing that this life of hers was hard and would continue to be hard.

She reached over and traced a light touch with her finger along the raised white welts on his arm from the mountain lion scratches. The wounds were long scarred over. He rubbed in grease from animals cooked out on the range for many months after it happened. The four zig zag lines on his bare arms eventually turned from raw red to white and ropy looking. No one would ever call them pretty, though some might consider it a sort of art.

"You have it too." She added, "Light gets in now."

"What?"

She explained further. "Only in the broken parts can the light get in. But not all can know this. They can't let go of the broken...so they stay broken."

He thought about his broken parts...and the light that could not get in. She shyly stuck out her hand and he took it in his, feeling the little bones underneath his clasp. They said goodbye like that.

Now, standing at the entrance to the Blue House, he shook that memory aside and gazed at the pageant unfolding before him. The Blue House on a Saturday night meant cowboys, local townsfolk and miscellaneous others mixing together, releasing the shackles of the work, real or imagined, that kept them bound. It played out on a nightly basis with the characters interchangeable. The constant was the drinks that flowed and the all-pervasive air of frivolity that followed.

He looked out into the crowd of faces. Many were known faces, some were brand-new. It was the ones that were not there anymore that he thought about all of a sudden...hungry ghosts of Colusa's past hanging about the place.

As he waded through, it started up. "Emmet!" "Lookee here, he's back!, "Well, you are a sight!" Comments and claps on the back, big bear hugs and all the rest. A couple of drinks in for Emmet fueled the hilarity that came with all the talk. Trading tales with Smitty and the guys, the laughter bubbled up inside him and spilled over when Smitty imitated a mating dance between bison he encountered out on the range. The story was told with a different twist at every telling and never got old.

Finally, he made his way back to Madam Charlotte's corner table where she sat with her deck of cards. She grinned wide and stood up. "Come here," she said with arms outstretched, "Gimme some sugar!"

He took in her whole package. She was dressed as usual in her full plumage complete with a feathered headband and makeup thick on her skin. Her décolletage was carefully displayed and powdered down in white. She smacked him with kisses on both cheeks and he could feel the lipstick residue left behind.

"Look at you! You're a sight. A full-grown man now no less..." She shook her head and clucked her tongue. "Sit, sit. Let's catch up."

As she filled him with the goings-on, he let her chatter wash over him along with the other sights and sounds in the space. It took him right back to earlier times, comforting times sitting in the same exact seat as a young lad. As she wound down, she smiled again and gazed at him with her still beautiful, light-colored eyes. "So...you haven't asked me yet."

"What?"

"You know what."

"Haven't given me a chance to get a word in, have you?"

She swatted at him playfully and sat back. "She's still here. And I know she'll be tickled pink to see you."

Emmet felt a lightness come over him that Bonita was nearby. He looked around the room and, not seeing her, said, "So...is she..."

"She'll be down shortly," the Madam said, which Emmet knew meant that Bonita was with a customer. "Sit a little longer here with me."

They talked some more, one upping each other with funny happenings. As Madam Charlotte wiped tears from her eyes from laughing, she said, "Okay, you win. You got me..."

The Madam cut off what she was saying as Emmet's eyes became riveted to the staircase. Bonita didn't see him as she walked down looking as ethereal as ever, her wisps of white blonde hair drifting around her face, framing it and keeping it soft. He asked himself if she looked older but he didn't think so. The toll of her working nights was not evident outwardly anyway...yet.

Finally, she felt his gaze upon her and her eyes met his. She blinked hard and her face automatically creased into a smile. When she walked towards the table, he stood. She offered him a hand and said, "Mr. Campbell."

He took the hand offered, so weightless in his and lifted it up to his lips, staring at her the whole time. The Madam cackled behind him and said, "Well, look who picked up some tricks on the road."

But Emmet barely heard her as it felt like all other activity in the House had come to a standstill. It seemed everyone in the place directed their energy to the reunion of these two: Bonita and Emmet.

He looked over at the Madam and asked, "Mind if I take her down to the river for a walk?"

Madam Charlotte was at a momentary loss for words by the two of them in front of her. She cleared her throat and motioned for them to go with one hand, a sly grin coming over her face.

They didn't say anything as they walked out the back door of the House and cut through the alley to Fifth Street which took them directly to the river. Side by side, her scent wafted in the air and took him right back to those times she had taught him to play the guitar. He had not realized at the time how much that would stay with him: those times, this girl.

There was enough moonlight so that her eyes reflected back at him, luminous and big in her face. He felt almost an electricity vibrating off of her. He didn't know what it was exactly but knew it was coming off him too.

They stood on top of the levee at the river, and looked below. She spoke first. "You play guitar any while you were gone?"

He nodded. "I did...a guy at the bunkhouse had one."

"You get any better?"

"You can figure that out...you still have the Martin?"

"'Course."

He felt some more laughter erupting from deep down in his belly and he let it rise up and out. They stood and didn't need to say anything else as they watched the river move with its strong current.

Chapter Twenty-eight

The courthouse square filled up with folks coming in for the founding fathers' harvest festival, a tradition in early November. Folks too busy during the summer and early fall months now reveled in the opportunity to trade tales and swap goods and services. A tented space was set up for dining where all would partake of the shared goodness brought into town from farms in the outlying area. Emmet made his way into town for the occasion from Lee Wakefield's ranch where he had procured employment and lodging.

Walking through the square, the courthouse building dominated Emmet's view. It brought up dark memories of the trial and the sharp pangs that always came with the recollection of it. But Colusa had called him back and, within a couple of weeks, he worked his way back into its folds.

Chatting with folks he passed by and receiving claps on the back and "welcome home" from many that he knew, he eventually skirted his way off to the side of the square away from the crowd for a breather, a place to be alone. Propping against a tree, he struck a match to light his smoke. Contentment ran through him to be there as he looked out at all the people, the decorations hanging from tree to tree and the fall flowers flowing out of containers.

The celebration of sorts would go on all day long and later spill over into the saloons (and the brothels too) in keeping with tradition. He idly observed the scene that unfolded in front of him. Some folks strolling around he had known all his life; others, new faces.

His vision suddenly narrowed when he saw the three of them walking in. Ann was in the middle, flanked by his half-brother on one side and his step-sister on the other. As they got nearer, he could see that John William and Mary Ann were actually supporting Ann, maybe even holding her up.

All three carried determined looks on their faces and people parted to let them forward although no one in particular seemed to greet them. From his private spot, he studied them. Their clothing and finery spoke to the riches they had backing them. But...but...closer observation showed that Ann was almost double in size since he had last seen her and her heavily powdered face could not disguise the thick lines etched into it. The age on her stunned him.

From his hidden vantage at the tree, he kept his eyes trained on them, fascinated by the sight. Mary Ann and John William found a seat for their mother and helped her into it. Mary Ann went off to fix her a plate as John William sat next to her, no light weight himself. Ann's eyes darted around like a nervous bird, looking for something. No one approached where the trio sat to dine with them or to even bid them a hello.

He didn't realize how much they had been pushed to the margins of Colusan society. It had to have been the trial and its outcome. The town picked him as the victor despite what the Judge decreed. It should have made him feel good. But it didn't. Instead, he just felt the loss and the shame of all of it. A shame he shared with the three that he was watching.

Eventually, a rancher named Johnson approached them and Emmet saw Ann's jowly face light up. She fluffed up her skirt and conversed with the man as Mary Ann and John William sat next to her, staying quiet and diminished. Emmet drifted away from the tree and from the trio who had once been his family of a sort.

Emmet, bleary eyed after some drinks in, sat on a barstool at the Mount Hood, his father's old saloon. When the harvest festival had wound down, the pull of nostalgia had tugged him to the saloon he knew so well. Looking down into the clear liquid in front of him, he mulled over what he couldn't shake. The sight of his stepmother.

The ranch was uppermost on his mind since getting back to Colusa. Seeing it abandoned and untended gnawed at him. He needed to approach her about it. He just didn't know how yet. Seeing her physical condition made him think he might have an edge. Yet he didn't know if that would be the case. Or not.

There was no getting around it...he had to visit and meet her face to face. He felt sick at the thought but he would do it. Now it wasn't just him back on the ranch...he knew he wanted Bonita there by his side. He realized that Bonita was the missing piece.

With all the thoughts about the ranch swirling around, he jolted when he heard the voice in his ear. "Lemme set you up here, Emmet. I owe you one." Dudley Shepardson sidled his way next to him.

Emmet sized up the man offering him the drink. Shepardson. He never trusted him as a child and the instinct had held true at the time of the trial.

Shepardson stared right back. "Don't look at me like that. I've known you your whole life almost. We ain't strangers."

Emmet gave a nod to the drink and Shepardson gestured with an imperial wave of his hand to the barkeep. "Scottie, set us up with two Kentucky bourbons and branch water here."

Once the drinks were in play, the two men sipped in silence. Emmet stared down into the glass, now with an amber hue.

"Have you visited your stepmother since you got back?" Shepardson asked.

"Nope."

Shepardson's gaze drifted off and he said, "She keeps to herself these days. Sometimes I think..."

He stopped mid-sentence and Emmet prodded him. "What?"

Shepardson shrugged off whatever he was going to say and said, "Nothing. Bottoms up, son." He lifted his drink and slugged it back.

The drinks loosened Emmet's tongue and it slipped out before he could stop himself. "I'm getting the ranch back from her. My father's ranch."

Shepardson let out a low belch. "Huh...you know some of it was sold off, right?"

"Yeah, but I hear she still owns the main piece of it."

Shepardson picked up his empty glass and moved it side to side. "Well, you could certainly try. You could certainly try."

He abruptly stood up from his perch on the barstool and placed a strong grip on Emmet's shoulder. "Anyway, welcome back, Emmet. Welcome home."

Emmet watched Shepardson saunter through the crowd, dropping comments and quips to those he passed by, before leaving the Mount Hood. He regretted telling Shepardson his plan and knew it had been a mistake. Slamming the last of his bourbon down, he got up on unsteady pegs to find his own way out.

Emmet knew that the three other Campbells had moved into town while he was gone. Word had it that Ann picked up a house for a song that a local builder, J. B. Danner, needed to unload due to financial losses.

After downing a drink for courage at the Mount Hood, he walked down to the corner of Fourth and Parkhill Streets. He stared at the house in front of him, made of brick and standing squat on its lot. A funny shaped tower on one side gave it a lopsided appearance. Their new house was not grand or imposing. In fact, it was odd.

When he couldn't put it off any longer, he rapped on the door with his knuckles. After a moment, it opened and Mary Ann stood in shadow looking out at him. "I need to talk to Ann," he said without preamble.

She studied him for a moment and then said, "Emmet. We heard you were back. Wait...here."

The door stayed ajar and he could hear her movements towards the back of the house. He heard low murmurs of voices, one higher pitched than the other.

Eventually, she came back and said, "Yes, Emmet. Mother will see you now."

He followed Mary Ann into the dark house barely making out the cluttered entry that led into an even more cluttered formal parlor. A cursory glance had him recognizing a lot of items from the ranch house.

Her treasured pianoforte, some fancy floor lamps and various paintings were jarring to see out of context. The smell in the air was the same though. Cooking odors mixed together with the underlying scent of menthol.

They continued past the formal parlor and into a back room. There Ann sat on a cushioned lounger with her feet propped up on an ottoman at the end. A newspaper lay on her lap and a half-eaten piece of cake on a plate was by her side. Peering at him over the half glasses on the bridge of her nose, he saw the same grey eyes now housed in a face puffy and sallow in color. Her body, as he noted at the courthouse square, ballooned outwards and her ankles and calves looked especially swollen.

No one said a word until Ann broke the silence stiffly. "Take a seat, Emmet." She gestured to a nearby sofa.

"I'll stand," he said.

"All right...to what do we owe the pleasure? You've been back how long now?"

"Several weeks, I reckon."

She sniffed and said, "And just now getting around to a visit. Huh." She looked over at Mary Ann directing her next words just to her. "My suspicion is that he is probably here to ask for something."

Mary Ann averted her eyes, not comfortable with being in the middle of the interaction.

"But before you do that, let's have a drink for old time's sake. How about it, young Emmet?"

Emmet was frozen in his skin. He was taken right back to his younger days when he had squirmed under her thumb, under her control. He mentally shook himself. He was a grown ass man now. He had seen as much of life as her. Maybe more. "All right," he answered.

A surprised flicker of a smile passed over her face. "Very well. Join me with a sherry?"

"You got any whiskey?"

She nodded. "Mary Ann, could you set us up with one sherry and one whiskey?" She asked Emmet, "Neat, I presume?" He gave a nod.

There was silence as Emmet gazed around the space, remembering. He knew Ann was observing him while he did so. Memories came flooding back with every stick of furniture and nick-nack from the ranch. He focused in on the old grandfather clock.

"It still keeps good time like it always has," Ann said as she caught him looking at it.

"That right?" He recalled that day when the men from the next town over had delivered it out to the ranch and the excitement in her that day. She almost seemed happy even. The only other time he saw her happy was when she coddled John William as a baby. He spent so much of his younger years puzzling over this woman and trying to figure her out. It had been a wasted effort.

Mary Ann walked back into the room holding a tray with a decanter and a bottle of whiskey. Emmet caught the label on the whiskey and recalled it was the same stuff that Shepardson always drank. Maybe that was why it wasn't Emmet's whisky of choice. Not by a long shot.

As Mary Ann poured the drinks, he asked, "Shepardson still come around to visit you folks?"

Ann shifted her substantial girth forward to pick up her glass of sherry. It threw him to see all the weight on her, how much she had expanded since he had last seen her person. He saw a grimace pass over her face and he could also see that she was not well. Not at all. This close, he could make out the lines in her face that spoke of nights in pain and something else. Cake crumbs were stuck in the creases around her mouth.

She took a sip from the sherry glass before answering. "Yes, Dudley and Winnie come over now and again."

Emmet studied the amber color in his glass and then slammed it down in one gulp. The silence came back between the three of them. Ann broke it by saying, "So maybe Mary Ann should make us something to eat. Return of the prodigal son and all that..." she let out a stilted laugh. She was uncomfortable, that much was clear to Emmet. He was unused to seeing her uncomfortable. She had always been in charge at the ranch.

But they all knew she wasn't in charge of him anymore. He had no fear of her left. Just the anger. "Nah...I'm not much of a Bible reader but I do know I ain't your prodigal son."

Her mouth formed an ugly line. "So why is it that you are here then?"

He hesitated, gauging how best to make his intentions known. He knew that Shepardson probably already clued her in so there was no reason to play cat and mouse.

He came right out with it and said, "I'm back in Colusa for good now and...and...I intend to farm the ranch. The Campbell ranch."

She chuckled softly under her breath and said, "Emmet...most of the land was sold a long while back. Didn't your good buddy, Powell, explain that to you?"

"I know that. But I'm going to buy it all back and piece it together. Including...including the piece you still have. That's why I'm here."

She stared at him with an indiscernible look.

"I don't have the money pulled together yet. But when I do, I want you to sell it to me." He wanted to say "buy it back" but he knew that may get her dander up. He was walking a fine line.

She gazed off to one side of the room and the only noise was the ticking of the grandfather clock. Finally, she turned back to look at him and said, "We can certainly discuss an arrangement when that happens."

"So you'll sell me the land?"

"Like I said, once you have the money---fair market value, of course--we can discuss an arrangement."

"All right then..." he hesitated before adding, "I know we haven't seen eye to eye much. But that land means everything to me. I'll do whatever it takes..."

She narrowed her eyes and said, "Indeed, Emmet. Indeed."

He left the stuffy dark house with a feeling of relief, in part to be away from her and in part because she said she would sell the land to him. At least...had she said that? He turned back and looked at the house. A shade was swiftly pushed back in place by one of them watching his departure.

They had become an even stranger family as time had gone on. Maybe it was because she came from a foreign land or maybe it was because of something else but it was of no matter to him anymore. As soon as the land was his, he would shake all the strangeness off forever.

Chapter Twenty-nine

He sat in the dark room in the tunnels next to Old Man Chung. Often, after getting the supplies the old man needed and setting them up, they would sit in silence. Not needing to exchange words, just presence.

This night, Old Man Chung struggled more than usual with the pain. Emmet could tell by the pinching around his lips. It was hard to watch. He suddenly surprised Emmet by saying, "Tell me story...I need...I need to leave my head."

Emmet sat back in the chair as he considered the request. There were so many stories to tell. So many stories that happened to him along the way back to Colusa. He closed his eyes to try and latch onto one.

He began. "So...I had been out on my own for a while before I got work...just wandering trying to figure out what was next. And I came upon this place..."

His mind snapped back to that homestead, the images suddenly crisp and sharp. The sun beat down hard and bright on Emmet and his horse as they made their trek out east of Sacramento. He rode too many miles without watering the horse and needed to stop.

He headed for a place on the pony express map with a drawing of buttes. Once closer, all he could see was a windmill in the near distance, no buttes. But the windmill meant a homestead and a water source so he gave the horse a kick to ride up to the summit of a slight incline.

Venturing nearer, he could make out a gaggle of children and a couple of women in the yard which was loosely squared in by an old ragged fence. Swinging off his horse, he tossed out a hello. He got blank looks all around in return.

One of the women scurried quickly indoors and soon a large man with a substantial belly and a long flowing beard came out on the porch.

Standing with arms on hips, he said loudly, "What brings you here, stranger?"

Emmet could not recall being called stranger before and it struck an odd note. "On the road and needing some water for my horse if you can provide," he answered.

The man nodded and headed over to his well which was right next to the windmill. Emmet walked his horse over as the children stayed put, mouths gaped open.

"Don't get many folks to these parts. What brings you through?"

"I'm following the old express route to go east."

"You got a ways to go?" the man asked as he pumped the well water into the trough.

Emmet patted his horse's flank and said, "I guess I do."

"Come on inside and the wives will fix you up with some vittles."

Emmet followed the man indoors. Inside, there were more children and one more woman. A big pot of something was bubbling on a stove and there was a general air of chaos to the place. It was hard for Emmet to process it all in one go.

The man spoke and said, "Wife Betty, fix up a plate for the young man here. He's got a hunger from riding all day."

The woman gave a nod and bustled over to the stove.

He looked at one of the other women and said, "Wife Sarah, go take some feed to his hoss out at the trough please."

Emmet's head spun round to see one of the other women do the man's bidding.

Next, the man said, "Wife Rebecca, fetch me my spectacles for the Bible reading."

Again, Emmet swung his head to get a glimpse of the third woman called wife.

He had never met a man married to more than one wife before. He had heard about them. There was one reputed to be living over in Grass Valley not too far from Colusa but he had never been around one himself. He would have thought one woman would be enough to have lassoed around a man's neck, much less two, three or four. It was hard for him to cotton to the idea of it. It must keep a man busy at night though ...

He had seen his fair share of spats between working girls over Johns that were considered desirable and yet they were not even married to the men. How did these women put up with each other and not get green eyes about it? Folks never ceased to amaze with their doings.

The man pulled Emmet out of his thoughts and said, "You'll stay with us 'course for the reading." It was not a question but more of a command. Emmet realized he was eating the man's food and it was a small, albeit annoying, price to pay.

He looked down at the food on the plate in front of him and concentrated on what was there: a tasty meat stew with fresh bread next to it. A home cooked meal like this was a rarity along his journey. In fact, he had not had one since Malinda Cooper's table.

The man—who introduced himself as Joseph—and Emmet had a mostly one-sided conversation with Joseph filling him in on the goings on in the area and Emmet occasionally answering questions about his journey.

A closed door creaked open and another woman came out into the room, her body swollen with child as though she might burst open at any moment. "Ah, there you are, Wife Naomi. I figured you were trying to get out of your duties," Joseph said playfully.

A sick grimace passed over the woman's—really, young girl's—face and Emmet felt a wave of compassion for her. She looked too young to be in this man's bed. She also looked too young to be in her current condition.

Joseph turned his attention back to Emmet. "So do you follow the teachings of our Brigham Young then?"

Emmet shook his head but added, "I have heard about him though."

The other man nodded and said, "You always have a chance to enter into the fold. Remember that."

Emmet cast a look about the place and ventured the question. "So... you have four wives then?"

189

The man beamed with pride and said, "And I am hankering for a fifth, I don't mind saying. Plural marriage is a hallmark of our religion and the ultimate way to honor God's grace on us."

Emmet again looked around at the disheveled condition of the place and all the blank looks on the faces. The women around him did not seem too "graced" in Emmet's estimation. Silent, even sullen, they all seemed marked by hard, hard labor.

"All righty now, let's gather round for our reading."

Children seemed to run out from hidden corners and soon enough the room felt swelled in size from the number of people in it. Emmet did a quick head count like he did on the range counting cattle. In total, there were sixteen children and four wives. All blond and blue eyed seemingly mirror images of each other. Emmet began to itch to escape from it.

The man droned on with the reading about honoring God and this and that. Emmet tuned it out just like when Ann made him sit through the Roman services and later when Jerry Powell had him and the Indian orphans sit through it at his church. He never had an interest in serving their Gods nor did he have an interest in serving this man's God either.

The children were still and obedient through the reading, waiting until the final Amen before leaving the room and going back to whatever they were made to do during the day. Emmet extended his thanks to the man and said he would be on his way. He tried to catch the eyes of the women to thank them as well but all of them made a point of looking away.

Out by the trough, he bridled up his horse and led it out of the ranch yard. Nearing the corner, he heard a noise. "Psst...psst." He looked over to see the pregnant girl, Wife Naomi, huddled under a cottonwood tree. He looked back to see if Joseph was looking then went closer to her.

She said with desperation in a raspy voice, "Take me with you." Her eyes bore holes in his with their pleading.

"What?"

Tears pooled in her eyes. "Please. Just take me."

"I don't..." Emmet began before a holler came from the house and stopped him.

A resigned look fell over the girl's face. Brushing a hand across her eyes, she trudged back towards the house without looking at Emmet again.

He felt undone. Not knowing if he should have grabbed her and put her on the horse with him, pregnant belly and all. How would that work? It wouldn't, he thought, as he stared after her. Joseph came out and stood on the porch with his arms akimbo, a stern look on his face as the girl got closer. At times like this, Emmet did not know what was wrong and what was right but he did know he felt badly about that girl.

As he rode hard away from the place with nary a backward glance, dust whipping around the horse, he was thankful for being spared that religion. Their line of thinking made no sense to him. He thought that some things, maybe many things, may have been worse for him than what he had. So much in life was not straight on. Like the eyes of that girl which would haunt him for a long time...he knew that.

As he got further away from the ranch, he concentrated on the scenery that unfolded before him. The buttes, the ones indicated on the old route map, got closer and closer on the horizon. They made patterns against the skyline in an accordion fashion. The blue sky accentuated them with perfection and, in this, he could see a hand of God, not back there in that man's house. It might serve them all better to come out here on the plains and just stare at this, Emmet thought, rather than read from that book the man had.

A couple days of hard riding put enough time and distance between Emmet and the homestead to clear it out of his head. When night fell after the third day, he found a suitably sheltered place to set up camp. He stared into the campfire after eating some victuals and realized he had to go back. He couldn't get the girl out of his mind. He couldn't leave it.

When dawn broke, he saddled up and headed back in the direction from where he had just been. The Spanish horse seemed to sense the change in direction and neighed in an expression of displeasure at going backwards, losing all that hard earned ground. But he settled down and obeyed his master after a few swift kicks to the belly.

Once back near the ranch, he tied off the horse at a nearby creek so water would be available. He had no idea how long he would be gone. Edging closer to the ranch on foot, he spotted a hummock not too far from the fence line which gave him a vantage point. His eyes, eagle sharp, were well trained through years of picking up anything in motion on the plains. He hunkered down to begin the watch.

His patience wore down but, in late afternoon, the girl came out to the same cottonwood tree where she had talked to Emmet before. She stood and stared off into the land, almost as though looking for him. He waited some more but no one came out for her so he started a low crawl to get closer.

After he gave a bird whistle to get her attention, she made a startled movement and then narrowed her eyes, spotting him. She stood statue still. He worked his way closer, taking his time so that he didn't make any noise. She took slow mincing steps towards him until she was at the fence. Once they were close enough to talk, he could see there was less of her. The baby had been born. Her face was wan, almost colorless.

"You still wanna leave?" he asked. She gave a slight nod.

"What about the baby?" She shook her head no.

He paused at that and then said, "I'll come back at night to get you. After they're all asleep. Be ready." She gave the same slight nod of acquiescence.

He crawled back the way he had come until it was safe to rise up and move back to the creek bed. He made himself comfortable and settled in for the long wait until the darkest time of night. He wrestled with the idea of what he was doing as he waited for that cloak of darkness.

As it got close to the middle of the night based on what he could see in the stars, he walked his horse to the hummock and waited some more. The moon was half in, half out and he had enough light to see that she was alone. Wearing a light-colored dress, she drifted over through the ranch yard to the cottonwood tree and then to the fence.

Moving quickly, he reached a hand over to lift her up. A satchel was slung around her neck but there was no baby, just her, light in his arms. They ran together back to the horse saying nothing.

He lifted her up on the horse, positioning himself behind her. The ranch was silent and he kicked the horse into a gallop to get distance as soon as possible. As they rode into the night, his nostrils picked up the scent of iron mixed with desperation rising off the figure snugly tucked against him. Again, he didn't know if it was right or not.

Before dawn, they stopped in a protected place surrounded by stone boulders where Emmet had camped one of the other nights. The girl fell to the ground into an immediate slumber. Emmet did the same.

Upon waking several hours later, he looked over at her. Both hands were nestled under one of her cheeks, child-like. It occurred to him that despite having given birth a couple days prior, she was still a child. He nudged her once to wake up and then did it again. She stirred and lifted herself up to a seat wincing as she did so. They stared at each other.

Before he even realized what he was asking, he said, "You sorry to leave your baby there?"

Her eyes shifted away from him and said, "Baby's got three mothers still. More to come too."

"I can get you to the next town. That's it."

She nodded and for the first time Emmet could see a brightness in her eyes. He recognized that brightness. It was hope. The girl spoke again. "It was a boy. He'll be raised to be a prophet."

She stared down at the ground and said, "I'd be sorry if it were a girl I left back there. Ain't a life worth living..."

Emmet mulled over what she said and realized she was right.

The ride to Carson took another day with Emmet continuing to look over his shoulder to make sure the man had not sent a posse after him. But they were left alone and encountered no one. Still, when they passed through any crossroads, they skirted through backcountry to avoid any encounters. At night, the girl tended to the fire while Emmet found squirrel to kill and cook up. They worked in silence, side by side.

The girl cut through the silence. "Where are you from anyway?"

"Colusa."

She shook her head and said, "I don't know it...haven't been many places. Just Cold Spring once. To see the bishop."

"It's out west. In California."

He wanted to ask her again how it felt to leave her baby behind but he stayed silent. She would likely be asking herself that question for the rest of her life. It was no business of his.

She looked up at him suddenly and said, "Why'd you come back for me?"

He shrugged. "I don't really know why. Felt like I had to...felt like I didn't have a choice."

She nodded. "I'm glad to be quit of it. I don't know what's going to happen to me but I'm glad to be quit of it."

When they entered the town of Carson, the girl's head swiveled one way and the other, taking it all in. Emmet knew it was probably a sight for her to take in a town of that size. She hadn't seen much in her life. Yet, in other ways, she had seen more than enough.

He had formulated a plan in his mind about what to do with the girl. He was going to drop her off at a church. He was hoping to find one of those Papist mission style buildings. If there was one thing his stepmother had taught him, it was that her religion had a mission to care for the sick and the needy. He deemed the girl as needy so she should fit right in.

They rode from one end of town to the other and Emmet did not see anything resembling a church, Papist or otherwise. He felt some sweat drip off his brow and headed to the back end of the town, finally locating one. A simple stone building adorned with a tall cross, it had a carved wood sign. He looked back at the girl and said, "What's that sign say?"

She took a look and shrugged. "Can't read none."

He drew in the reins to come to a stop. His eyes flitted over until he found the giveaway, a statue of a white cloaked woman placed on a bed of rocks off to the side. His stepmother had one just like it. "This is it," he announced to the girl.

"What?" she asked.

"You're going in here. Ask them to help you. They'll sort you out."

She looked over at the entrance and drew in a shaky breath. He hopped off and helped her down. She drew her satchel tighter over her bony shoulder. Looking at him square in the eye, she said, "Thank you."

He doffed his hat. Feeling a twinge of something at leaving her, he said, "You'll be all right."

"I know," she answered.

She watched as he swung back on top of the horse. Breaking her gaze away from Emmet, she turned to face the church. Squaring her shoulders, she walked towards it and Emmet knew he was watching bravery in action. She opened the door of the church and entered. He stared at the closed door for a moment before gently nudging the horse into leaving.

Having finished up his story, Emmet fell silent. He watched the sparks of the nearby cooking fire spit and hiss. He thought about the girl, Naomi, and what she was doing now. He hoped that he had given her the chance to find her own way. Everyone deserved at least that. Himself included.

Looking over at Old Man Chung, he found that the old man's chin had fallen to his chest and slight snores were coming from him. Maybe Chung could rest now.

Chapter Thirty

Emmet tied the horse off at the well-worn hitching post and held out a hand to help Bonita down. She straightened her dress and looked around at the disarray of run down outbuildings with the ranch house off to the middle. Earlier, he had swung by the Blue House on a day that Bonita had free from her work and they rode away on his horse, her arms wrapped around his waist. A hard blowing north wind made talk impossible as they rode out the three miles south of town.

"What is this place?" she asked.

"Campbell Ranch. Where my daddy started out. A long time ago now..." Emmet said.

"You grow up in that house?" She pointed to the ranch house off to the north.

He nodded. "For a time. Until..."

"Until?"

"He died."

"Oh, right."

She gazed around again, taking the whole place in. He could not hold it in any longer so he came right out with it. "Bonita, this is what I am working for. Getting all this back."

She nodded and said, "Good. I hope you do, Emmet. I really do."

"Do you think I can do it?"

"'Course I do...You can do anything you set your mind to."

Looking around now at the ranch and his buttes, he longed for the day that she would be here and could leave her line of work forever. "Someday..." he started. She looked at him with a curious expression. He wanted to say that she would be here with him. He would tell her that. Just not yet.

Instead, he lifted his saddle bags off the horse and said, "Follow me..." They walked over to his favorite hummock where he lifted out a

196

horse blanket and then laid it out. He pulled out items out for a picnic that included a cold bottle of cider. He looked up to see her watching him with a little smile playing at her lips.

Emmet gestured for her to sit. As they ate the meal, he couldn't help staring at her. There was just something about her. It felt like an age-old connection, something from way before their very first meeting. Everything else, her big green eyes, her delicate features and her golden white wispy hair was just extra to him really.

He realized he had been staring too much when she looked up at him and said, "What? I got something on my face?" She wiped around her mouth with one finger.

"Nah...I was just...just thinking."

"Hmmm...where'd you get all this anyways?"

"Went over to Sussmont's before I come to git you."

He thought back to when he had been carefully picking all the provisions out and Mr. Sussmont had called him out on it saying, "Someone special you're courting?"

He answered, "Maybe I am...and, yeah, she's pretty special..." Sussmont didn't press him any further on the topic.

As they ate in silence, sounds filled up the space around them. Insects ramped up with their various songs of the season. Emmet's horse snorted. Bird calls overlaid one another, reminding Emmet, with a sting, of Sarshel. Smells too...smells of springtime moving in, fresh and clean. Most of Emmet's attention, though, was on the familiar scent drifting over from Bonita which had his every sense on fire. Something electric was happening between the two of them.

Despite her occupation and despite him spending a lot of time at the Blue House, they had never been together in this particular way before. Waiting this long gave it gravity, something Emmet had not experienced with other women he had bed down with. He had never waited for any length of time to be with a woman.... with the exception of Mary Benicia.

She reached across the blanket and touched his hand. Then she unfolded each finger one by one. When she got to the last one, she leaned closer towards him and he grabbed her wrist tugging her closer. They filled up any space between them and a long-awaited dance began to unfurl. With their bodies tucked into one another, he wanted to stop the moment right then and there. Make it last forever. She was the one to finally press her face as close as possible and to place her lips on top of his.

He loosened the clasp that held her hair back and it flowed down in long strands like bird feathers entwined through his fingers. Something he had wanted to do since he first laid eyes on her. The rest happened in a flurry with items of clothing flung off until they were skin to skin under the blue, blue California sky

With their bodies locked into one another, they moved in an ancient rhythm of connection. His lips traced the outline of her face as her fingers danced along his spine. Once spent but far from satisfied, they lay on their backs, the plaid blanket still mostly underneath them.

She looked over at him and said, "This blanket itches."

"Yeah," he replied and then he rolled on top to tickle her saying, "You just need to move around some more..."

She let out a peal of laughter as she struggled underneath him until they both went still, her green eyes staring into his blue. He felt all of it in the core of his being.... the buttes, the sun, the sky, the ranch and Bonita, especially Bonita, underneath him gazing at him with a pure sense of something.

Chapter Thirty-one

The day of the burial it rained. Emmet and a small group of Chinamen stood over the freshly turned earth while Feng, now the unofficial head of the community, spoke utterances in his native tongue. Emmet caught the gist of it and found it not too unlike the Christian burials he had attended. The universal response to death being the same in all tongues and religions in the end.

Emmet purchased a burial plot for Old Man Chung in the new Colusa Community Cemetery. All the Chinese in town who could afford a proper burial were placed near each other in the far western corner of the cemetery. Emmet did not do right by Sarshel but he could do right by Old Man Chung.

Afterwards, Emmet headed back to Lee Wakefield's ranch in Williams where he had lived for almost a year. Away from the cemetery and out of town brought Emmet into the big open sky country which worked on easing his frazzled nerves.

Closer to Williams, Wakefield's ranch came into view. It looked like the picture postcards of farms that Emmet had seen in the general stores, not a blade of grass was out of turn. Lee Wakefield hailed from Tennessee, leaving there while young with nary a whisker yet. After he put in the hard work, Wakefield accumulated a sizable amount of land and a full herd of cattle. It was not lost on Emmet that this was what his father had done...and, to some degree, this was what Emmet had lost.

Wakefield brought in a few men including Emmet to help him out with the operation. They all lived in a separate bunk house on the property. Emmet made his way into the bunkhouse after taking his horse to the stable. He sat heavily on his lower bunk.

The memories from Old Man Chung's last days hit hard with a gut punch all over again. Though it had been Chung dying, it brought up the painful days of his father's demise too. As he sat with the idea of the old man being gone, the new cowboy in the bunk house, Ed Morgan, sauntered in and stopped short in front of him. "You going into town tonight?" he asked.

Distracted by his thoughts, Emmet looked up and focused on Morgan. A wiry sort with a muscular leanness that bordered on menacing, Wakefield had taken him on as a bet it seemed like. He showed up at the ranch as skittery as a wild hare. Hot-headed in nature, he was always at the ready to pick a fight for no good reason. The others steered clear, giving him a wide berth. But not Emmet. Emmet found a way around the rough edges. A way to live alongside this angry man.

There had been a poker game where he and Morgan finally made a connection. Emmet was known around Colusa to be the most fair and honest cowboy there was and many a night those who had too much tipple handed their winnings to Emmet for safekeeping. Each and every one of them got every penny back the next day or so when they were right in their heads again. Some didn't even remember what they had won and almost lost.

Morgan, out of his head on liquor, had thrown his winnings all around as he twirled in a circle. Emmet gathered them all up and placed them in a cloth bag. The next morning when he gave the bag to Morgan, the man looked at him in utter surprise and said, "You really gonna give me this?"

"It's your money. I don't keep others' monies." Ever since that night, Morgan and he got along easy.

Emmet now said to the man, "What?"

Morgan looked at him with impatience and repeated the question, "I said you going to town tonight or what?" It had become a regular thing that the cowboys from the bunkhouse ended up together at the Blue House on a Saturday night.

Some nights Morgan was more loaded for bear than others. Emmet got the sense that this was one of those nights. "Nah. Not tonight..."

Skinny Red came into the bunk house and caught the tail end of the conversation. "Come on now, Campbell. You gotta show up tonight..."

Both men continued to work him over until he finally consented. In the end, the idea of staying put on the ranch and thinking about Chung made Emmet too unsettled. He wouldn't mind seeing Bonita's face either---even if the price was seeing her with her customers.

Eventually, the boys from Wakefield's ranch all banded together to ride into town: Skinny Red, George, Slim, Ed Morgan and Emmet. The weather had turned and held the promise that spring holds on such nights. Emmet used to stay in town in the tunnels after the revelries were over to check in with Old Man Chung. This night would be different...maybe this would be the night he could stay with Bonita for the entire night. He had worked on the Madam about this but she was slow to give him a decision on it.

The bunk house crew all hung loosely together at one end of the bar counter. Emmet felt a flash of affection for these new comrades. He felt the same for the others he had known for years. He even felt it for those in the Blue House he didn't even know.

Emmet's eyes wandered over to Bonita and feasted at the sight of her...still so young, so fresh. Creamy colored skin, bright green eyes. She calmly looked out into the room, waiting. He tamped down the angry feelings, almost violent feelings, about Bonita with the other men. He knew she was just doing her job but it was wearing at him, making him edgy.

As Emmet took a step to go to her, a figure moved in and blocked his view of her. It was Ed Morgan and Emmet's entire body immediately tensed. Morgan crowded in on Bonita like a hawk swooping down onto prey.

He trained his gaze on them and did not move a muscle as Morgan began to sweet talk the girl Emmet considered his. After some time went by, Emmet could see agitation in Morgan's jerky movements. He stood and loomed over her and a look of something that Emmet could not discern flitted across her face. It wasn't fear, rather it seemed to be an all too worldly awareness of rough and ready cowboys. The look saddened Emmet.

When Morgan's voice rose and he roughly grabbed her by the arm, Emmet acted in a flash crossing over the room to them. Morgan's head leaned close to Bonita's face, hissing at her.

She spoke up in a clear voice, "Let me go."

Emmet pulled out his pistol and brandished it in front of Morgan's face as a caution to the man, saying "Back off the lady, Morgan."

Morgan took his hand off the girl and went to grab the pistol. Emmet held it aloft, just out of his reach, and said, "No, you don't."

The rest of the crowd instantly became silent as the two men stared each other out for several long moments. All stepped back from the trio giving them a wide berth. Bonita broke the spell and said, "Give it to me, Emmet. I'll keep it."

Without his eyes leaving Morgan's face, Emmet said, "I'm handing the gun to Bonita for safekeeping and we'll carry on. Got it?"

Bonita opened up her hand to grab the pistol and tucked it deftly under her lace drenched petticoats. As Emmet handed it to her, he breathed in her lilac laden scent.

Morgan's visage broke into a sudden, strange grin and he clapped Emmet on the shoulder with a resounding thud. Surprised it had been that easy, Emmet asked, "We good?"

"Oh yeah. Just lost my head for a moment. Just playing. You know me..."

The Blue House settled back to where it had been....the conversations starting up, the bartender pulling the ales and the threat of violence dissipating into the night. Emmet retreated back to the corner where he kept Bonita in sight. Still watchful. Still waiting.

A half hour later, he again felt the same clap on his shoulder from Ed Morgan who stood next to him. "Need some fresh air, cowboy."

Emmet narrowed one eye, sizing up the man. He seemed back on even keel and Emmet shrugged saying, "Not a bad idea, Morgan. Not a bad idea at all."

The two swung through the doors of the Blue House and made their way outside into the cool spring air, leaving the fug of cigar smoke and all the rest behind. Morgan again clapped Emmet on the back as they crossed Market at Fourth Street. "Good night, eh?"

As Emmet shifted to look at the other man, he saw the flash and, in that millisecond before the bullet came crashing into his body, sensed that everything in his entire life had led him to this exact, precise point in time. He landed on his back from the impact in front of the Odd Fellows Lodge Building. From dazed eyes, he stared up at the beautiful, milky black sky dotted with its bright stars never looking more brilliant.

People poured out from the Blue House and the other saloons nearby as well at the sound of gunfire. In a tinny noise that sounded far, far away, he could hear someone say: "Emmet Campbell's done been shot through the heart."

Chapter Thirty-two

When he came out of the all-encompassing fog of pain, he found himself in a bed unknown to him. His voice sputtered out, "Hey...Hey..."

Bonita walked into the room and looked down at him for a moment. "You shouldn't have done it for me."

Emmet croaked out slowly, "Yeah, I should have. And I'd do it again."

Bonita shook her head. "Sheriff Arnold's been waiting on you to wake up. You ready to talk to him?'

"Where'd Morgan go?"

"They got him locked up in jail. I'll get Arnold."

Bonita turned back and asked, "Who is this Mary Bernice you keep asking for in your sleep?"

Stunned, Emmet answered, "Mary Benicia. She's..."

Bonita stood in a half-turn, waiting for his answer. He finished by saying, "She's...an old friend." Bonita stared at him a little longer before leaving the room.

As he waited for the sheriff, Emmet listened to the church bells ring over across Market and almost to Tenth. When he opened his eyes, Sheriff Arnold was looking down on him, shaking his head. "Only you, Emmet Campbell. Only you."

"What?"

"Only you could take a bullet that barely skimmed by your heart. You got lucky, son. You sure did."

"You call this lucky?" Emmet said as his face creased into a pained smile.

"Nice to see you got your humor bone still in you. Doc said if the bullet had even slightly altered its path you and I wouldn't be having this conversation."

204

"Okay, yeah then. Call me lucky."

Arnold settled his girth into the hard backed chair next to the bed. "Now why don't you tell me why Ed Morgan tried to kill you last night?"

Emmet had been mulling it over while listening to the church bells chime. Ed Morgan was really another side of the same coin as him. He needed more breaks in this life than he had gotten. The two of them shared the common vein of those forgotten and forsaken.

He turned tired eyes back to Arnold and said, "Jus' a misunderstanding is all. He didn't intend to do it....didn't intend to kill me."

"Huh? That's not the word here at the Blue House. Folks claimed you and he got into it over this gal, Bonita."

"Nah. That weren't no big thing."

Arnold shook his head. "You know we can't keep him if you don't press charges against him."

Emmet nodded. "Set him free then."

The sheriff stood up and made a tsking noise. "Are you courting this Bonita or something?"

Emmet gave a slight shrug and said, "What if I am? What of it?"

"Well...she..."

"What?"

"Nothing. Seems like a nice gal."

He started to walk out but paused. Turning back, he said, "I don't know about you, Emmet. I don't know."

"Yeah...you'll never figure me out. Don't even try."

Sleep came and went just like every day and night since he had been shot. Emmet was pulled around with the pain, vaguely aware of the noises of regular life going on despite him. The rumblings in the Blue House carried out until the wee hours eventually reaching a moment of stillness. If he was awake for it, it was the loneliest moment of all, the darkest of night, right before the dawn.

Fevers passed through his body leaving him chilled and shaking afterward. With the fevers came the night stories that his dreams told...stories so fantastical he would shake himself to wake up, not able to handle their disturbing messages.

One memory of his time out on the range kept coming back to him. A cough had started as a tickle and became something bigger as he crossed into north country. Emmet figured it was headwinds that had done it but he didn't know for sure. His breath became raspy with it.

He finally had to leave the rest of the cowboys and go to the nearest town one day, a crossroads town called La Bonte. He took a room at a saloon and fell into the bed. Later, he managed his way down to the saloon for some food. He could only take some broth as it turned out, his stomach curling at the idea of ale or whiskey.

The saloon keeper studied him across the counter and said, "What's ailing you, cowboy?"

Emmet's voice came out like a croak, partly from what had made him sick but partly from not using it for many days. "Think the winds drove it into me."

"You need to go see the medicine woman," the other man said.

"Where's she at?"

"Go down at the end of the road and, when the buildings end, you'll see a big old cottonwood. Biggest one you've seen in a while I'd wager. There's a cabin tucked behind it. That's where she is. Tell her I sent you." He added, "She goes by the name of Georgine. The only doctoring we have here in La Bonte."

"What's that mean anyway? 'La Bonte'?"

"If I had a copperhead for every time I get asked...La Bonte means wealth, goodness, kindness. You get the idea. I thought the best kind of people would be here."

"Are they?"

"Some yes, some no. Just like most other places I guess." He continued, "It's French and I suspect that's why Georgine is here. Never asked her point blank though so I could be wrong."

Just as the saloon keeper said, a big cottonwood waited for him at the end of the road to the medicine woman's cabin. Stopping several times to catch his breath, he couldn't recall a cough taking him ill like this. A shiver went through him at the remembrance of his father's cough but he shook it off, lifting his face into the sunny day.

There was a well-trod path leading to the door of the cabin. She sat outside in the sun herself, eyeing him as he approached. Emmet almost had to look away from the bright and colorful cloth she was attired in. There seemed to be a layer of color atop another layer of color. The crowning touch was a ruby red scarf wrapped around her head.

"Ma'am, the bartender at the White Sun Saloon sent me your way. Says you could help with this cough I got out on the plains."

She motioned with a hand for him to walk closer. Pointing to the stool next to her, she said, "Sit. If Floyd sent you my way, that's okay then. Sends a lot of folks out here."

Once Emmet sat, she put her hand out. Emmet didn't know what she wanted and asked, "You need coin?"

She made an irritated sound and said, "Your hand. Give me your hand."

Her voice had an accent that he could not place. Didn't sound French to his ears but must be some country over that way. The thought crossed his mind that at some point she must have crossed the same areas his stepmother had. Whenever the thought of Ann came into his mind, he banished it quickly, not wanting it to leave its shadow.

Georgine held his hand in one of hers with his palm up. She took her other hand and rubbed it slowly across its rough, beat up surface and the embedded grooves from the lion's scratches too.

"You are ailing. I can feel it."

"Yes, like I said, it's a cough—"

"Shush. Let me listen." She closed her eyes and her hand stopped rubbing and stayed still on top of his.

Emmet felt unnerved by her touch but did as she asked, still trying to catch his breath from the walk out to her place. What he really needed was a doctor rather than this woman with her hands on his but he was hard pressed to find one until back in Sacramento.

Her eyes popped open and she looked at him in a way that felt too personal. "There is so much pain...so much pain."

Emmet shifted, uncomfortable with the woman's eyes on him and her hand too. "I don't know that I am in that much pain."

"But it will end sooner than you know..."

She stared at him again with a sadness on her face that he didn't understand.

"Well, can you give me anything for it?"

"For it? The cough...yes, yes, I have tea for it. Wait and I will get it."

Emmet watched as she rose in a flow of color and went into her cabin. Returning, she handed him a muslin bag and explained that he would make tea two times a day and it would fix the cough.

He nodded and said, "Thank you, ma'am. How much do I..."

"No, no. No money from you."

"Well...thank you, ma'am," he said again, rising to stand.

She looked at him with that same funny look and bit her lower lip with a tooth. "You...you must take each day."

"Take each day?"

"Take each day and make it mean something."

Emmet did not know how to respond so he just nodded and walked away. When he gazed back over one shoulder, he could see that she was staring at him with a frown on her face. It gave him a bad feeling. He did not understand the encounter with her and probably never would.

Back at the saloon, he brewed the tea which smelled extremely vile but tasted passable. She had said to take it each day and he would do that. Not too unlike the teas he had drunk in the Chinatown tunnels. Not exactly the same either.

That night, after a pot of Georgine's tea revived him somewhat, he went down to sit at the bar. Floyd, as Georgine had called him, eventually worked his way towards Emmet, making deft movements with a bar towel as he did so.

"How you fare, cowboy? You go see Georgine?"

"I did. She gave me some tea and it helped some."

Floyd nodded. "I told you she'd fix you up."

"So...she seemed to be double talking me a bit. Talking about what ails me but then maybe about other things too."

Floyd nodded again and said, "Yep. She knows about things."

"How so?"

"She's one of those that can see ahead like. See ahead into the future. Things that are going to happen to folks. But she won't ever tell you ahead of time. She just gives you a clue or two."

"Huh." Emmet thought on that for a bit. "How do you know this?"

The bartender studied the rag under his hand. "I lost my woman shortly after we got here. She hinted to me it was going to happen...I reckon to help me get ready. "

He looked up at Emmet and said, "Some people just know things, I guess. Don't know if it's a gift or a curse. I wouldn't want to have it. I do know that."

Floyd moved down the counter to tend to another customer. Emmet gazed off into space debating if he should go see the woman again. Ask her exactly what she had meant about him. A funny sensation rested in his gut as he thought back over her words...take each day.

Chapter Thirty-three

In the mornings, Emmet kept his eyes screwed tight against the sunlight brightening the room until Bonita came in carrying a tray. She would sit and watch as he got food into his mouth. Some days, his eyes remained shut and it was not clear to him or to Bonita whether he was asleep or awake. She would carefully unfurl his clenched fingers and, with a feather light touch, massage each finger and then his entire hand.

After a couple of weeks of struggle, he knew he had to get up and put mind over matter. Madam Charlotte wouldn't let him lounge around Blue House forever. He had to get better. Get back out into the world. Three weeks in, Bonita walked in the room one morning and he said, "Help me out of this bed, Bonita."

She said nothing, just bit on her lower lip and reached behind him to support his back as he worked on the slow, slow process of sitting upright. He breathed in a jagged breath. Placing one hand down on the bed, he pulled himself up to a stance. His whole body shook from the crown of his head down but he did it. He felt a slight rush of euphoria that he was finally up and standing again.

"What are you going to do?" Bonita asked.

"I'm going to go out and walk down the street."

She nodded. Gathering his street clothes, she helped him to dress and pull himself together. He had been housed in a room on the first level close to the rear exit. The rear exit was in place for girls who needed to get out of the place quick if there was trouble afoot. Bonita opened the door and supported Emmet as he got down the two stair steps to ground level.

"You need me to come with you?" she said, handing over his Stetson.

"Nope," he said, positioning the hat on his head. Taking small steps, he made his way to the front of the building and started a slow, careful walk down Market. He took one look back to see Bonita staring after him, her face furrowed with worry.

As he passed by folks, he would get a nod or a "How you doing, Emmet?" every few feet or so. He kept a grin plastered on his face, masking the sensations ripping through his body. His benchmark was Market and Eighth and then he would turn and walk back.

Sweat pooled down his face and his breathing became more labored with each step. He persevered to put on the good show all the while feeling a mere fraction of his former self. It felt like the bullet had taken all his stuffings out and he wondered how he would ever get them back....

The next day, Bonita came in and took a seat. Snapping the *Colusa Morning Sun* out flat, she read aloud: "'Out. Emmet Campbell shot through the body just above the heart, by Ed Morgan on the evening of May 12th after a night of scuffling and skylarking, was out on the street on Wednesday.'"

She looked up from the paper at him and said, "So it sounds like you're the picture of health out on the street, don't it?"

He snorted. "Yeah, that's me."

She looked at the paper again thoughtfully and then said, "Well, you fooled them all anyhow."

He breathed in and felt the barbed pain that always happened with every breath now, day and night since that May night. It had to die down sooner or later, he kept telling himself. He began to cuss a blue streak as was his habit.

Bonita put a hand up for him to stop and said, "Oh, it hurts my ears when you do that, it surely does."

She studied him seeing the angst cross his face as he kept silent with it. "A distraction is what you need." He raised his eyebrows at her suggestion.

"Nah. Not that. But I got an idea. ..."

When she came back later to change his dressings, she had the Martin in hand.

He protested. "I jus' need to sleep a bit...maybe later..."

Bonita propped the guitar on his lap carefully just as she had done that first time. He moved his hands over the strings but didn't have much spirit left to do any more than that.

He looked over at her and saw her frown. He rallied, moving the instrument into place but wincing at what it cost him to do so. Her face brightened and she said, "Show me what you got."

At some point in his travels, it had suddenly clicked into place. Like the feeling when a horse was finally broke and took a rider on a saddle. It seemed sudden but he knew it had built up over time with him chipping away at it, the practice. All those times when it felt like there was no way through, no way for it ever to come to him. Slowly, very slowly, it had been like something from far off coming into view closer and closer. It clicked...in a way that letters and words never had.

He strummed out the chords with a slow hand. The chords he finally mastered after the years on the road. Not only the musical notes but the words too which he sang under his breath, holding back the coughing fit that wanted to come up. He picked up his pace and the song came together, the Night Herding Song:

Oh say, little doggies, why don't you lay down? You've wandered and trampled all over the ground Lay down, little doggies, lay down

I've cross-herded, circle-herded, trail-herded too but to keep you together, that's what I can't do Bunch up, little doggies, bunch up

My horse is leg-weary and I'm awful tired but if I let you get away, I'm sure to get fired Bunch up, little doggies, bunch up

His fingers strummed the last note of the song and he let his hand rest where it was. After some time, he looked up to see Bonita's face wreathed in a huge smile. Maybe the biggest smile he had ever seen there. He was taken aback. "What?" he said.

"You can really play." There was some awe in her voice.

He set the instrument aside, holding back a gasp of pain as he did so. "I guess I can...although it's not going to help me much with walking now."

He gave her a crooked smile then stared at her intently from his awkward lounge in the bed. "What if you didn't do this anymore?"

She looked at him with some confusion. "Playing the guitar?"

"No...I mean...this. The Blue House. Or any other place like it."

She stared down at her hands not saying anything.

"What if you came out with me to the ranch...when I get it, I mean?"

"Like...you would keep me out there for you?"

"No..." He shook his head, frustrated that she didn't read his intent. Then he came right out with it. "I'd marry you...and we would have the ranch together."

"Oh, Emmet." She gazed around the room taking in the bottles of liquids and pills that Doc Calhoun had left and all the other needs that came with being sick. His eyes followed hers and he knew what she was thinking.

"I'm going to get better, Bonita. This is just...just a bump in the road. It's not going to keep me down. It's not going to keep me from getting the ranch. You know me. You know I'll kick this."

After his torrent of words, the cough crept up his throat and outward so that he could not catch his breath. He fell back onto the bed.

"Okay, okay..." she laid a hand on his chest gently with some alarm in her eyes. "Just rest for now...."

Chapter Thirty-four

The sun hit him square in the face and he wanted to claw his eyes out. Four months in, Emmet stood on the corner of Market and Seventh at high noon wondering how the hell he had gotten there. Lack of sleep most nights led to this....him not knowing what or where he was doing sometimes.

He felt a surge of rage. At the sun, at the street, at everything but, especially, at the unrelenting pain. He tried to remember if he had slept at all the previous night. Probably not was his guess. A lot of nights went by when he did not sleep at all. Although Bonita said that was impossible. That he wouldn't be a human anymore if that were the case. But he lay at night in the bath of pain, wide awake more nights than not by his estimation.

It was the anger that made him pick up the wood stake lying on the side of Market Street, left over from some road repair being done. The town of Colusa had just recently installed several of the new-fangled gas fueled lamp posts at various points on Market. Emmet swung the stake up and down until the nice, shiny gas lamp post in his path trembled. The action of swinging the stake and the satisfying thud it made as it struck the lamp post gave him focus, gave him purpose.

It took him out of everything else just for the moments he was doing it. He kept at it until it started to topple. Until the lamp fell completely to the ground, lying still with glass shattered on the street on one side like an abandoned kiddie toy. Only then did he stop, throwing the stake down. A voice behind him somewhere said, "What'd you do that for?"

Emmet was dimly aware that several folks had collected around him. Then he heard another voice behind him---this one, a baritone timbre with authority---say, "Son, come on over here now."

Sheriff Arnold. Emmet looked over at the sheriff under heavy lidded eyes and the man blurred in front of him. The sheriff spoke

214

again. "Come on. We're going to the station house." He grabbed Emmet by the arm. Emmet didn't balk at being led away from the lamp post and the townsfolk gawking with open stares.

Emmet stumbled into the station house with the sheriff keeping a vise-like grip on his arm. He could barely register the coolness of the indoors or the barren, sterile hallway. At the entrance desk, the town clerk raised eyebrows at the sight of the two men as Arnold said he needed to get Emmet signed in.

The clerk shook his head saying, "Judge Hatch ain't in town today. Nothing to be done for it until the Judge gets back. Take him over to Doc Calhoun."

Arnold let out an exasperated breath before tugging on Emmet's arm to go back outdoors. Out on the street, he placed his massive hands on Emmet's shoulders and stared him down. "Look at me in the eye, son."

Emmet struggled to meet the man's gaze but finally did so.

"These high jinks need to stop, you hear?"

Emmet gave one nod. Satisfied with that response, Arnold continued. "Now, I know Doc is out towards Williams today helping birth Jessie Coulter's new baby. Until he gets back in, which may be tomorrow sometime, I'm letting this go. But you behave yourself now. You hear me?"

Emmet twisted his head in what might have passed for another nod. The Sheriff couldn't be bothered to verify it one way or another and the two men parted ways on the street near the front of the Colusa Courthouse.

That night, Emmet left the backroom where he had spent the past several months and headed to the front saloon area. The Madam had told him a couple days earlier that his time was up, he needed to clear out. He had no idea where he was going to go.

A voice hailed him as he walked in. "Hey, there he is. Look here, boys. It's Emmet." Lee Wakefield clapped him on the shoulder and pulled him into the small group of men that hung loosely together, Skinny Red, George and a couple of others. The new guys probably had replaced him and Ed Morgan. Ed Morgan, at last report, had hightailed it out of Colusa after Judge Hatch released him in early August.

After Wakefield bought him a drink, Emmet stared down into it and reflected back to that day in court when Morgan had been discharged. Emmet had rallied and made it over to testify. His testimony left out most of it so that Morgan would not be kept behind bars. When given an opportunity to speak, Morgan said he intended to go to the state of Nevada and be an orderly and peaceable citizen. He stared right at Emmet directly and said he was very sorry for what he did and if he ever found out there was an opportunity to do Emmet Campbell a service, he would do so no matter what it may cost him. Of course, after that, he left town and no word had been heard of him since. Emmet figured no word or good service would ever be heard or done from Morgan. It sat okay with him though. The man was free...

But Emmet wasn't free...not free from pain and it did not appear he ever would be. Not free of other things too. Lee Wakefield and the guys sat around him having their wind-up time and trying to cajole him out of his funk, but Emmet sunk deeper into it, the alcohol helping the way along.

The same rage he felt earlier at the street lamp post overcame him again. He could feel it building up inside and churning around in his guts. The feeling became too much, smothering and choking out all else. He sprung up from the bar stool, not able to sit a second longer. He felt around in his pocket for his bowie knife, the one he had won in a poker game out east and kept close ever since.

"I'm done," he said in a low voice to no one in particular. He pulled the knife out. Tilting his neck to one side, he placed the knife firmly on the taut arc of muscle.

Wakefield, spotting the glimmer of steel in the light of the saloon, leapt over the other men and grabbed Emmet's hand. He hauled it away from Emmet's neck while Emmet attempted to bring it back in place. Both men fought for the knife in a tug of war like tousle. Others pulled on Emmet from behind to give Wakefield leverage.

Finally, Wakefield got a hold of the knife and the others grabbed Emmet by both arms, taking him out of the Blue House. Emmet struggled to get loose of the men, yelling profanities as they dragged him over to the Sheriff's.

Sheriff Arnold stood up as the men walked into the jail. He turned on heel and opened the one jail cell in the building that had seen varied and illustrious traffic throughout Colusa's short history. "Throw him right in here, boys." Wakefield and his guys did as they were told.

As an afterthought, the Sheriff yelled back at Emmet as he walked away. "You'll be safe enough here 'til Doc Calhoun comes back tomorrow."

The next morning, Emmet stirred at the sound of clanking metal bars and a key opening the lock. He looked over from the cot that sat low to the dank floor and saw Doc Calhoun with the Sheriff. Both doleful and serious.

"He's all yours, Doc," the Sheriff said.

The elderly man sat down on the edge of the cot and sighed big. "What is it Emmet? I've never known you to be like this. What's happened?"

Emmet grabbed his shirt collar and pulled down on it exposing the angry red and welted scar where the bullet had gone in. "This happened."

The two men sat in silence until Emmet spoke up again. "Not fit to work anymore. Won't be able to get the ranch back. What's the point of living?"

"Now, now. We can figure this out between the two of us. Let me get your vitals and we'll figure it out."

Emmet stared down at the floor as Doc Calhoun listened to his heart with his stethoscope. Emmet vaguely took in the stale cigarette smoke emanating from the elderly man whose own breath was almost as raspy as Emmet's. He remembered the Doc coming out to the ranch to tend to his father as the new doctor in town. Now he tended to Emmet.

"Breathe in for me...there you go."

"So, what is it? Have I done lost my mind you think?"

Doc stared at him hard. "You got circles under your eyes bigger than a 'coon's. You been sleeping at all?"

Emmet shook his head.

"You ain't crazy. You just been in pain too long. And you missed out on too much sleep because of it."

"How do I get beyond it, Doc?"

"I'm going to get you a sleeping draught but you gotta be careful with it. Otherwise, you may get in too deep...you understand what I mean?"

Emmet's thoughts flickered back to the tunnels where some of the Chinamen could not keep away from their smoking pipes of what he now knew was opium.

"Yeah, I know what you mean."

He slapped Emmet on the thigh. "Alrighty then. We'll get you fixed up good."

Emmet slung himself back down on the cot and kept one arm over his face. In the Sheriff's office, he could hear the two men talking.

"That new town magistrate with a bug up his bottom is calling for a suit to pay for the lamp post. Town vs. Emmet Campbell."

"The boy can't work none. How's he supposed to pay that?" Doc Calhoun asked.

"They want to know from you if he should be sent to Napa."

Doc snorted in disgust. "Napa? Hell no. He needs sleep first and foremost. I'm going to get him straightened out."

Emmet dug back into the recesses of his mind and pulled out the image of that castle set back off the road that ran between Napa and Healdsburg. Napa Asylum of the Insane. It had been in operation for several years though he didn't know anyone who had gone in there. He did know folks that maybe should be there. Emmet didn't think he was one of those though...even now with his problems.

He drifted off into an uneasy slumber, the only kind of slumber that came to him in these times. He awoke again to the tell-tale lilac scent of

218

Bonita's perfume. He could now sniff it many yards away. It was followed by the sound of the key clanking in its lock.

She held the Colusa Sun in hand and she tapped it on her petticoat. "What?" he said as he worked himself up to a seat.

"You. In the paper again."

"What's it say?"

Bonita read it aloud: "'CRAZY- Emmet Campbell has been acting rather odd for the last few days and on Thursday evening tried to kill himself with a knife but was prevented by Lee Wakefield and others. Since he recovered from the wound given to him by Morgan, he has been despondent and says he is not fit to work and doesn't want to live. Campbell will be examined and perhaps sent to the Asylum.'"

He thought about the title of it: Crazy. Maybe he had always been just that. Crazy. Certainly that is what the boys who bullied him around town used to say. Others probably too. His own father even. Definitely her. His stepmother.

Bonita breathed in deep. "What is going on with you, Emmet?"

He shook his head and stared down at the floor. He just didn't know how to fix it. He couldn't work. Couldn't sleep. His personality had been taken over by the pain. He had become someone different. Someone not himself. His bad-tempered ways were alienating the people that cared about him, like Bonita. But he couldn't help himself. Was that the definition of crazy?

When he didn't answer, she continued, "I worked with a girl who was sent there. The Napa Asylum. She couldn't take it and ran off. She ended up...well, she ended up doing... doing what I do instead." Her gaze ventured over towards Blue House.

She looked back at him. "Anyway, the point is you need to make sure they don't send you there. Say whatever. But don't end up there."

He exhaled some air. "Do you believe in fate, Bonita?"

She thought about it for a moment. "No...not fate. But I do believe in luck...and sometimes...sometimes we gotta make our own. Our own luck."

Chapter Thirty-five

When Sheriff Arnold opened up the jail cell door wide, he said, "Git outta here. You got a court date coming due in a week. For the damage to the lamp post. Be ready for it...."

Out on the street, Emmet stood in front of the jail taking measure of the outside. Then he headed towards Market. When he passed the *Colusa Sun's* building, its owner, Will Green, stepped out the door as though he had been waiting for him. "Come on in, Emmet."

He held out an arm to usher Emmet into the one-story cottage painted green. He distinguished his appearance with a trademark suede vest and small round spectacles along with a wiry brush of a beard. He kept his hair on the longish side. Emmet always figured Green cut the figure of a typical newsman, not that he had encountered too many others first hand.

Once inside the tight room, Emmet took it in as almost identical to C.D. Semple's one room law office next door which made sense since Semple was Will's uncle. Emmet had spent a lot of time in Semple's room before, during and after the court case against Ann. That time would always be a stain at the edges of his mind.

"Take a seat boy. Let's have a talk." While Emmet sat, the smell of newspaper ink rose up and permeated the room. He looked at Green's desk which was littered with the effects of a newsman's life. A half empty bottle of whiskey and a shot glass along with stacks of papers.

Green, the source of all information Colusan, gazed at Emmet with astute, light-colored eyes, sizing him and his situation up in one go. "We need to get you squared away. Here's the thing...the last place you want to be is Napa. I can promise you that. I've been in there and it's...well, it's... the stories about that place would make your hair curl."

Emmet looked sharply at the other man. Green was seldom at a loss for words so it must be a pretty terrible place. He put his hands up.

"Okay, okay. I'll get myself together...Doc says it's maybe sleep dep...dep something."

"Deprivation."

"Yeah, that's it."

"Now, in the meantime, Mr. Sussmont has been kind enough to offer you the back storeroom as a place to stay. Temporary like. In return, you're going to be like his watchdog. He likes the idea of that, having somebody there at all times. So, head on over there and square it with him."

Emmet stood, knowing Green was looking out for his best interests and knowing that he had to make do with what was on offer. He might have felt uncomfortable by Green's interference. But he didn't. He felt reassured as he left and headed right to the corner of Main and Fifth.

He stared at the sign that read M. L. Sussmont's. Just like every other time, the sight of the building took him right back to the days with his father. To the early days. All the hours he had spent right in this place. All the hours...

Sussmont stood behind the counter and did not bat an eye when he saw Emmet. He knew that Emmet would be walking through that door. The invisible net of Colusa had tightened and formed a secure web for Emmet. This was a part of it.

"Good day to you, Emmet Campbell." His voice was always thick with his German inflection.

Emmet cleared his throat before beginning. "Mr. Green sent me over...he said..."

Sussmont interrupted him and said, "Yes, yes. Let me show you."

The man walked to the back storeroom. A place Emmet knew well. A place he had hidden away many times. His safe place.

The storeroom was reconfigured and taken over with German efficiency and organization. Shelves were in place where there had been none before. White washing on the walls kept it fresh and clean. With a flourish of his hand, Sussmont waved to the space and said, "So, it is here. Space for a bedroll maybe and what you have, yah?"

Emmet nodded slowly, looking at the man's kind eyes.

Sussmont continued, "I like for you to be here. To watch the store." He gazed at Emmet as though taking a measurement of some sort and added, "You know, you can never feel too safe in this life, my friend." Emmet nodded again. He wouldn't say the man was half wrong.

Briskly, Sussmont laid out the arrangement. In return for the space, Emmet would also perform odd jobs as needed. At the end, Sussmont tacked on "until you recover."

"Thank you. Thank you for this," Emmet said, not able to look at Sussmont directly and, instead, looking down at the widely spaced plank flooring.

"Bah. It is not much. Besides, you are helping me too. Remember that."

Bonita helped him bring over the few scant possessions he had from his time on earth, several items from being a wrangler (bedroll, lasso, saddle, spurs), two sets of clothing, his Stetson, his father's Bible (his stepmother being Papist wanted no parts of it) and the Martin guitar. They placed everything on his bedroll. After Bonita left, he stared at the sparse collection, wondering if he should have more things.

He sat down and tested how hard the wood floor was going to be. He stared at the one other item next to his bedroll, the murky liquid sitting in a glass bottle. The sleeping draught that Doc Calhoun had given him. He would use it but he did not intend on overusing it. He thought back to the sweetness on his stepmother's breath after she took a nip of her medicine back on the ranch. She had a problem with it as much as the men in the tunnels with their smoking pipes.

If it let him sleep, he would use it just enough to take the edge off. To slip into slumber. Other than that, he told himself, he would go no further with it. Not deeper into the dark places that the Chinamen and maybe his stepmother went.

He resolved to fight this thing on his own terms and no one else's. The murky liquid in the bottle would not be the way out of it. Maybe it was true what Bonita had said: it was time to make his own luck.

Several days later, he lounged on his pallet during the daytime, the hustle and bustle of store activities right beyond the storeroom door. He could not recall a time ever in his whole life that he had laid around so much during daylight. But his energy drained out by mid-day it seemed like and it left him like this, lounging on his pallet. Sussmont let him be, not hassling him about it. But still...he struggled with the feeling of letting the man down somehow.

At a rap on the door, he startled and then worked his way up painfully to a seat. "Come in," he said.

The door opened and his stepsister, Mary Ann, stood in the threshold, staring down at him. He looked up at her, taking her in. Short and stout, she was no more attractive than a mud hen. The eyes that looked down at him were Ann's eyes, dark gray and appraising. The two of them were strangers now even though they lived in the same house as children. One favored and cosseted; the other made to feel like a pariah.

Her hands gripped a basket handle which was covered with a white cloth. He flung one hand in its direction and said, "Don't need no charity."

"Emmet...I...Mother..."

"Whatever it is, just take it back."

She drew herself up, almost puffing herself out. "Mother wanted to send you some scones and her jelly. To let you know we all wish you the best in your recovery."

Emmet gave a bark of laughter. "Didn't see fit to visit me at the Blue House, huh?"

Mary Ann drew in a breath. "She doesn't get around too much these days so..." She left out the part unsaid. That respectable folk in Colusa wouldn't be caught seen in the Blue House.

"What's she got wrong, anyways?" Emmet was curious about this since that visit to their house in town.

"It's the malaria that she picked up on the trail. It never left her."

A long buried memory rose up in Emmet's mind. "I thought she came out by the isthmus, down south. Not the trail."

"No, no...it was the trail." A flicker of confusion passed over Mary Ann's features but she said again, "It was the trail."

The mysteries of his stepmother...ever present. Mary Ann spoke up again. "These are her favorite scones...of course, I make them now..." Her voice trailed off.

"What?" Emmet said, still thinking of the past, cobwebs on his brain. "Oh, all right. Just...put them down I guess." He let out a cough, wincing.

Mary Ann frowned. "I think you misunderstand Mother. She wants nothing but the best for you. She tried to help you, Emmet. She tried all those years."

Emmet closed his eyes and opened them after a moment. "Maybe she did," he murmured to the nearly grown woman in front of him. "Maybe she did."

As the silence grew wider between them, he waved a hand her way. "Off with you now. I'm busy...getting ready to head out for some work on the range."

She bit her lower lip. "I will be on my way then. And I'll give your regards to Mother."

He watched as she turned and left, leaving the door open behind her. He let out another raspy cough.

Chapter Thirty-six

As Emmet moved the broom across the jailhouse floor, the ache in his shoulder hindered his movement and the sweeping was kept to short strokes. Emmet had found some work at the jail to tide him over along with other odd jobs around town. When he could fully get back in the saddle, he had every intention of going back to Wakefield's ranch and saving up again to buy the Campbell ranch. As he maneuvered his shoulder back and winced, he reassured himself it was just going to take some more time.

It was almost a year to the day that he had avoided being sent to the Asylum. Sheer dint of will kept him from slipping away into that dark place. Instead, he filled his time with random tasks in town. Whether it was cutting green grass behind the showy picket fences that were now popular in Colusa or hitching up an elderly person's carriage, Emmet became known as the man that could do all the miscellaneous chores. Often, they were tasks left undone by the man of the house for whatever reason. In this way, he cobbled together a living as best possible while limiting any burden he placed on others. He didn't want to owe anyone. Although he did owe people...he owed them his thanks.

Along the way, he also became privy to secrets about folks, secrets he kept closely guarded. Not unlike how he kept the purse winnings from card game sweeps that cowboys at the saloons handed over to him to protect. People counted on Emmet with their confidences and their trust was well-founded.

At the end of the hall in the last jail cell sat Dudley Shepardson. Since his early years in Colusa, Shepardson veered more towards the darker sides of his personality and was quick to lash out, often unprovoked. He feuded bitterly with Sheriff Arnold for years over some unknown slight or another. It finally led him to calling the sheriff out in public to a duel.

The whole town was on tenterhooks over it and Arnold, a sensible man who served Colusa well, made it clear that, while he would not be bullied, he also would not cave in to Shepardson. He managed to sidestep Shepardson's tomfoolery until that last day. Shepardson caught him out on the street and, with no warning, shot Arnold straight through the heart.

As Emmet's broom got closer to the dank jail cell where Shepardson had been whiling the days before trial, Emmet thought about the funny ways life could twist and turn. Looking over into the cell, he saw Shepardson staring right at him. He nodded and went back to the sweeping.

Emmet had never seen the man like this, quiet with some of his bluster taken out of him. Shepardson seemed to think he could get away with shooting the much beloved Sheriff Arnold right out on the street in broad daylight and just carry on. He learned that was not the case.

Shepardson spoke up. "You know what I never thought was right?"

Emmet paused and placed a hand over the broom top. "What's that?"

"That Ann never let you take on that land. We all knew you wanted to be on that land. She should have honored that..."

Emmet shook his head, holding back any comment he might say on the topic. Instead, he asked, "You ever regret any of your choices, Dudley?"

Without missing a beat, Shepardson said, "Nah...I don't ever look back. That's just who I am..."

"Huh...maybe you should though."

Emmet took up with the broom again. After he got to the other end of the hall, Shepardson yelled out to him. "Hear that gal Bonita left town on you. That right?"

Emmet went still with his broom. He thought back to the day the previous month when Bonita told him she was leaving. He had struggled to keep his face together as she told him she had to go back to

Tennessee because her sister was ailing. She said, "I'm not leaving you, you know that right?"

He stayed silent until she had added, "Come with me. You can get a fresh start..."

"Leave Colusa? Can't do that. The ranch...."

She grabbed his hand and lifted out one finger at a time before putting it back in a fist and bringing it up to her lips. He knew she would come back though just like he had come back to Colusa. She would not be able to stay away for too long....he knew this to be true deep in his heart.

He started to sweep again as Dudley grumbled to himself in his cell. He couldn't make much sense of it. It didn't matter anyway----he had pushed Dudley into the recesses of his mind a long while back, just as he had Ann.

Several days later, Emmet sat at the Mount Hood Saloon, nursing a whiskey and missing Bonita. He nursed them on days he could drink; his days of chugging long done. Looking down into his whiskey, it was more the ritual of holding the drink in his hand that he enjoyed rather than the drink itself.

He came into the saloon to escape all the talk out on the street about Shepardson. How he had been fully exonerated for shooting Sheriff Arnold dead. It pulled at Emmet, the injustice of it all. But seeing Dudley like that in the jail cell...he thought there was something bigger afoot. The shooting changed the man anyway, punishment or not.

He also came in to escape the memory of his recent visit to Doc Calhoun. The doctor saw patients in the office attached to the residence on Main Street just as Doc Robinson had. Unlike the days when Emmet had herded Doc Robinson back after nights out carousing, the place was all straight edges and squared away.

Emmet had sat on the examining table and looked at the various glass bottles lined up on the counter, all different heights with the light reflecting off the fluids held within. He probably had been through every last one of them but none had the fix for what his body was enduring. It was becoming clear as crystal that there was no fix to be had.

Doc Calhoun walked in and Emmet could see right away by the man's stance and the look in his eye that the results of recent tests were not in Emmet's favor. Luck was not on his side after all. The man cleared his throat and placed a hand on Emmet's shoulder.

Emmet had the passing thought that it must be hard to deliver bad news to folks all the time. Took some bravery in fact. Doc faced it head on though and looked down at Emmet straight into his eyes.

"Son, it's consumption. Not much to do about it. Other than what you have been doing. Rest up."

Emmet nodded. He already knew what the beast was. Had known for some time. The wasting away of his body so that it was almost skeletal. The cough that just wouldn't give up and sometimes led to blood on his handkerchief. The pallor of his skin, whiter than he had ever been. Consumption---he had heard it once called the "White Plague."

Madam Charlotte, never one to mince words, pinned it down one night at the Blue House for what it was. She came over to where he now had the habit of sitting and watching at the back corner table and said, "Oh Emmet. Look at you. You're just a shadow of yourself, ain't you?" She was right. He had become a shadow.

Doc continued by explaining why it had happened. "The gunshot wound is the root cause of it. Left you vulnerable and the germ got in there. Into your lungs."

His look was sorrowful and Emmet immediately tried to change that. Again, feeling for this man who had to face giving out the truths like this.

"It's all right, Doc. You done what you could. Don't you worry about me. I'll be all right."

As Emmet gave his head a shake to clear his thoughts, a rancher who looked vaguely familiar tipped his hat at him from the other end of the bar. The rancher raised his voice enough for Emmet to hear him. "Sorry for your news, Emmet."

Emmet's face must have shown his confusion because the rancher added, "She was a fine woman."

He felt a sharp twist in his gut at the thought that something had happened to Bonita. He and, as far as he knew, no one else had heard from her in months. "Who?"

The rancher, taken aback, said, "Your mother. Who do you think I'm talking about?"

"You mean Ann?"

"Yes, Ann Campbell. She's your mother, ain't she?"

"Well...what about her?"

"Sorry to hear of her passing is what I mean."

Emmet looked away from the man and stared into his drink before shooting it back in one gulp. He got up and left Mount Hood, throwing some coin on the counter.

He blindly walked through town without even thinking about a destination. He ended up at Old Man Chung's cemetery plot, the one he took meticulous care of. It stood out among others that were not as well tended. He took his hat off and worked it between his hands. "Chung, she's dead," he said. His only answer back was a whisper of wind.

Chapter Thirty-seven

Emmet walked with his half limp out to the Catholic cemetery on the edge of Colusa. It was no easy stretch for him anymore but he did it. He needed to see it happening. Her being buried.

He lived in the same town with her for almost his entire thirty years. He managed to avoid her for the past thirteen since his father died. He couldn't seem to take in that she was really gone. He remembered all the times he dreamed of it, imagined it and wanted it but never thought it could happen. He had fought her in his head for so long.

He stood at the side of the cemetery where a row of oak trees formed a terse line. He felt the searing in his lungs as he breathed in a sip of air...just sips, he discovered, kept the pain in check. He missed breathing in deep.

The small group, all draped in their black garb, stood several yards away from him. Squinting one eye under the broad brim of his Stetson hat, he picked out who was who in the gathering. He ended up mainly staring at his stepsister and his half-brother, the heir apparent.

As he watched the casket being lowered into the ground, a hollow feeling settled into his gut. A feeling maybe worse than all the others, knowing he would never get her to acknowledge what she had done to him.

As the group broke up and walked away from the mound of California earth that was Ann Campbell's gravesite, Mary Ann looked over and set her piercing eyes on him. As she made her way towards him, he remained still where he was.

"Emmet," she said when she was within talking distance. He again studied her looks. He doubted she would be able to find a husband despite holding the purse strings to the Campbell fortune. "Did you come to pay your respects?" she asked.

He eyed her carefully before responding. "In a way. I guess you could say that."

Mary Ann did not flinch a whit at his words. Instead, she said, "She always worried about you, Emmet. You know that, right? Right 'til the end."

She sniffed into a handkerchief and he took in the red rimmed eyes under her spectacles. She was young to lose her mama at twenty-two by his reckoning. But then he had lost his even younger.

"Did she?" he asked and it hung between them.

"I wish you could have seen fit to visit her before...before..."

"Didn't see how that woulda done much."

"Well, it would have helped her."

"Helped her? Helped her to feel better about what she had done?"

Mary Ann's face flushed with heat and she said sharply, "I won't listen to anything bad about Mother. Especially today." A sob broke into her words and then she collected herself and said, "She always did her best."

"Did she?".

"Oh, you're impossible. You always were, you know."

"Maybe so...maybe so..."

Then he asked what he needed to find out. "What about the ranch land, Mary Ann? She said she would sell it to me."

Mary Ann looked at him with pity coming over her mottled features. "Oh Emmet...she never said that. That will always be John William's ranch. Even if he doesn't farm it or put cattle on it. It's his to do as he wants."

He closed his eyes as her mouth continued to move, the words washing over him. She was never going to let him buy the land back. She continued, "Even if you did have the money. That land stays with John William. It's his inheritance."

"She said...you were there..."

"She never had any such intention. You heard what she was saying wrong." She let out a big sigh and then added, "I might as well tell you

231

now. Mr. Goad, the solicitor, will bring it to you to sign off on soon. She left you fifty gold coins."

Emmet stared at the woman in front of him and saw that she showed no signs of embarrassment or chagrin upon telling him this. From all the riches his father accumulated, fifty gold coins was to be his lot.

He turned away from her and limped back along the edge of the cemetery. Back the way he had come. He had not found what he had been looking for and he now realized he never would.

On an October day with unseasonal warmth, Emmet went back to the Catholic cemetery. He found the new monument placed on her grave to be a substantial obelisk with verse along each side. His reading still wasn't much and his writing worse. She had tried to work with him on that---he had to give her due for it. He could just barely pull out some of the words of the inscription that read:

"...a tender mother...parental kindness..."

He let out a loud guffaw after picking out, "parental kindness." The laugh quickly turned into the hacking cough that dogged him day and night. He raised his blue eyes upwards to the sky and shook his fist. She had the last say.

Now, not too unlike his stepmother, Emmet's body was slowing down bit by bit. Like the parts of a machine, each piece beginning to give out. He understood it for what it was and planned accordingly. He put a little aside here and there for the day that he would need to be put six feet under. Will Green was keeping it for him and knew exactly what it was for. But not here. Not near her.

Strangely, he felt a sudden and surprising gasp of energy surge through his being. He stepped away from the cemetery and headed outside of town to his favorite stand of cottonwoods to see the grand show of their fall colors. He remembered an Indian telling him about how sacred his people considered cottonwoods to be. Something about them providing all the answers if listened to hard enough.

The view beyond the stand of trees was Sutter Buttes. Looking exactly like they had when he and his father had made their way towards Colusa. They entranced him then and still did. He breathed in a couple of jagged breaths and felt the California air sift through his body. He could just about smell the scent of future harvests of threshed winter wheat with those overriding aromas long after he would be gone.

Stretching his hands out in front of him, he extended each finger fully except for the one that had been broken along the way. The bones of his hands were outlined by sunlight, almost see-through. He drew upon his last reserves of strength, making fists with each hand. Opening them up wide again, Emmet lifted his gaze up to the clouds moving fast across the great big Colusa sky, taking it all in.

10 November 1883, Colusa Weekly Sun

A DIAMOND IN THE ROUGH—On Tuesday last Emmet Campbell passed away. If ever the appellation "rough diamond" applied to anyone, it applied to Emmet. His father, John Campbell, brought him here a baby nearly thirty years ago. His mother died on the plains and, like Topsy, he was not raised, but "growed." The consequence was, he was rough, delighted in rough language and kept rough company at times, but his heart was always right, and we wish that the actions of every man in high-toned society turned on as nice points of honor. The sick, the weak, the friendless, always found a stout heart and a willing hand in Emmet. He knew nearly all the men in the county, and many a night he has stayed up to watch someone in his cups to prevent his being bled. Such men have given him purses containing hundreds of dollars and every time the return was straight. When he was shot through the breast, a few years ago, he withheld much of his testimony as possible to prevent the punishment of his would-be slayer, whom he forgave. He died of consumption, the wound being the cause. May He who judges all things unerringly, find the brightness of the interior diamond to outweigh the rough exterior. A very large number of the most respectable ladies and gentlemen of Colusa attended his funeral and saw him decently interred. He had enough means laid by to cover all expenses of his illness and burial. He always dreaded being a burden or a charge to anyone.

Author's Note

This story is anchored by the Ernest Hemingway quote in the beginning of the novel ("Every man has two deaths, when he is buried in the ground and the last time someone says his name...) and by the real life Emmet Campbell's obituary, **A DIAMOND IN THE ROUGH,** from the Colusa Sun included at the end of the novel. My hope is that the reader of this tale makes the connection between those two "anchors."

There is always a story behind the story and here is this one:

Eleven years ago in 2011, I came upon one of those genealogical discoveries that would fall under the category of "you may find out about something you don't want to find out." The discovery was a court case that read stranger than fiction. It left me in pieces over the injustice served up for a boy named Emmet Campbell in Colusa, California. The irony: this injustice was meted out by my ancestor, Ann Campbell. I am a relation to the perpetrator of this injustice.

It can be a heavy burden to fill in the blanks. It can also be a heavy burden to tell a story about someone cast aside and forgotten. But once I uncovered and learned it, I couldn't "unlearn" it. I couldn't "not know" it anymore. I felt compelled to right this wrong in the only way I knew how: tell the tale. An ancestral debt of sorts...

Because there are more blanks than not, the tale is fiction based on the particulars of a real life person. The actual court transcript from the probate file in the Colusa County records is the basis of the story. Other firsthand documents are used to piece together Emmet's life wherever possible. But imagination served as the best way to fill in the idea of Emmet as a person, how he lived and what he endured.

It was my good fortune to be able to travel to the town of Colusa in April 2017. Colusa is a throwback town from an earlier version of America. It has a local dairy bar where shakes, burgers and fries are ordered at a walk-up outdoor window. Its former high school is a majestic Mediterranean Revival style building still in use as an alternative school. Its downtown, while shabby around the edges and a bit vacant, is a reminder of what America's main streets used to be. Ghosts linger there...some of them are my ghosts.

My primary goal was to find Emmet's grave---the one that the obituary says he paid for himself---and to honor him somehow. Sadly, the original Colusa Community Cemetery was moved a couple of years after Emmet's passing so that land could be made into a park. Family members were given a chance to move bodies in the summer of 1885 but, for Emmet, this did not happen.

It is estimated there are still over 75 bodies buried underneath what is now the Will Semple Green Park on 8th Street between Webster and Parkhill Streets. In hot weather, it is said the indentations of the graves can be seen in the park. As best I know, Emmet is in one of those graves. This is the final post note to Emmet's tale...the burial place he set up for himself was erased and made anonymous.

When I discovered this, it spurred me on even more to finish a manuscript that, by that point, had gone through several point of views and countless versions. I finally got out of my way enough so that the final result is in your hands right now.

Like with so many other events of the past, I will never know the real story behind Emmet just as I will never know who he really was. But I do know this: he didn't live in vain and his second death has not happened yet because I, for one, am still talking about him.

Campbell's Boy is a story from my heart.